Dear Diary,

Matt took me and Mommy and Casey out for pizza tonight. Casey picked off all the little fishy things, but me and Matt think they're good.

Matt likes baseball, almost as much as me. He gave me a present last week, a ball that Ernie Banks hit a home run with. And he said he's gonna take me to a Mariners game pretty soon. Boy, I can't wait!

Matt's not mean like Daddy was. He looks at Mommy a lot. And Mommy looks at him a lot, too. I didn't want to like him, not at first, 'cause Casey thinks he's Mommy's boyfriend. But I like him. I like him a lot. And I think Mommy does, too....

KIM

Please address questions and book requests to: Harlequin Reader Service
U.S.: 3010 Walden Ave., P.O. Box 1325, Buffalo, NY 14269
CAN.: P.O. Box 609, Fort Erie, Ont. L2A 5X3

Born in the USA
WASHINGTON

SANDRA JAMES

Belonging

Harlequin Books

TORONTO • NEW YORK • LONDON
AMSTERDAM • PARIS • SYDNEY • HAMBURG
STOCKHOLM • ATHENS • TOKYO • MILAN
• WARSAW • BUDAPEST • AUCKLAND

HARLEQUIN BOOKS
225 Duncan Mill Road, Don Mills,
Ontario, Canada M3B 3K9

ISBN 0-373-47197-1

BELONGING

Copyright © 1987 by Sandra Kleinschmit

Printed in U.S.A.

CHAPTER ONE

A BLINDING FLASH of light accompanied the click of the camera. A lone woman stood poised on the small platform. In stark contrast with the sterile gray walls of the pocket-sized auditorium, she was tall and feminine, her features finely sculpted. Her upswept flaxen hair caught the sharp glare of overhead lights and, oddly enough, was transformed into a halo of molten gold.

Despite the businesslike hairstyle and the conservatively cut white linen suit, there was no denying that this was a woman in full bloom, a woman who would turn heads whenever she walked into a room. And her beauty was only enhanced by the aura of dignity, efficiency and control she projected.

It was an image the woman was aware of, though not one that she intentionally cultivated, at least on a conscious level. Although neither came as readily or as often as they once had, laughter and gaiety were not unknown to her.

But this cramped auditorium was really no place for either. Angela Hall had a meeting to preside over. During her six months as mayor of Westridge, Washington, she had initiated a practice of holding a monthly press conference to discuss recent events, goals and concerns. The media loved it, though Angie was the first to admit she was sometimes put on the spot. But the meetings bolstered her reputation for frankness and openness with both the press and the community.

As she readied herself to speak, cameras whirred once more, lights blazed and tape recorders were hurriedly checked to see that they were still in motion. Angie's slender hands rested on the edge of the podium as she scanned the assemblage before her.

"As some of you may know," she said, enunciating her words clearly, "a citizens' committee was formed several months ago to study the feasibility of constructing a new city hall."

"Have a sudden windfall, Mayor?" someone called out.

Angie smiled slightly, not surprised at the scrutiny. Already the issue had proved to be a sensitive one. There were several council members who believed the prospect had merit while others expressed the opinion that it was a frivolous venture. Consequently, Angie suspected she would have a fight on her hands. John Curtis in particular had been rather vehement, as usual, in his support of a new building.

"No windfall," she replied, "but the city's revenue projections are certainly more optimistic than they've been the last few years. And at least we're not looking at another site, so purchase of property wouldn't be a factor."

"How do you feel about this plan, Mayor? Is it one you endorse?"

The question came from Blair Andrews, a reporter for the *Westridge Bulletin.* Her beat ran the gamut from city politics to a weekly social column. She and Blair weren't the best of friends; in fact, they weren't friends at all. Angie had opposed Blair's uncle in the mayoral election, and even before incumbent Bob Andrews's sound defeat, Blair had put Angie in the line of fire as often as she possibly could.

Angie took a deep breath. In her opinion, building a new city hall was an ambitious project and an unnecessary expense. But she also felt it wouldn't be right to undermine the committee's work by voicing her opposition before their report was wrapped up.

"First of all," she told her audience, "the committee's recommendations won't be known until next Monday's council meeting. Second, I'd like to clarify that there is no formal plan yet to construct a new building. The committee has also been looking into the cost of renovating the existing building since there can be no question about the building's historic value."

She let the words sink in before she continued. "Cost savings would be substantial, and the possibility exists for expanding some of the city's services with the excess funds." In addition to expanding the transit system and replacing a number of city buses, the creation of a women's shelter was also being bandied about. But since nothing was really clear-cut, she thought it was best not to go into too many details.

There was a hushed murmur among the group, and sensing another barrage of questions, she decided to wrap up the meeting quickly. "But the fact remains," she stated firmly, "that as far as city hall is concerned, freezing in the winter, boiling in the summer and contending with a leaky roof year-round hardly make for the best of working conditions.'' Her tone indicated that there was little more to be said.

But before Angie had a chance to make her closing remarks, Blair Andrews's voice rang out once more. It was smooth and silky, with an air of smugness that put Angie's teeth on edge. ''Rumor has it our new police chief, Matthew Richardson, wasn't your first choice to replace Sam Nelson. Would you care to comment, Mayor Hall?''

Angie resisted the impulse to glare at the woman. Though she firmly believed in her open-door policy, she was wise enough to recognize that not everything that went on in city hall was for public consumption. But one thing was certain. With Blair Andrews always out and about, Angie had to watch where she stepped—as well as how, with whom and why.

It was, she reaffirmed on a sour note, a typical beginning of the month, thanks to Blair. Even the name Matthew Richardson dredged up an odd feeling in the pit of her stomach. An image of dark hair, surprisingly light gray eyes and tanned skin flashed into her mind. She wasn't sure how her newly hired chief would take the news that he was second choice, especially when hearing it from a secondhand source. Now it appeared Blair had left her no alternative. She was going to have to tell him herself that he hadn't been first pick.

She pursed her lips for a fraction of a second, choosing her words carefully. ''Naturally, the possibilities were narrowed down to several candidates, all of whom were certainly qualified for the job. While it's true the first choice declined our offer, I'm sure Chief Richardson will do a perfectly adequate job of seeing to our police protection.''

With that Angie lifted slender tawny brows and scanned the room to see if there were any more questions. When there were none, she smiled graciously and thanked the participants, but not before her eyes locked with those of Blair Andrews. The woman's generous red lips were set in the self-satisfied smirk of the proverbial cat who has swallowed the canary. Angie couldn't help but wonder about that look as she turned and walked from the auditorium.

She didn't see the man standing at the rear of the room, nor was she aware of the narrowed gray gaze that followed her graceful exit.

MATT RICHARDSON'S JAW thrust forward as he strode across the carpeted floor of the small reception area that led to his office. He briefly noted the woman sitting at the desk—what the hell was her name? Maggie? Yes, that was it, Maggie. His mind again registered her appearance, almost without his being conscious of it. He put her age at somewhere near fifty. Rather dour-looking, she was thin to the point of being downright skinny.

Yet he couldn't help but be distracted at the speed with which her long, thin fingers traveled across the keyboard of her Selectric. He looked on for a moment in utter amazement.

Realizing he didn't want to make a bad impression his first day on the job, he gave his secretary a cursory nod. She spared him the briefest of acknowledgments before turning back to her typing. His secretary, it seemed, wasn't any more talkative than he was—at least at the moment. But then again, she hadn't been loquacious this morning when they'd first been introduced.

His mood had softened a little by the time he entered his office and seated himself in the comfortable leather chair behind the massive mahogany desk. The chair creaked as he turned and looked though the narrow glass window behind him. From his fifth-story vantage point, Matt had a splendid view of the city and surrounding countryside.

Westridge was nestled in a rich pocket of wilderness a hundred miles south of Seattle. It spread out against the base of the foothills that led to the Cascade Mountains. Dense forests covered the gently sloping hills and sharply jutting mountains beyond, an endless carpet of lush green woodland that blended with the bright blue of the sky.

His gaze drifted to the city that was now his home. With ninety thousand inhabitants, Westridge was a bustling center for nearby timber and dairy communities, a city that was home to ranchers, farmers and businessmen alike. In fact, he'd thought more than once since he'd settled in last week that he might have been standing in the middle of a Chicago suburb if it wasn't for the profusion of cowboy hats, boots and pickup trucks that continually caught his eye.

Yes, he'd left the slums, the tenements, the countless art galleries and awe-inspiring museums—all that was Chicago—behind him. He couldn't really say when the nagging restlessness that had plagued him had started. A year ago. Perhaps more. He'd been to hell and back and quite a few places in between, and maybe it had finally taken its toll.

Or was he getting old? Edging too near the demon known as the ripe old age of forty? Maybe. He'd been tired. Bored. Burned-out was how cops and everyone else referred to the feeling.

Life had lost its challenge, and so had his job. He'd felt he was competing with a never-ending stream of corruption and dead ends without even the smallest scrap of hope. He was a man used to fighting for what he wanted and fighting hard; it was the only way to survive on Chicago's South Side. But he'd known it was time for a change when he'd stopped looking forward to the next day ahead.

So he had packed up lock, stock and barrel and left the only home he had ever known. A tough, streetwise guy from the big city, he'd left everything behind for...what? For the wide-open spaces of the West? He leaned back in his chair and grinned, almost in spite of himself. Certainly not for a peaceful, tranquil job where all he had to do was prop his feet on his desk and hobnob with the owner of the local gas station. He'd never have been satisfied with that in the first place.

Perhaps he wasn't growing old after all. He still craved a little action, a little excitement. Yes, Westridge was just what he wanted. Not too big, not too small.

"But this is one hell of a way to start a new job," Matt grumbled aloud. His grin faded as he thought of Angela Hall's statement. *I'm sure Chief Richardson will do a perfectly adequate job of seeing to our police protection.* A wave of indignation swept through him. Seventeen years on Chicago's police force had taught him to do much more than an *adequate* job.

But was that what was really bothering him? No. Instead, it was the knowledge that he'd been second choice. That was something he hadn't known, nor had he even considered the possibility. The city's police chief had retired. Westridge had offered him the post; he'd wanted it and he'd accepted. It wasn't as if he'd wanted to be king of the hill, but nonetheless, the realization that Mayor Angela Hall had thought someone else more capable than he was rankled.

"Hell," he muttered, then repeated it. *"Hell!"*

He got up and paced around the office, then finally dropped back into his chair and pressed the button on the intercom, feeling the need to hear a voice other than his own. Even Maggie's. "Maggie?"

The voice, when it finally came, was rather stilted. "The name is Margie, sir."

"Margie," he echoed, then cleared his throat. He was a little embarrassed that he hadn't remembered her name. "Margie, would you please get me a copy of last year's annual report to the city council?"

This time there was little pause. "The annual report, sir, is in the filing cabinet next to your desk. Filed under—"

Matt reached out his other hand. "I see it. Uh, thanks, Margie."

He released the intercom but made no move to retrieve the document he'd requested. He already knew most of the statistics and information detailed in the report, anyway. He'd made it a point to know what he was getting into before he'd accepted the job. Instead, he just sat there, his big hands resting for a moment on the desktop.

Damn! Why was it he suddenly felt like a kid on his first day of school? Strange. Alone. Out of place. He got up and paced around the office again. He halted, his eyes sweeping upward to linger reflectively on the stained and yellowed ceiling tile. Matt guessed the entire building must date back to the thirties, if not earlier. It was old, a little on the dilapidated side, but city hall, like the rest of the town, had a kind of rustic appeal.

At least his office was quiet and roomy, a far cry from his quarters in Chicago. There he'd shared a cramped hole-in-the-wall with the second-in-command of Missing Persons. He'd gone home more times than he could count with his ears still ringing from the steady drone of voices the paper-thin walls failed to shut out.

Was that what this feeling was? Transplant shock? One corner of his mouth turned up wryly at the thought. He was, after all, thirty-eight years old and not a six-year-old on his first night away from home.

He eased back into his chair, then finally picked up the annual report and thumbed through it. He'd no more than idly flipped it open to the first page than the intercom buzzed.

"Sir?"

It was Margie. "Yes?" Absently he toyed with a pencil.

"You have a staff meeting in the conference room in ten minutes. And at three this afternoon a meeting with the mayor. I just wanted to remind you."

Cool and efficient, just like Mayor Hall. An image of Angela as she'd appeared that morning flashed into his mind, and he experienced a spurt of irritation. There could be no doubt that she was one extremely attractive woman, but she seemed so cold, so formal. Unless he was mistaken—and thankfully that wasn't often—she was a woman who had business on her mind and little else. But fast on the heels of that image was another—the malicious triumph he'd glimpsed on the reporter's face when she had divulged that he'd been second choice.

He threw the pencil down on his desk. Mayor Hall. That damn reporter. Magg—Margie. Did all the women in this town have ice in their veins?

"Thanks, Margie." He paused. "I don't suppose there's any coffee around?"

The mild inquiry had no sooner been voiced than her response came, short and sweet. Sweet? Who the hell was he kidding? "There certainly is," she informed him stiffly. "Down the hall, past the records section, first door to the right in the lunchroom...sir."

In other words, get it yourself. Matt quirked an eyebrow as he levered himself up from his desk once more. As he ambled past Margie, a faint touch of dry humor colored his thoughts as again he wondered just what he'd gotten himself into. His boss was a lady, a lady that he knew instinctively didn't particularly care for him, even though she'd hired him. The same went for his secretary, a woman who was clearly independent as hell. Well, maybe he should have expected it. This was, after all, the twentieth century. And hadn't he wanted a change?

Contrary to what he'd encountered already that morning, the staff meeting went off without a hitch. Former Chief Nelson, it seemed, had been a capable administrator, and Matt decided he was content to let things ride for the time being. The last thing he wanted was for his staff to think that as an ex-cop from Chicago his only intent was to show them the ropes. No, he didn't want to earn a reputation as a mover and shaker and end up inspiring a lot of discontent and morale problems.

Matt was, in fact, feeling rather pleased when he returned to his office an hour later. Surely he could handle his secretary, and even his new boss, by whatever means it took. He'd been a cop long enough to learn that strong-arm tactics weren't the only way to pull someone over to the other side of the fence. He perched on the edge of Margie's desk and smiled at her.

Margie stopped her busywork and looked at him as if he were an annoying speck of dust on her desktop.

"Have you worked here long, Margie?" he inquired congenially.

"Over thirty years, sir."

The reply was brief, even terse, but he detected a hint of wariness in the tilt of her chin as she looked up at him. "That's quite a while," he observed. "All that time for the police department?"

She nodded, but this time there was a flash of pride in her eyes. He whistled. "You and Chief Nelson must have gone back a ways."

Again she nodded. Ah, Matt thought. It was probably loyalty to Sam Nelson that prompted her leeriness of him. Well, that was understandable. She probably considered him an outsider.

"You know, Margie," he remarked conversationally, "that I'm from Chicago."

"I'm well aware of that, sir!"

Matt ignored her waspish tone and gave an encompassing glance around the office. "To tell you the truth, things were a lot different there. The people were different," he mused in a deliberately casual tone. "There were a lot of times when you had to watch out for yourself because no one else would do it for you." He noticed from the corner of his eye that she was listening intently.

Margie's head bobbed up and down in agreement. "I had a friend who moved to Chicago years ago. I went to visit her once." She sniffed disdainfully. "I've never seen a more uppity bunch of people in my life!"

Uppity? Matt had to resist the urge to laugh. At least he hadn't lost his sense of humor. Not only was his own private version of "uppity" sitting right in front of him, the name Angela Hall came immediately to mind, as well.

"You know, you're right," he agreed. "Why, in the week I've been here, I've wished more than once I'd moved here years ago." He flashed his most disarming smile. "To tell you the truth, Margie, I could use a friend. What do you say you show me around the department, and then the two of us can go to lunch?"

"Lunch?" She looked astonished at the suggestion.

Matt shrugged. "Why not? I imagine it'll be close to noon by the time we're finished. And I can't think of anyone more qualified than you to show me the ropes."

Margie's look of surprise changed to one of beaming pleasure. "Why, thank you." She flashed the first genuine smile he'd seen. "I think I'd like that. But, Chief—" she waved a finger insistently "—only if we go Dutch."

Having come this far, Matt wasn't about to argue—especially

since he'd progressed from "sir" to "Chief." He liked the sound of it too much. Though he'd never considered himself the least bit chauvinistic—he wouldn't have accepted a job working for a woman if he was—he hadn't pegged Margie for the women's-lib type. But at least she wasn't immune to a little old-fashioned male charm.

He was reminded of his meeting with Mayor Angela Hall that afternoon. One down, one to go, he couldn't help thinking. Would the same tactic work with her? At the thought a wry smile curved his lips.

Where Angela Hall was concerned, he had the feeling it wouldn't hurt to sharpen his ax.

CHAPTER TWO

As MUCH AS HE WISHED he could blithely brush aside the incident that morning, Matt experienced a twinge of annoyance every time he recalled that he hadn't been the number one choice for police chief. He knew it was his pride chafing. He also knew that he wasn't going to feel a damn bit better until he'd gotten the whole issue off his chest once and for all.

So it was that there was a certain tension in the air as Matt entered Angie's office early that afternoon. The steely eyes that rested on her were keen, a little too penetrating for her peace of mind. Angie couldn't help but be aware of them as she rounded her desk to clasp Matt's hand in a brief handshake, a move she made graciously if reluctantly.

Their fingers merely brushed; she deliberately made the contact minimal. Yet it was oddly unsettling that he removed his hand first.

She moved back to her chair, wishing she weren't quite so conscious of his stare drilling into the slender lines of her back.

"I can't tell you how glad everyone is to have you on board," she told him, schooling her features into a faint smile as she sat down. "Westridge is very lucky to have someone with your experience."

He inclined his head. "I was just thinking the same thing not long ago."

A hollow silence followed. As polite as his tone was, there was something less than friendly about the way he'd said the words, just the slightest suggestion of sarcasm. She couldn't help but wonder if he had something else on his mind, a bone to pick with her perhaps.

Angie hesitated. She hadn't been looking forward to this meeting, not really. Even before the incident with Blair had come up this morning, something about Matthew Richardson made her uncomfortably aware of each and every thing about him. Shimmering June sunlight shone through the glass window beside him, casting the roughly carved features before her into stark relief. High cheekbones accented a strong jawline, a thin but firmly contoured mouth. Dark brows arched over flinty gray eyes. It didn't take a second look to ascertain that beneath the navy suit were lean but extremely well-developed muscles—and Angie was trying very hard not to be quite so conscious of the fact. It reminded her of days gone by...days that were best forgotten.

But she had learned over the years to know exactly what she was dealing with. Matthew Richardson possessed an intensely masculine aura, an aura that hinted of controlled strength. This was a man who would be at ease, yet in control, of any situation.

Strangely enough, however, intimidating was not a word Angie would use to describe him. Exciting? To other women perhaps. But not to Angie Hall.

When she had scheduled this meeting, Angie intended to talk dollars and cents about the police department's budget. But when she tried to summon the statistics and figures that always came so quickly to mind, they were hardly the ones she expected. Six foot. Narrow hipped with the shoulders of a linebacker. She had to mentally shake herself to quell the renegade meanderings of her mind. She dealt with men on a professional level every day. Was this one really any different? They both had a job to do, and it was time she did hers.

"So," she said finally, "I assume you've had a chance to review the budget material we sent you." The police department's budget was coming up for ratification by the city council in mid-July, some six weeks away.

"Indeed I have, Ms Mayor."

Ms Mayor? Angie had been called a few things during her term, some nice, some not so nice, but his address was slightly irritating.

Business as usual, she reminded herself. Brushing the feeling aside, she clasped her hands on the desktop in front of her. "Any changes or recommendations you'd like to make?"

Matt lifted an eyebrow. "Is it too late to plead for more money?" Her brisk, no-nonsense manner didn't surprise him. It was on a par with the way she'd handled the press conference that morning. He had brains enough to recognize an intelligent woman when he saw one, and he had no doubt she would demand as much of someone else as she did of herself. Everything neat, tidy and in its place.

Exactly the way she looked. Even now, at three in the afternoon, there wasn't a hair out of place, not a wrinkle in her cloth-
ing, not even a shine on her delicately formed nose. The perfect
woman. For just a moment he was reminded of Linda, whom he
hadn't thought of in years.

But to his surprise Angie laughed. The sound was pure and
sweet, and so unlike the impression he'd just formed in his mind
that for a moment Matt was startled.

"That," she commented dryly, "is a question I think I've
heard from every department head. And the only answer I can
give is that the city's budget has been increased over and above
last year's already. Any further increase and I'm afraid we'd have
a tax revolt on our hands."

It was no more than he'd expected. But Matt could live with
the budget as it was, though he planned to do a little juggling
before it was submitted to the council in final form. The dispatching system could stand to be further automated, and he wanted
to increase public awareness of crime prevention through security
surveys and neighborhood watch associations.

"Sam did his best to make the proposal something the next
chief could live with," she added.

The next chief? Her choice of words reminded Matt once more
that he wasn't the one she had wanted in the position. "Sam
seems to have done an excellent job," he remarked. "Very well
liked, I'd say." He shifted in his chair, aware of the speculative
blue eyes focused on his face. "It was thoughtful of you to send
me the budget proposal in the first place," he continued. Just to
throw her off balance, he gave her a slight smile. "But no one
likes having the bomb dropped on him at the last minute."

There it was again—the feeling that this conversation was dou-
ble-edged. Angie's eyes narrowed. She wasn't the type to avoid
a confrontation—if that's what the two of them were having. She
had the distinct impression it was.

Raising fine arched brows, she leaned back in her chair. "Is
there something else on your mind?"

The directness of the question caught him off guard, but Matt
was growing accustomed to her cool, calm tone. Somehow it only
reinforced his impression that she had about as much warmth in
her veins as an iceberg at the North Pole. He seriously doubted
that Mayor Angie Hall had a loving bone in her body!

Not that he'd known an overabundance of that emotion himself,
Matt thought dryly. He certainly hadn't while he was growing up

in Chicago's South Side. He suspected he'd known even less while he was married to Linda. Still, although he'd grown rather cynical over the years, he'd never thought of himself as being incapable of loving. He wasn't sure who was worse—the woman sitting primly in front of him or the old battle-ax who stood guard outside her door.

"We can't all be top dog like you, Ms Mayor," he said mildly, crossing his long legs at the knee, he gave her back stare for stare. "But politicians are generally known for their ability to do quite well at double-talk."

"So I've heard." Her tone was flat. "You're not looking at one, however."

Matt smiled.

Angie began to steam. She could almost suspect that he knew....

"Your point, Chief Richardson," she said through tightly compressed lips. "You do have one?"

Chief Richardson. Somehow it didn't sound nearly as satisfying coming from her lips as it had from Margie's. Matt shrugged and looked up into his boss's snapping eyes. On one plane of thought, he realized that it was getting harder for him to think of this cold but lovely creature as the mayor of Westridge, let alone his boss. On another, it occurred to him that, as a cop who'd indulged in more than a few brawls and heartily enjoyed it, there was nothing he liked better than a good fight. Good, but fair.

He straightened abruptly. "I was at your press conference this morning," he said evenly. "Needless to say, I was there when a certain reporter started asking a few questions about your new appointment to police chief."

There was no need to go on. Matt could see from her expression that she understood him perfectly. *Perfect.* It was a word that came to mind rather often with her around.

He could also see he had discomfited her, and he derived a grim satisfaction from that.

"I see," Angie said slowly. And she did. Matt Richardson wasn't the type of man who would like coming in second. Until Blair Andrews had brought up the subject this morning, she really hadn't planned to tell him. But after the press conference she had realized it couldn't be avoided unless she wanted him to learn about it in the morning edition of the *Bulletin.* And she'd planned to let him know casually at the end of this meeting, to lead into it as gently as she could. Much as she didn't think she liked Matt

Richardson as a person, she didn't want him to quit after only
one day on the job.

"I had no idea you were there this morning," she said finally.
She mulled over her words a few seconds longer, thinking grimly
that once again Blair Andrews had succeeded in making waves.
"I didn't tell you earlier because I didn't feel it had any bearing
on the job. As for now...well, I just didn't have the chance. But
I can assure you, the fact that you weren't my first choice has no
reflection on your qualifications."

"I've no doubt about that," Matt intoned quite pleasantly. "I
am, however, rather curious about the man who beat me out."

Angie's gaze sharpened. The expression on his face was indeed
curious, but there was also a steely demand reflected in his eyes
that set her on edge. She couldn't deny he'd been polite to a fault
from the moment he'd walked into her office, but beneath the
civil facade lurked a very tough, hard man. And wasn't that why
she hadn't chosen him in the first place? Angie credited herself
with being professional enough to put her personal feelings aside
and concentrate on choosing the best person for the job. But the
fact remained she really hadn't liked Matt Richardson from the
start, and she was beginning to understand why.

"Beat you out?" she repeated dryly. "That's an odd way to
put it when you're the one who got the job."

"I think you know what I mean, Ms Mayor."

This time there was no denying the harshness of his tone. Angie
had the strange sensation she was being interrogated—and Matt
Richardson would be a master at getting whatever information he
wanted. He'd spent years as a homicide detective for the Chicago
Police Department.

She tapped a pencil on her desk for a few seconds. "All right,"
she said suddenly. "I wanted to hire an undersheriff from Marion
County in Oregon. The county seat there is much the same size
as Westridge, and like Westridge, it's surrounded by a largely
rural area. The budget there is on a par, as well. We may be a
growing center of business, but we have a number of residents
who have lived in the area for generations. I felt we needed a
certain—" she hesitated, searching for the right word "—cama-
raderie with the people. An ability to relate to the community."

Matt's mouth twisted. "And that's where I fell out of the running."

Angie bit her lip. The explanation hadn't come out quite the
way she'd intended. She had sounded just a little lofty, and she

really hadn't meant to. It wasn't as if he had fallen out of the running precisely. He'd just dropped one rung down the ladder.

"You have to admit Westridge and Chicago are worlds apart."

So he'd heard, and only that morning from Margie. In a town like Westridge, big-time cops from Chicago just didn't fit in. Matt opened his mouth, but before he had a chance to speak, he heard her voice again.

"The fact remains," she was saying, "that I wouldn't have hired you if I hadn't thought you had your nose to the ground in Chicago."

While hers was turned up in the air here in Washington? He recalled thinking something only that morning about hobnobbing at the local service station. He'd seen Angela Hall pull into the city lot driving a Mercedes this morning shortly before her press conference. Yet here she was, sitting before him in a suit that might well have come from a fashionable boutique on Michigan Avenue and obviously living high on the hog, telling him she was afraid he'd have a communication problem! He wasn't sure if he was more angry or amused.

She folded her hands in front of her on the desk and spoke crisply. "You have an impressive record, Chief Richardson, one that you can be proud of." Angie mentally reviewed his accomplishments. He hadn't earned the rank of lieutenant merely walking a beat. He'd worked in homicide, internal affairs and the organized crime division in Chicago. He'd also been appointed by the superintendent to serve on several special task forces and he'd been decorated several times.

But there was no denying she'd felt Matt wasn't quite right for the job, which was why she had wanted to hire Undersheriff Dennis Morgan. It was all water under the bridge, however. Now it seemed she and Matthew Richardson were stuck with each other since Dennis Morgan had ultimately decided working for a woman wasn't his cup of tea.

Almost as if he could read her mind, Matt voiced the question. "Your undersheriff turned you down, I take it?"

Angie nodded.

"May I ask why?"

He could ask, but that didn't mean he would receive. The sharp retort almost slipped out, but then she suddenly remembered what he'd said about politicians and double-talk.

"He decided he didn't want to work for a woman," she told him shortly. "A problem you obviously don't have."

"Obviously." His reply was bland, but Matt had actually harbored a few reservations before he'd finally accepted the offer. During his seventeen years on the force, he'd never had a female partner and hadn't really wanted one, either. Only the certainty that Angela Hall was just as capable of handling her own job had convinced him that the sex of his boss shouldn't influence his decision. He'd wanted a change; a change was what he got. So he couldn't complain, could he?

At least she'd been honest in her reasoning. He couldn't fault her for that. Yet there was something, some small scrap of pride, that made him rise to his feet and say, "At any rate, maybe I should be glad you decided I was better than nothing."

The slight sarcasm in his tone wasn't lost on her. Angie's eyes flashed upward. Her usual calm deserted her when she snapped, "We obviously had to have a police chief."

His laugh grated on her further. "I'm surprised you didn't take on the job yourself. You strike me as the type of woman who can handle just about anything."

"You've decided not to tender your resignation, then?" There was a definite coolness in her tone. Her blue eyes followed him as he moved across the room toward the doorway.

There he paused, one big hand resting casually on the doorknob. "Oh, don't worry," he said with a shrug. "I've never been one to scare easily. So like it or not, Ms Mayor, you're stuck with me. And you can rest assured I won't disappoint you." The smile directed over one broad shoulder might have been beguiling under any other circumstances—and to any other woman. "Who knows?" he added conversationally. "I may even buy a pickup and a pair of cowboy boots."

Angie was too busy gritting her teeth to think of a snappy comeback. Maybe he was right she thought with vexation, staring at the closed door a moment later. Maybe she *should* have taken on the job of police chief.

She had the feeling Matthew Richardson wasn't going to make life any easier for her; in fact, he had a rather unpleasant effect on her. It reminded her of a pill stuck in her throat—necessary, but not very easy to swallow.

IT WASN'T THE BEST WAY to begin a working relationship, but Angie had little time to think of Matt Richardson during the next few days. There were the usual day-to-day meetings and activities, a luncheon address at the Women's Civic Club on Wednesday, the dedication of the new wing of the children's section at the city library.

Most people would have said that serving as mayor wouldn't leave much room for a personal life, but Angie was very careful to squeeze the most mileage out of her workday. Over the past three years she had learned to stand on her own two feet. As a widow with two young daughters she'd had no other choice. From the time she had started working outside the home, she did her best to keep her career separate from her home life. Granted, there were a few times when she was up doing paperwork at midnight, long after Kim and Casey had been tucked into bed for the night. And occasionally her presence was required for an evening appearance, but she tried her best to keep them to a minimum, and for the most part she succeeded.

But this particular Friday was not one to be side-stepped, as she soon discovered.

It was just past one when Georgia opened the door and came in, carrying a cup of tea and a sandwich. Angie's assistant was in her forties and just this side of plump. The half lenses she wore would have given her a studious look if she didn't perpetually have them arched precariously on top of her head. They were rarely in place at the end of her nose where they should have been. Angie often thought with amusement that the glasses served a better purpose keeping Georgia's wiry brown hair off her forehead.

"Eat," the woman grunted in her familiar gritty voice. She set the plate on the desktop, then remained where she was, her arms crossed over her ample breasts, eyebrows raised threateningly.

Angie hid a smile and pushed aside the cumbersome budget printout she'd spent the morning poring over. The age difference between herself and Georgia wasn't all that much, yet the older woman treated her with a gruff but motherly concern.

As usual, Georgia's clothes were a mess. The sleeves of her blouse were rumpled from repeatedly being thrust above her elbows. There was a run in her nylons, and the toes of her shoes were scuffed and worn.

Angie loved her dearly. Despite her haphazard appearance, she was sharp as a tack. Managing the office and keeping track of all the mayoral concerns was no small task, but Georgia pulled it off without a hitch. In Angie's eyes she was invaluable. More, she was a friend.

When the last bite of sandwich had been eaten, the last drop of tea drained from the cup, Georgia's ominous expression softened. "That's better," she said briskly. In a rare moment of relaxation, Georgia sat down in the comfortable leather chair. "At least I don't have to worry about you eating tonight. Not with the spread they'll have at the Sheraton."

Angie was used to Georgia clucking over her like a mother hen. She'd even gotten rather good at tuning in what was important and tuning out what wasn't. "Now, Georgia," she began, "you know I always make sure the girls and I eat a good dinner—" Suddenly she stopped short as Georgia's words finally penetrated. "The Sheraton?" she echoed, then frowned. "What's going on at the Sheraton?"

Georgia's eyes contained a measure of surprise. Slipups by Angie were few and far between. "Don't tell me you forgot. There's a big bash tonight at the Sheraton. In honor of our new police chief."

This last piece of information was added with a sidelong glance at Angie. Though the public saw the image of a beautiful but successful and hardworking individual, Georgia knew the woman beneath the elegant exterior, the woman of integrity and very real emotions. Once, those feelings had been clearly visible. Now, though they were still there and thriving, they were much more insulated, far less exposed. Life had taught her well, Georgia sometimes reflected, a little too well.

The two women had been through a lot together. She'd seen Angie grow in strength, self-confidence and esteem. She had witnessed the private torment she had undergone when she lost her husband, a torment that Georgia somehow suspected wasn't solely due to grief.

But even Georgia didn't know everything about Angie.

She had started to work for Angie almost four years ago when Angie had joined the investment firm Georgia was with. Though she was in her late twenties, it was Angie's first real bout at tackling the career she'd spent years preparing for. Georgia had thought it was a shame that a woman with Angie's abilities had been sitting at home with a husband and two children since shortly after college. She and Angie had taken to each other like ivy to an oak tree, and Georgia sometimes reflected that perhaps it was because she could see a part of herself in Angie.

No two women could have been more different in physical appearance, but they were, in fact, alike in a number of other ways. Neither one found it very easy to display her inner feelings, though Georgia admitted her own were a little more volatile and vocal. And like Angie, she, too, had cherished hopes and dreams and aspirations. Unlike Angie, Georgia hadn't had the education to build those dreams, and as the years passed, they faded. These days they surfaced only seldom.

Neither one had the support of a husband. Georgia had never even *had* a husband. As for Angie...well, Georgia sometimes thought she'd have been better off without him.

Oh, Angie had never said so in so many words, but Georgia had known. She'd recognized the signs, but even if she hadn't, her intuition would have told her. There had been days when Angie's smile had been too bright, her laughter a little too forced. As her career had taken off and thrived, the situation at home had disintegrated.

It was, Georgia had long ago decided, the reason Angie was so determined to keep her professional life separate from her home life. Mayor Angela Hall was a far cry from mother Angie Hall. Even Georgia wondered how Angie managed to balance both career and home.

Secrets of the heart? Yes, Angie had a few. But Georgia, like Angie, had learned her own lesson from life and knew when not to pry.

After all this time she also knew what she could get away with and what she couldn't. She'd seen the furious glint in her boss's eyes after her meeting with the new police chief the other day. She'd also heard a few drawers being rattled and slammed. She'd held her peace until today, though.

"Don't see how you could forget about tonight," Georgia commented. Getting up, she pulled a cloth from Angie's bottom drawer and began to idly swipe at the desktop. "Not when it's in honor of our illustrious new police chief," she continued. A rare smile lit her face. "Now there's a man not many women could forget."

Angie darted her a sharp look. It wasn't so much a matter of forgetting as simply not wanting to remember. Instead of replying to Georgia's statement she asked, "Since when have you started taking inventory of every man who walks in and out of this office?"

"I'd do it a little more if they all looked like him," Georgia told her brashly. "To tell you the truth, if I were twenty years younger..."

Angie snorted. Matt Richardson might be passably good-looking...well, perhaps more than passable. There were probably some women who would find his roughly hewn features quite compelling. But Georgia? Angie had never known her assistant to look twice at any man since she'd known her.

"Who are you trying to kid!" she exclaimed. "Why, you're no more interested in having a man in your life than I am."

Georgia's grin faded, and her hand stilled for a second. "Maybe you should be. When you get to be my age, things start looking pretty lonely," she said slowly. She stood in front of Angie, her arms akimbo on her hips. "Maybe you should be," she repeated.

Angie said the first thing that popped into her mind. "If I did ever want a man in my life again, it wouldn't be Matthew Richardson!"

This time it was Georgia's turn to snort. "Who, then? That smart-aleck Todd Austin who's always sniffing around your heels?" The way she rolled her eyes heavenward expressed her feelings more clearly than words.

Angie sighed. Todd Austin was the Westridge city manager. She'd met him shortly before Evan's death when she had served as a member of the district school board, and it had been at Todd's urging that she had decided to run for city council a year later. Since that time Todd had accompanied her to various official functions, and she'd always appreciated that Todd respected her for her intellect. Of late, however, he'd made it clear he would like to deepen their relationship, a desire she didn't share.

Her body cramped from the long hours in her chair, she got up and stretched, then walked to the window nearby. She stood for a moment, looking down at the deep pink rhododendrons and leafy foliage that edged the sidewalk.

"Todd and I are friends," she said after a brief pause. Unfortunately, the same couldn't be said of Georgia and Todd. From the first they had taken to each other like oil and water. "No more, no less," she told her assistant firmly. "Just friends. And as for our new police chief, I'm much more interested in the way he does his job than the way he looks."

Georgia said nothing. Glancing over her shoulder, Angie saw that Georgia's thin lips were tightly compressed as she began collecting the cup and plate and loading them onto the small tray.

Angie turned around. "Are you coming tonight?" she asked softly.

"No."

She sighed. She hadn't expected Georgia to say yes. As the older woman always put it, she preferred to leave the "woman of the hour" and social duties totally in Angie's hands. Angie didn't really mind since Georgia was so dependable in other ways. But the last thing she wanted was a rift between herself and her assistant, no matter how small. Especially one sparked by the new chief of police.

"You're going to let me face the hungry masses all alone?" she chided gently.

This earned a reluctant smile. Georgia turned to face her, tray in hand. "You, Mayor Hall, can handle just about anything."

Angie laughed, relieved to note the familiar sparkle was back in Georgia's eyes. "With one hand tied behind my back?"

"Not quite," Georgia retorted airily. "Even you need a helping hand once in a while." Turning, she began to leave.

Angie couldn't resist calling after her, "What would I do without you, Georgia?"

She heard a crackling laugh from the outer office. "Starve," came the muffled response a second later. Angie smiled and shook her head. She could tell Georgia was once again buried in her work. Her assistant could talk all she wanted. She had no more room in her life for a man than Angie did.

CHAPTER THREE

GEORGIA WASN'T the only woman who had seen Angie through a drastic period of change in her life. Janice Crawford had known Angie for nearly eight years. When they had first become neighbors, Angie was in her sixth month of carrying Kim, and Janice had just delivered a daughter. Janice was the one Angie had always come to when she wanted to borrow a cup of sugar, or when she simply wanted to talk.

But Angie hadn't done much talking the last year of her marriage. And as Janice sometimes told her husband, Bill, there was much that Angie held inside—too much. The Angie the Crawfords had first met hadn't been terribly outgoing, but her warmth and enthusiasm showed in the sparkle of her eyes. The woman they knew now was the same and yet somehow different. This Angie was much more protective of herself and her children.

It was almost three o'clock when Janice walked into her kitchen to find Angie's slim figure just stepping through the back door.

"Hi," she greeted her. "Take off early?"

Angie nodded and stopped for a second. Closing her eyes, she took a deep breath.

Janice laughed as she saw her sag against the doorframe. "Tea?" she asked knowingly.

"Sounds great." Angie opened her eyes and smiled at Janice. She dropped her purse on the bench in the breakfast nook. "Just let me say hi to the girls and I'll be right back."

"They're in the yard," Janice called after her, running water into the teakettle. "Playing in the pool."

Angie smiled as she stepped into the enclosed backyard. The small plastic pool had been upended and leaned against a tree, and the children had turned their attention to spraying each other with the hose instead.

Four-year-old Casey was the first to spy her. "Mommy!" she

squealed and ran over. She threw her arms around her mother's legs. When Angie bent down to hug her, she planted a wet kiss on her cheek before running off once more. Kim did the same, as well as Janice's daughter, Nancy.

Sixteen-month-old Eric had apparently decided he'd had enough of the water and pandemonium. Eric had the same round face and dark hair as his mother. At the sight of a familiar, sympathetic adult face, his hands lifted in a pleading gesture, and he toddled toward her.

"What! Are they drowning you?" Angie laughed. Lifting him onto her hip, she turned to go back into the house.

"Oh, no!" Janice's eyes grew wide, and she rushed over to retrieve the baby. "He'll get you all wet!"

Chuckling, she gave him back into his mother's care, unmindful of the wet spots on the cap-sleeved dress she wore. "Wash-and-wear has been around for some time now. It *will* dry, you know."

After Janice had put Eric in dry clothes, she settled the baby in his high chair and sat down across from Angie. "All ready for the game tomorrow?" Janice laid a graham cracker in front of Eric, who wasted no time stuffing it into his mouth.

Angie nodded, a smile touching her lips. Kim and Nancy had both joined a girls' summer baseball league. Baseball was one of the few things that quiet Kim grew excited over, and it warmed Angie's heart to see her happy and eager again. Both she and Janice were coaches for the team, and like the girls they supervised, they brought a good deal of enthusiasm, if not know-how, to the team.

But she shook her head at the thought of what would come before tomorrow. "What I'm not ready for," she mused aloud, "is tonight."

Janice spooned a generous amount of sugar into her tea. "What's going on tonight?"

"There's a dinner for the new police chief," Angie told her. "I'd rather sit through a dozen chamber of commerce luncheons, but I'm afraid if I didn't go, Blair Andrews would have a field day with it." At Janice's inquiring look, she explained how she'd been put on the spot, both at the press conference earlier in the week and later that same day when Matthew Richardson discovered he hadn't been her primary choice.

When she had finished, Janice rested her chin on her hands, her brown eyes sparkling merrily. "Just think—a cop from Chi-

cago here in Westridge! It's like having Kojak in town or something!''

"Kojak!'' Against her will, Angie felt her lips twitch as she
thought of Matt Richardson's dark good looks. As for possessing
the suave, smooth manner of the TV detective...well, that remained to be seen. But Kojak had been a little on the tough side,
too, she recalled. Maybe it wasn't such an inappropriate comparison after all.

She turned her attention back to Janice. "Anyway," the other
woman was saying, "I can't believe you'd rather stay home than
go to a party—''

"Party?'' Angie recalled the brief encounter she'd had with
Matthew Richardson earlier in the week. If it wasn't for the fact
that dozens of other people would be present, she might even
consider the dinner something of an ordeal. "I can guarantee this
isn't going to be 'Some Enchanted Evening,''' she told Janice
with a slight smile. "All anyone does at these functions is talk
shop.''

"Then make something happen! With all the local big shots in
attendance, I can't think of a better place to snag a rich husband!''
The words were delivered with Janice's usual zeal. Her short dark
curls danced as she bobbed her head emphatically. Janice was
very open and honest, unafraid to show her feelings.

Angie's eyes grew wistful. She had once been like Janice,
though perhaps never quite so buoyant. But that had been a long
time ago.

"You know I don't need the money, Jan," she said with a
shake of her head. She had made some excellent investments
during the past few years, and she was thankful that she had no
financial worries. But there was a time, and not so long ago, when
money had been both a curse and a blessing. "As for finding a
husband—'' her laugh was forced ''—I'll leave that to someone
else.'' Rising, she busied herself with pouring another cup of tea.

She knew by the small silence that followed that she hadn't
fooled Janice. She heard the click of the high chair as Janice lifted
Eric out and set him on his feet. A second later she heard the
screen door slam behind Janice as she took the baby out to his
sister.

Angie was still standing motionless at the counter when Janice
returned. "Evan really did a number on you, didn't he?" she
asked softly.

Angie closed her eyes. Her ten-year marriage to Evan—one

that had started with endless days of sunshine—had ended in shadows. Through a will born of desperation and a very real need to save her own sanity, she had spent the first year after his death trying to forget. Even now, when she could remember without all the old bitterness and hurt creeping through her, the good memories were tainted by the bad. Evan had killed their love as surely as he himself was dead.

For just a moment the tea bag hung limply suspended from Angie's hand. It was the only sign that Janice's words had disturbed her as her mind traveled fleetingly backward.

It was four years earlier that Angie's life had undergone a radical change. She had exchanged her role as full-time wife and mother for that of a full-time career woman, a move that had initially been made solely for financial reasons.

Evan had been employed by one of the local banks since his graduation from college. Over the years he had worked his way up to vice president. But shortly after Casey had been born, the bank had been declared insolvent and he had lost his job. For a man who thrived on success, it had been a deep blow—a very deep blow indeed.

"We don't have any choice," she'd reasoned with Evan as she prepared to go on her own job search. "We have a family to feed and a mortgage to pay. Besides, you'll find something else in no time. It doesn't really matter which one of us brings home the paycheck, as long as it's there."

But it *had* mattered to Evan. It had mattered far too much as she'd discovered during the bleak months that followed.

"Evan resented me," she finally said to Janice. She didn't bother to turn around. "After he lost his job, he resented the fact that I supported the family, and he was jealous because I had no trouble landing that job as a financial advisor with Pacific Investments. And he was jealous because I made just as much money as he ever had." When she returned to the table, her face was as expressionless as her voice had been.

"He was wrong," Janice said bluntly. "He had no right to be jealous of your success. All the while he was climbing the ladder, you were there—behind him all the way."

Her words were no less than the truth. Angie had been proudly supportive of Evan. Busy with a home to run and a small child to raise, she really hadn't had time to regret not making use of her education. And Evan had really preferred that she stay at home.

"It certainly wasn't your fault that no one wanted to take a chance on him because the bank folded," Janice continued hotly. "If anyone—or anything—is to blame, it's the good old U.S. economy. With the decline in the housing industry and the cut-backs in the lumber industry, the whole state of Washington was hit hard. Bill was even laid off for a while."

Angie ran a finger around the rim of her cup. "At least before he was rehired, he had enough sense to keep looking for a job," she recalled quietly. "Evan just...gave up."

It was then that the situation at home had worsened. Evan had come from an old-fashioned family, and Angie had always se-cretly thought of his father as rather domineering. Very much a man's man, interested in hunting, fishing and sports of all kinds, Evan had found it frustrating that he was no longer the chief breadwinner. He had become jealous and resentful of her success, bitter at the world and everyone around him.

Especially Angie—Angie whom he had promised to love, honor and cherish. The fabric of their marriage had been in tatters. Evan had become angry and surly. Countless times Angie had returned home from a hectic day at the office, nearly dropping on her feet, to find the house a mess and Evan nursing a six-pack of beer, his eyes glued to the television set. She hadn't been able to fault his care of the children, but no matter what she did or didn't say, did or didn't do, Evan had sniped at her, yelled at her, screamed at her.

Angie's nerves had begun to fall apart with the strain she was under. She loved Evan, but she simply hadn't been able to stand the present situation any longer. "Evan, this can't go on," she had told him quietly one night after the girls had been tucked into bed.

Another argument had ensued. Angie had tried to reason with him, calm him. Too late she had realized the amount of liquor he had consumed. Then it happened.

He had been as shocked as she was by what he had done. "God, Angie," he'd cried hoarsely. "I didn't mean to hit you, I swear." They had wept in each other's arms then while he begged forgiveness.

She supposed she was lucky it had only happened twice...*twice.* Yet even if he had only struck her once, she couldn't have been more shattered.

She took a deep, cleansing breath, trying to control the sudden churning of her insides. Something of her thoughts must have shown in her face. Her eyes flickered to Janice, who watched her closely.

"I'm sorry, Angie," her neighbor said gently. "Maybe we shouldn't even be talking about Evan, especially when I know how bad things were for the two of you."

Bad? Angie fought to control a mocking laugh. That was far too mild a word to describe the hell Evan had put her through. Evan had hurt her so much, robbed her of her dignity, her sense of self-worth.

But it hadn't been just his physical abuse, the abuse she had hidden from everyone, including Janice. She'd been so eager, so vibrantly aware of her own sensuality when her marriage had begun. It hadn't ended that way—far from it. She shook off the shadow of memory and forced herself to concentrate on Janice's voice.

"There are a lot of nice men out there," she was saying.

"And I've done quite well without one for two years now." This time Angie couldn't prevent the faint note of bitterness that crept into her voice. "I'm happy with my life as it is, and I'd like to keep it that way."

They had been friends too long for Janice to take offense. And if it hadn't been for the durability of their friendship, she was aware she'd have been testing its limits with the line of her questioning. "You're old enough to know what you want, Angie," she said evenly. "But you have Kim and Casey to think about, as well."

Angie knew Janice was talking about the lack of a father figure in their lives. For a second she almost wished she could pretend she hadn't heard her. But she found her eyes drawn to the scene just outside the kitchen window.

Bill Crawford had just pulled into the driveway. A big, robust man with a thatch of reddish-gold hair, he worked as a purchasing agent at a nearby lumber mill. Apparently he had heard the commotion in the backyard. Nancy and Casey were laughing and giggling, huddling around his feet. As she watched, Eric toddled across the patio and launched himself at his father's legs.

The only one absent, as Angie had already known she would be, was Kim. Her eight-year-old body all arms and legs in her swimsuit, she had moved away to sit on the edge of the picnic table. She saw Bill smile and call out something to her, but Kim only nodded and drew her towel more tightly around her thin shoulders.

The child's shyness around men was something that hadn't appeared until after Evan's death. It bothered Angie more than she cared to admit. She supposed Janice was right: it was, in part, due to the lack of a male presence in the home. But there wasn't an easy solution.

She didn't say anything for the longest time. Then her gaze swung back to meet Janice's. "I know," she said quietly. "Casey was only two when Evan died, so she doesn't really remember him. But Kim...well, she's even shy with Bill and she's known him for years." She mulled over the implication of her words. "Can you imagine what she would do if I brought someone home and said 'Look, sweetie, here's your new daddy.' You know how she idolized Evan. I think she would resent any man who wasn't her father."

There was a sympathetic look in Janice's eyes as she nodded. Then she hesitated. "Kim and Casey aren't the only ones I'm concerned about." A frown appeared between her dark eyebrows. "What about you, Angie? I know how you value your career, but you have so much else to give. Children are fine, but sooner or later they leave the nest. I hate to think of you spending the rest of your life alone."

Angie injected a light tone into her voice. "You and Georgia must be in league together. She was telling me the same thing just this afternoon." At the concern she saw reflected in Janice's eyes, she found herself yielding. It was strictly for her friend's benefit, but she heard herself say, "Maybe someday, Jan. Maybe someday." *But not now,* she added silently. *And maybe not ever.*

JUST AROUND THE CORNER from the Crawfords was Angie's house. The neighborhood was an old one, though over the years the streets had been widened and sidewalks added. Dainty flowering plum trees bordered the walkway in the block where Angie lived, and in the next stately oak trees shielded the thoroughfare.

Her house was a rambling Victorian structure flanked by a wide veranda. A sun porch had been added shortly before she and Evan had purchased it, and while Evan had thought it made the house appear slightly unbalanced, Angie had thought it lent a certain charm.

"You look pretty, Mommy," a little voice piped.

"Thank you, sweetie, so do you." Angie turned to smile at the small figure perched on the side of the wide brass bed. Aside from the one blond pigtail that had escaped its confining band and the trail of spaghetti sauce at one corner of her mouth, Casey did indeed look very pretty in her pink gingham sundress, which was tied at each shoulder.

She frowned over at her youngest daughter. "Casey, didn't you wash your face after dinner?"

"Nope." Impish blue eyes sparkled.

"And you didn't brush your teeth, either, I suppose."

The child looked at her as if she'd never heard of a toothbrush. Angie sighed and pointed her in the direction of the bathroom. "Go, young lady. And make sure you remember to turn off the water after you rinse." Two weeks earlier she had walked into the bathroom to find it nearly flooded after Casey had been inside to wash and to brush her teeth. She'd left the facecloth in the sink, and it had blocked the drain.

Five minutes later, Angie had finally managed to shoo Casey in the right direction. She braided her hair into a sleek coronet atop her head, and after dusting a light coat of powder over her face, she stopped to give herself a brief but critical glance in the mirror mounted behind the door.

The dress she wore was a simple ivory sheath shot through with silver threads. Slim, tapered sleeves fell to just below her elbow. The design was simple, almost plain, but on Angie the effect was sheer elegance. A single strand of silver gleamed against her throat, and matching studs glittered at her ears. The jewelry and the silver-heeled shoes were the only concession to her sex. She was, after all, in the business of running a city and she had chosen the majority of her wardrobe to create an effect that was more businesslike than womanly. Yet even if she wasn't mayor, she wouldn't have been inclined to buy frilly, fancy clothes.

Satisfied with her appearance, she moved to pick up her purse from the top of the bureau. It was then that she noticed Kim, dressed in shorts and a tank top, hovering near the doorway. Her eldest had Evan's thick, chestnut hair and deep brown eyes, and Angie suspected she would be tall like him, as well.

"What's on your mind, hon?" Angie crossed the polished oak floor and pressed a brief kiss on her daughter's forehead.

Kim smiled up at her. "Mrs. Johnson's here—" The sound of a cupboard door slamming downstairs brought her up short. She jumped, and for an instant there was a faint look of alarm in her eyes.

Sudden noises always affected her like that. They had for quite some time now. Angie knew better than to make an issue of it, however. She knew from experience that Kim would only clam up and retreat into that somber mood that disturbed her mother so.

Instead, she shook her head. "Casey must be into the cookies again. Try to keep her out of them so Mrs. Johnson doesn't have to do too much cleaning up after her, okay?" Mrs. Johnson lived next door and stayed with the girls in the evening if Angie had to be away. She was a spry and active sixty-year-old, the type who was there with a cloth before a drop of water could ever hit the floor. She was wonderful with the girls, but Angie worried about Casey wearing her out.

Kim nodded obediently. One bare toe nudged a braided rug in an oddly uncertain gesture that tugged at Angie's heart. She sensed that Kim hadn't come solely to tell her Mrs. Johnson had arrived.

"All right, young lady, out with it," Angie said cheerfully. She pulled Kim over to the bed, then sat down beside her.

At Kim's silence she squeezed her daughter's shoulder reassuringly. "Hon, you can tell me anything." Angie lowered her head and added in a conspiratorial whisper, "Mommy doesn't bite like Spooky does." Spooky was the family cat, a silver tabby who was rather independent and aloof. Nonetheless, Kim and Casey adored her. When she was in the right mood, she didn't mind the girls playing with her. But when she wasn't, she didn't hesitate to let them know. And unlike other cats, instead of scratching she tried to bite.

Angie's words earned a tentative smile. Then wide brown eyes turned up to her. "Mommy, is Todd coming here to pick you up?"

Her anxious whisper wasn't lost on Angie. If Todd and Angie were going to the same social function, he often picked her up at home beforehand and drove her home afterward. Sometimes he stayed for coffee.

But the concern Angie had felt such a short time ago at Janice's surfaced once more. "No," she explained, "Todd's been on vacation all week." Knowing Kim's normal reaction to men, Angie really hadn't thought much of her behavior. But for the first time she wondered if the child hadn't been more withdrawn than usual around Todd. She almost asked her if she disliked him and why, but Kim's face had lost its worried expression.

Angie's eyes lingered speculatively on Kim as she moved from the bed. At the dressing table she picked up a bottle of perfume and shyly asked if she could use it.

"Of course you can," Angie replied readily.

When she left the house a short time later, however, she couldn't help but be reminded of the child Kim had once been—so lively and vivacious, much like Casey. But after Evan died, Kim had retreated into her own little world, a shadow of her former self. It was so bad for a time that Angie had considered taking her to a child psychologist. Then, little by little, Kim had begun to respond once again. But she wasn't the same child she'd been before Evan's death. Angie suspected much of it stemmed from the sense of loss she'd felt over losing her father. It saddened her that both of them, mother and daughter, carried scars because of Evan.

For a moment she almost hated her dead husband. Even from the grave he hadn't lost his ability to hurt her.

MATT STOOD in the shadows just outside the French doors that led to the terrace. There was a thoughtful air about him as he leaned one broad shoulder against the doorframe and gazed into the crowded banquet room.

He hated affairs like this; they triggered unwelcome memories of the endless parties Linda had always insisted he attend with her, parties filled with frivolous chatter and plastic people. Granted, this wasn't on the same grand scale and the people weren't all affluent Chicago blue bloods. But the fact remained: if he wasn't the guest of honor, he wouldn't have come tonight. He'd have much preferred to spend the evening lounging around at home, dressed in jeans and a sweatshirt and watching the late movie on TV, instead of being trussed up in a three-piece suit and pretending he was having a good time. And it was exactly what he intended to do as soon as he left.

But something—some*one*—was keeping him here. He had scarcely been able to take his eyes off her since she had first entered the room. The dress she wore highlighted her blond beauty but, if anything, made her appear even more aloof. He had no trouble picturing her driving up in her Mercedes and handing her keys to the parking valet without a word. No doubt she lived in an apartment, probably decorated in sterile whites and cool glass, something like the one he and Linda had shared for the three years they'd been married. God, how he'd hated coming home, feeling he couldn't even relax by putting his feet up on the ottoman for fear of getting it dirty.

Yet with her quiet elegance, the golden wreath of her hair and her slender gracefulness, he couldn't deny the sensual image Angela Hall projected. Nor could he repress the memory of his long-ago fascination for the ever-elusive Linda. Linda, who had promised everything…and given nothing. She had used her sensuality as a weapon, something to be given or withheld as the mood struck her.

Apparently he hadn't learned his lesson as well as he might have hoped. He couldn't deny that Angela Hall's icy demeanor both repelled and attracted him.

His mouth turned up in a self-deprecating smile. A know-it-all psychiatrist would probably say he was regressing to his childhood, always wanting what he couldn't have.

Just as he was about to step inside, he caught her movement in the crowd once more. In a minute he told himself. Just one more minute….

Again it struck him that, even while she was talking, laughing, the mayor maintained a certain distance, a cool detachment. Yet people liked and respected her, not only for her poise and polish but also for her accomplishments during her relatively short time in office. He'd learned that much in the week he'd been on the job. The thought was still with him as he watched a man come up to her and slip an arm around her shoulders. The gesture was friendly. There was nothing overly sexual about it. She was even smiling. Then gracefully, deftly, she slipped away and turned to someone else.

Matt's eyes narrowed. His mind sharpened. She was subtle about it, so subtle he doubted anyone else would have noticed. But it slowly dawned on Matt that this wasn't the first time tonight he'd seen it happen, and he could draw only one conclusion.

Angela Hall didn't like to be touched.

ANGIE SPENT an obligatory few minutes chatting with one of the county commissioners. She felt as if her lips would crack as she continued to smile and nod politely, but at this point his voice was a faint buzz in her head. Her feet hurt from the unaccustomed height of her heels, and she could feel a headache coming on. More than ever she wished she were home.

The commissioner finally wandered off, but Angie had no sooner turned than she saw Blair Andrews coming toward her.

Under any other circumstances, Angie wouldn't have minded butting horns with her, but right now she was simply too tired. She ducked for the nearest door—in this case, two—and breathed a heartfelt sigh of relief when, from the corner of her eye, she saw someone grab Blair's arm.

The doors led to a small, enclosed terrace. Angie stepped across the flagstoned surface to rest her hands against the railing of the balcony. Inhaling deeply, she filled her lungs with the cool evening air, and, unable to resist, she bent over to free her feet from their pinched confinement.

A low chuckle sounded behind her.

Angie whirled, startled by the unexpected sound. As an unfamiliar blush stained her cheeks, she was glad for the concealing cloak of darkness—especially when she saw that the voice belonged to Matthew Richardson.

Matt couldn't help it. His chuckle turned into a laugh at the sight of Mayor Angela Hall, flawlessly groomed as always and clutching a shoe in each hand.

Angie tried very hard to frown, but it was rather hard to maintain her dignity while she was standing barefoot. The humor of the situation suddenly struck her, and she gave in to a smile. "You're the guest of honor," she reprimanded lightly. "What are you doing hiding out here?"

"Getting a breath of fresh air?" he suggested.

It must have sounded like the feeble excuse it was. Her laughter came so readily and was so unlike the rest of her that Matt found himself studying her once more. There was both strength and softness in those fine-boned features, and he finally admitted to himself that there were some inconsistencies about this woman. And he couldn't have called himself a cop if he wasn't intrigued by the thought of investigating them further.

He also couldn't have called himself a man if he'd been totally unaware of exactly how lovely she really was. It both irritated and amused him that he found her desirable and alluring. To be singed by the flame once was excusable—twice was something only a fool would do. Apparently this was his day to make a fool of himself.

"To tell you the truth," he heard himself say, "I was just thinking I could use a cigarette. Unfortunately, I don't smoke."

A cigarette, not a lollipop? Angie couldn't quite hide her

amusement as she thought of Janice's comparison of this man to Kojak.

She also couldn't help thinking that he seemed a little more approachable tonight than on the previous occasions they'd met—the smile softened the blunt edges of his harsh masculinity. Before she had been distinctly on edge. Now she felt she could relax—almost. What was it Matt had said? Something about tonight being a stressful situation.

"I know the feeling," she returned softly. "Unfortunately, fading into the shadows isn't always possible."

"Or expected of the city's mayor," he remarked. There was a small silence before he added almost conversationally, "I suppose you'd rather be anywhere but here right now."

She felt an odd fluttering in her stomach as she watched him slip his hands into his trouser pockets. His hands were big, dark with a generous sprinkling of hair across the wide backs, the fingers long and lean. She shivered, unable to suppress an unwelcome memory of Evan's hands, warm and tender, hard and hurting.

Evan was the last person she wanted to think about now, or any other time for that matter. She forced her attention back to the present.

Moistening her lips, she took a deep breath. "If I say yes, will you believe I don't mean that personally?" She glanced up at him, wishing she could see his face a little better. "Unfortunately, I can't pretend I don't hear when duty calls." She sighed, then added, "But I'm really not very fond of get-togethers like this."

Surely she wasn't saying she was a homebody. Matt tried not to look surprised. It suddenly occurred to him that he'd thought all along that she would be in her element at something like this, just like Linda. But for some reason he was reluctant to call her a social butterfly, either.

"At last, a kindred spirit." His tone was teasing, but his mind had backtracked to the moment before. For just an instant there had been something vulnerable in her expression. But vulnerability was a facet he found difficult to reconcile with his impression of her as diamond hard.

His eyes dropped to the shoes that still dangled from her hands. "You look like Cinderella fleeing the ball," he observed.

She smiled, a rather secretive smile, Matt decided. He watched as she moved a few steps to sink into a wrought-iron chair, putting her high heels beneath it. Her feet, he noticed, were exactly like the rest of her—small, slender, dainty.

"More like Cinderella fleeing the wicked stepmother," she corrected with a thread of amusement in her voice. Tipping her head to one side, she looked up at him. She wasn't really sure why she felt more at ease with him, but the feeling was infinitely better than crossing swords with this man. She only hoped she wasn't about to shatter the truce.

"Do you remember the reporter from the press conference on Monday?" she asked. "The one who—" She paused, suddenly not quite sure how to phrase the question.

His eyes glinted. "Oh, yes. The one who enlightened me as to my—"

"That's the one," she broke in hastily. "Her name is Blair Andrews."

Matt nodded. "Don't tell me—you're not winning any popularity polls where she's concerned."

Angie shook her head. "That obvious, hmm?" She watched as he shrugged, then angled a chair next to hers and sat down. His posture seemed inviting, so she went on. "Actually, Blair's uncle was the last mayor. He was my opponent."

"And she's carrying a grudge because he wasn't reelected?" He hoped he didn't sound uninterested. But it was hard to pretend an absorption in her words when all he could really think of was how pretty she looked with the moonlight turning that golden halo of hair into silken threads of silver. Even those incredibly blue eyes of hers were flecked with silver.

Pretty? God, that didn't even begin to describe her. Gorgeous. She was absolutely gorgeous.

"Are you married?" He didn't recognize the voice as his until it was too late. Hell! Matt thought with annoyance. It sounded as if he were making a pass—and he wasn't. At least he didn't think he was. Not for an angelic-looking temptress with a heart of ice.

"I—" The question startled her. Angie wasn't quite sure why. Maybe it was because she didn't like divulging personal details to someone who was, after all, a stranger. But she suspected it had something to do with the rather intent expression in those intense eyes that swept over her body. It was a look that was much too thorough for her peace of mind—and much too male.

Her back was suddenly ramrod stiff in the chair. "That really isn't any of your business," she coolly informed him.

That icy tone was one he was already very familiar with. It

riled his defenses and made him madder than hell. But it also made him want to feel—just once—that he had gotten the long end of the stick.

"Are you?" he asked again.

She glared at him.

Matt grinned in satisfaction.

When she continued to stare at him in tight-lipped silence, he slipped his hands into his pockets. "I'm not," he offered casually. "At least not anymore."

"Do I dare ask why?" Her voice was slightly mocking. "A case of 'marry in haste and repent at leisure' perhaps?"

That was indeed a rather accurate description of Linda's actions when their marriage had ended nearly six years ago, but Matt didn't say so. Instead, he crossed his long legs, then turned so that their knees brushed.

Angie stiffened. This man had an amazing knack for putting her on the defensive. While it was a position she was used to assuming, somehow he made her feel as if she were floundering in deep, unknown waters. She knew she should get up and leave. Now. This instant. The whole conversation was absolutely ridiculous! But when a warm, faintly rough fingertip reached out to touch one of her hands where it lay curled around the thin arm of the chair, she felt a curiously debilitating sense of weakness wash over her. All she could do was focus on that long finger as it traced a random pattern over the back of her hand.

"Angela—" his voice was soft as silk and just as smooth "—you don't mind if I call you that, do you? Or do you prefer Angie?"

She flushed uncomfortably. "Angie," she heard herself confirm in a low voice.

"I was just wondering...is there anything in the city charter that forbids the mayor from fraternizing with the hired help?"

His hand still caressed her own. Caress. Why was she thinking of it like that? she wondered wildly. Even in the muted light she could see that the contrast between his dark skin and her own honey coloring was startling. Her eyes moved slightly to take in the figure next to her, but the sight that she met didn't ease the tight knot of awareness in her chest. The knee nudging her own was connected to a long, tautly muscled thigh. She felt both hot and cold, but she couldn't stop her gaze from journeying slowly upward. His hips were lean and trim; his jacket parted to reveal a broad expanse of chest.

It was almost a shock to realize that this man—infuriating as he was—touched an awareness inside her that she hadn't felt in a long, long time. She hadn't looked at a man—really looked at a man—since before her marriage. Certainly not after.

She snatched her hand from his and stood up abruptly. "Chief Richardson—" she began.

"Matt. Please call me Matt." He flashed an engaging grin. "Try to forget, just once, our differing stations in life."

He was baiting her. She knew it and she also knew she shouldn't let it disturb her. At the same instant she recalled exactly how thorough her own inspection of his blatant masculinity had been. And oddly, that thought angered her more than any of his roundabout suggestiveness.

"Chief Richardson," she stated with a calm she definitely didn't feel, "let me make one thing perfectly clear. *You* may be free, but *I'm* not interested." With that she turned on her heel and left him sitting in the dark.

Matt watched as she stalked inside the hotel, her head held regally high. It occurred to him then that he'd been trying to get more than just a cool, passive response from her—a response of any other kind would suffice. Experience had taught him to be wary of her type, but again he found himself admitting she was one damn attractive woman. And he couldn't deny that she made him feel more alive than he'd felt in years.

Looks like you got what you wanted, old man, he thought with a smile. *She's just as human as you are.*

He got to his feet, and as he glanced idly down, his smile was transformed into a full-blown laugh.

Cinderella had left her slippers.

CHAPTER FOUR

MATT FOUND he was still smiling when he stepped onto the porch of a white two-story house a short time later, Angie's shoes tucked under one arm. As his eyes traveled quickly around the darkened property, he experienced a swell of pride. Through the darkness he could just make out the shape of the huge rhododendrons that bordered the house on all sides. When Matt had bought the house a month earlier, he'd been totally entranced with the fragile pink blossoms that displayed frilly ruffles and pale blushes against a background of leathery green leaves. Coming from a man like himself, he'd found his reaction rather amusing, but it hadn't stopped him from vowing to plant a vegetable garden—for the first time in his life.

Inside the living room, sparsely but comfortably furnished, he eased himself into a recliner in front of the fireplace, not bothering to switch on a light. Stretching his long legs out in front of him, it suddenly occurred to him that he was encountering quite a few "firsts."

Buying this house had been a first, for instance. The first fifteen years of his life had been spent cooped up with his mother and his brother in a run-down apartment that wasn't much bigger than this room. Life with Linda had certainly been easier; although the financial rewards of his job had offered security and stability, living fifty floors up in the sterile surroundings she'd called home had been stifling. He had been on a perpetual merry-go-round, and the hell of it was he hadn't even realized it. Only lately had he finally found the way to stop and let himself off.

He wasn't a kid with a whole lifetime of dreams stretching before him. But for the first time in longer than he could remember, he felt free, unfettered by demands on his time, on his person.

And what he really craved, what he had longed for all his life, was the security of knowing that he belonged, that he was needed by someone.

Matt's smile retained just a touch of cynicism. For a man who'd been something of a loner since he was a child, it was an odd thing to want out of life. After all the years of emptiness and loneliness, of telling himself that it didn't really matter, was he going all soft and sentimental? Maybe. Yet, he sensed that it was all a part of the change he was going through.

It was odd. Very odd. Here he was, sitting in a darkened room steeped in solitude, but he didn't feel nearly as alone as he had all those years in Chicago.

Yes, he was glad he'd made the move here to Washington. And as his eyes lit on the pair of heels he'd dropped on the couch, he found himself admitting that Angie Hall was only one of the reasons.

But certainly not the least.

FILMY STREAMERS OF LIGHT found their way into Angie's bedroom the next morning, first in a pale gray haze that chased away the purple shadows of dawn, then in errant shafts of gold that filled the room with brightness.

Angie awoke slowly, savoring the sensation of waking on her own instead of to the insistent blare of the clock radio. Sleeping in an hour late on weekends was a luxury she'd indulged in only over the past year or so. The girls had been too young to supervise themselves before that time, but now Kim was usually able to entertain Casey by switching on Saturday morning cartoons. When Evan was alive, he had been the one allowed to sleep in.

Evan. Angie closed her eyes and steeled herself against an unwelcome surge of emotion. Then, realizing the futility of doing battle with the ghosts of her past, she took a deep breath and let the feelings sweep over her, wondering hopelessly if she could ever make peace with herself...and with him.

After all this time she still felt so many things when she thought of Evan. Pain. Despair. Bitterness. But love? She had entered their marriage with her heart so full of happiness she thought it would burst. At the last the fabric of their love had been so torn and tattered that not even the slightest thread of hope remained. No, there was no love left in her heart for Evan, just as there had been no tears shed when she had learned of his death.

Then there had been only a deep-seated sense of relief that at least she had been spared his anger. Evan had died not knowing that she intended to leave him—for good. And Angie still struggled with a guilt-ridden conscience. Not because she'd planned to divorce him but because she felt such relief that she hadn't been forced to tell him.

With a heavy sigh she rolled over, and it was then that last night's episode with Matt Richardson flooded her consciousness. His rugged face appeared before her, and she experienced a tingly sensation, not pleasant but not entirely unpleasant, either.

The smile that emerged surprised her. She had encountered Chuck Harris, the city's personnel director, the minute she'd marched back into the banquet room. She'd completely forgotten her shoeless state; Chuck's aghast expression had served as a rude reminder. With the aplomb that had served her so well, she'd directed a beaming smile at him but made haste to the nearest exit, thankfully only a few steps away.

Chuckling, she started to throw off the covers, then became aware of Kim snuggled into the space next to her. A warm feeling of pride washed over her but mingled with it was a prickly sense of unease. It wasn't unusual for Kim to steal into bed with her mother at some point during the night. It happened perhaps once a month. Angie quietly studied the peacefully sleeping child. Kim had often been plagued by nightmares following Evan's death, but they had tapered off during the past year. Had they started once more?

Kim stirred beneath her mother's thoughtful gaze. Then, opening her big brown eyes, she rubbed them sleepily.

"Hi, precious." Tenderly she brushed a tumbled curl from Kim's flushed cheek. "Have another bad dream?" Deliberately Angie tried not to sound too worried.

Kim shook her head.

"Was your sister kicking you again?" Angie forced a teasing note into her voice.

Again the little girl shook her head. "I didn't hear you come home last night," she finally admitted in a small voice. "I worry about you when you're late."

Angie's smile was bittersweet. Kim's concern for her was both touching and pathetic. "I wasn't late, sweetheart," she told her gently. "You and Casey were both asleep when I got home, and I did come in and kiss you good-night."

It saddened her that, for Kim, darkness brought with it the shadow of fear. For Angie, the fear had ended, but her daughter's had only begun. She supposed Kim's anxiety stemmed from the fear of finding herself alone. After all, she had already lost one parent, and it was understandable that she would be afraid of losing the other. It was for that reason that Angie had decided to put Kim and Casey in the same bed.

As if on cue, Casey came racing into the room, her eyes bright and sparkling as though she'd been up and around for hours. "Are you awake, Mommy? I'm hungry and Kim's not downstairs."

Angie felt her spirits rise. "That's because she's right here with me." Reaching out, she lifted her youngest onto the bed and proceeded to tickle both her and her sister until they shrieked with laughter.

"I'm hungry, Mom," Casey piped again when she slid off the bed a few minutes later. "Will you fix breakfast?"

"Sure, hon." Angie reached for the robe draped over the end of the bed and slipped into it. "What would you like?"

"Ice cream!" Casey immediately chortled.

Angie laughed and began to straighten the pale buttercup-printed comforter. "When was the last time you had ice cream for breakfast?" When the two girls exchanged conspiratorial glances, she groaned. "Now I know why you don't mind if I sleep late on Saturday!"

They settled for French toast dripping with syrup, then Angie spent the remainder of the morning doing household chores.

"Mommy!" Kim wore a frantic look as she ran into the dining room shortly after lunch. "I can't find my jersey and my shorts!"

Hiding a smile, Angie wordlessly handed her a neatly folded blue-and-white jersey and matching blue shorts from the pile of laundry she'd been folding. Kim's game didn't start until two-thirty, so they wouldn't be leaving until shortly before two, but Kim started getting anxious several hours ahead of time.

Ten minutes later she ran back into the room. "Mom, you're not even dressed yet!" she cried distressfully.

Angie shook her head, knowing that Kim wouldn't relax until she'd done so. "I'm going, I'm going," she told the child good-naturedly, abandoning the remainder of the laundry still lying in a heap on the dining room table.

"Can I call Nancy and see if they're ready?" Kim's voice followed her as she headed for the stairs.

Angie nodded. A few minutes later she returned downstairs. The doorbell sounded as her foot hit the last step. A little surprised that the Crawfords had managed to herd themselves together already, Angie grabbed her cap and threw open the front door.

"How on earth did you get here so soon—" she began laughingly.

Her voice dropped off abruptly. A pair of startled gray eyes mirrored her own shock at finding Matt Richardson on her doorstep.

For his part, Matt couldn't have been more pleased. A little stunned, perhaps, at finding this bewitching, ponytailed creature standing before him instead of the polished sophisticate he'd seen thus far. But, oh, yes, most definitely pleased. His gaze traveled appreciatively over slim, bare legs revealed by a pair of brief nylon shorts all the way to the long flaxen hair caught in a ponytail at the back of her head. It didn't stop until it reached the baseball cap she'd jammed on her head at the last second.

"Trying to throw me a curve ball again, aren't you?"

Very funny, Angie thought. Aware of the direction his eyes had taken, she reached up and removed the baseball cap, dropping it on the small table near the door. She could see that he was trying very hard not to smile, but somehow she wasn't as amused by his unexpected appearance as she'd been last night at the hotel. Nevertheless, she couldn't quite control the involuntary quickening of her heartbeat. Dressed casually in jeans and a blue denim shirt, he seemed less harsh and even more overwhelmingly masculine.

"Chief Richardson. What brings you here?" She strived for a formal note, for some reason needing to place that barrier, no matter how small or inconsequential, between them. Exactly why she felt that way she wasn't certain.

"The name is Matt, Angie. I thought we settled that last night." For all of his soft-spoken charm, there was a touch of insistence in his voice. "And speaking of last night—" he held up a pair of silver-heeled shoes and smiled "—Prince Charming to the rescue."

Angie felt a rush of betraying color warm her cheeks. Silently she took the shoes from him and turned away, hoping he didn't see it. The less said about last night, on *all* counts, the better. She didn't realize he had followed her inside the house until the door closed gently behind him.

"Coach?" Matt was referring to the white lettering emblazoned on the back of her royal-blue jersey. A half smile lifted his mouth as his inquisitive eyes flitted to her face. "You coach a baseball team?"

Hearing voices in the hallway, Kim and Casey came in to investigate. Angie placed an arm around both youngsters and drew them to her side. "These are my daughters, Kim and Casey," she told him coolly. "It's Kim's team that I help coach."

Daughters. Matt hadn't expected one, and certainly not two. Angie Hall was full of contradictions, he reminded himself dryly. Mayor of Westridge. Baseball coach. Mother of two. And what had happened to her husband? Had she, like Linda, eventually concluded that her husband wasn't good enough for her?

His mouth turned down for just an instant before he noticed the youngest child had turned bright eyes up to his. "Who're you?" she asked with more frankness than politeness. Unlike Kim, Casey wasn't the least bit cautious with strangers, even men.

"I'm Matt." He dropped down to one knee so that he was on the same level as the little girl. Even then she had to tilt her head to look at him. "Are you Kim?" he asked.

Blond pigtails shook furiously. "I'm Casey. That's Kim!" A chubby finger pointed at her sister, still standing at her mother's side.

"Ah. The baseball player." Matt turned his head to smile at Kim, who stared back at him warily and nudged closer to Angie's bare legs. Like mother, like daughter, he couldn't help thinking.

"Are you one of Mommy's boyfriends? Like Todd?" Casey blurted.

Boyfriends? Matt immediately recalled his observation that cool, aloof Angie didn't like to be touched. Some detective, he thought wryly. And who the hell was Todd?

"Todd isn't Mommy's boyfriend!" Kim stepped forward and faced her sister. Her small chin jutted forward, and her fists were balled at her sides.

Casey suddenly looked equally fierce. "Then why does she go to parties with him?"

"She didn't go with him last night, and when she does, it's only because he works with her! Todd is just...just a friend!"

And that was that, Matt decided wryly. So Todd was another devoted fan of Mayor Angie Hall. Somehow it would have been slightly more reassuring, and convincing, if it had come from Angie. But it was understandable, really. In the short time he'd known her, and especially the past twenty-four hours, he'd thought of her as a woman—a very desirable woman—far more than he'd thought of her as his boss.

His attention returned to the two angelic-looking cherubs still determined to butt heads. He found their mother had grasped each of them by a shoulder and stood between them.

"That's enough, both of you!" she said sharply. "And as I've told you before, Todd *is* just a friend." She addressed herself to both children.

Casey tipped her head to the side. "What about Matt?" she insisted once more. "Is he your friend?"

"Yes." Angie's tone was short. "Now why don't you two check to see that Spooky has food and water?" She watched as Casey ran from the room. Kim followed more slowly behind her.

Matt whistled softly when she turned to him again. "It's nice to see I've moved up in the world," he ventured teasingly. "Do I dare ask who Spooky is? Not, I presume, a friend?"

The flicker of amusement in his eyes, his easy manner with the girls...Angie couldn't help it. She felt her defenses slip a notch. The way he'd dropped to talk to Casey on her own level especially impressed her.

Her smile lit up her entire face, making her look open and unreserved. Matt found himself even more drawn to this Angie than the other he'd glimpsed all week long.

"Spooky is our cat," she explained. Then she seemed to hesitate. "Look, I apologize for the girls."

"Don't bother." He shrugged. "Kids will be kids. Besides, I think it bothered you a lot more than it did me."

Her laugh was a little nervous. Matt might have found it amusing, but she was still rather embarrassed.

Matt was too busy taking in his surroundings to really notice, though. He'd been a little disconcerted when he'd parked his car in front of the rambling Victorian house, so much so that he'd double-checked the address he'd scribbled down from the phone book.

But, as he was beginning to learn, nothing about Angie Hall fit the mold. Where were the sterile whites and the cold reflection of glass he'd convinced himself he would find? From the high-ceilinged entry, he glimpsed an old-fashioned but functional kitchen with touches of red brick. A wide arched doorway led into the living room, and he glanced inside. The room was filled with cherrywood antiques that he suspected had cost a pretty penny. Nonetheless, the pale yellow sprigged wallpaper, the warm, polished glow of wood and, particularly, the collection of dolls and doll clothes strewn across the sofa lent a warmth and coziness that he found tremendously appealing.

This was a home, a *real* home. Nothing at all like the museum he and Linda had occupied.

"This is a nice place," he commented, then found himself admitting, "Somehow I had you pegged as a cliff dweller."

Angie looked blank. "I beg your pardon?"

"I thought you'd live in an apartment building." His rueful smile was directed at himself. "You...well, to tell you the truth, you look like the high-rise type."

Angie raised her eyebrows and made a quick inspection of herself. "Really?" she asked dryly.

"Let me rephrase that. You *looked* like the high-rise type."

"In case you hadn't noticed, Westridge doesn't have any high rises." She smiled again, a slow, sweet smile that had Matt holding his breath and wishing he'd met her fifteen years ago. "Unless you count the *Bulletin* building," she added. "It's eight stories high."

Who the hell was Todd? he wondered again. And what, *really*, was he to her?

Whatever Matt had been about to say never materialized. There was a knock at the front door. Angie went to open it, and Matt heard a cheery "Hello, there! Sorry we took so long, but I had to change Eric at the last minute."

A petite brunette with a baby balanced on one hip filed inside, followed by a young girl wearing the same uniform as her mother, Angie and her daughters. A friendly-looking man brought up the rear as Angie quickly made the necessary introductions.

The baby was placed on his feet and immediately disappeared after Nancy, who had run off, Matt presumed, to find Angie's daughters.

"So you're our big-time police chief from Chicago." Janice Crawford turned to Matt, her dark eyes shining. "Do you like lollipops?" At his quizzical look she laughed and eyed Angie, who smiled weakly. "Never mind. It's just a joke." She hooked her arm through her husband's.

Bill picked up where she left off. "How do you like Westridge so far?" he asked. "Quite a change from Chicago, I'll bet."

It was Matt's turn to send a sidelong glance at Angie. "The more I see, the more I like," he murmured.

Angie wasn't quite sure how to take the remark, and judging from the unmistakable male gleam in his eyes, she wasn't sure she wanted to know. Now that he had done his duty and delivered her shoes, she had yet to figure out why he was staying. Checking her watch, she said apologetically, "I hate to cut this short, but I'm afraid Janice and I and the girls have a date at the baseball park." She paused, hoping Matt would pick up the hint and bow out gracefully.

Janice didn't even give him a chance. "Say, how would you like to come along?" She pretended not to see when a wide-eyed Angie sent her a warning look. "Bill gets a big kick out of watching the games, and you might, too."

Angie's heart sank when Matt seemed to consider the idea. Having him stop by for a few short minutes was one thing, but having him tag along to the girls' game was quite another. She knew full well what Janice was up to, and she also had the sneaking suspicion that Matt Richardson didn't mind in the least.

She quickly took advantage of the momentary lull. "Oh, I'm sure he has plenty of other things to do on a Saturday afternoon. Don't you, Matt?"

His eyes conveyed a rather wicked satisfaction as she finally called him by the abbreviated version of his name. She knew she was doomed the minute she saw it. "As a matter of fact, I can't think of a reason *not* to come."

Except one—Angie didn't really want him along. There was no doubt in his mind that what he was about to do wouldn't exactly endear him to her, but at the moment Matt wasn't feeling very sensible. Not sensible at all.

Janice positively beamed. "Great!" she said with her usual vibrancy. She called the other children. When they were all clustered around her, she lifted a finger and counted heads. "There's eight of us. Too many to fit in our car, even though it's a station wagon. Especially with the police chief along." She added coyly, "I seem to remember something about a law against driving while encumbered."

"I don't mind driving," he said easily. "As long as someone points me in the right direction."

"Angie can go with you, then," Janice said breezily. She thrust the baby into Bill's arms and quickly herded the other children out the front door, flashing a brief glance at Matt. "See you at the park!" she called over her shoulder.

Seeing the look Janice gave Matt, Angie muttered something under her breath. It was all she had time for before she was left alone with him.

Matt didn't have to hear what she was mumbling to know it

wasn't anything complimentary, and he couldn't hold back a grin at Angie's condemning stare.

"I plead not guilty." He held up both hands in a conciliatory gesture. "If Janice hadn't asked me along, I wouldn't be going. Although I'll admit it might have been nicer if *you* had asked me."

Angie said nothing. She stared at him for a moment longer, then shook her head with a resigned sigh.

Matt laughed. Reaching out, he retrieved the baseball cap she'd dropped on the table near the door. "Smile, Angie," he told her, dropping the cap on her head. "It's the neighborly thing to do."

CHAPTER FIVE

THE NEIGHBORLY THING to do.... It was a thought Angie tried to keep in mind during the drive to the baseball field in Matt's BMW. Matt Richardson was, after all, a stranger in town.

Which somehow brought to mind his teasing gibe last night that they were kindred spirits. The thought was oddly disconcerting, yet she found herself wondering if it was true. She'd always considered herself quiet but intense. And Matt? He struck her as a man who knew exactly what he wanted. A man who was somewhat of a loner, someone who blended in with the crowd around him and yet was different, separate.

The need for human comfort and warmth was a basic one, one that went hand in hand with trust, and Angie was not yet ready to trust again. She preferred to stand alone—proud but alone. It was safer, if not easier.

Matt was only barely cognizant of the lazy charm of the broad, tree-lined streets, the scent of freshly mowed grass drifting in through the open window. His eyes shifted away from the street toward the woman who sat on the other side of the car. He wondered at her thoughts as she stared silently out the window.

He felt like an intruder as he casually commented, "Your friends seem nice. Have you known them long?"

Angie turned her head slightly to look at him. "About eight years. Ever since we moved into the neighborhood from across town."

His mind zeroed in on her use of the word "we." Did she mean she and her daughters? Or she and her ex-husband? He had a sudden urgent compulsion to know everything about her. His instinct told him she wouldn't welcome an inquisition into her background. Angie Hall was one cautious woman, and he realized at the same moment that it was altogether possible that what he'd perceived as icy distance was no more than cautious restraint.

He settled for a gentle probing. "So you're a local, then?"

A faint smile curved her lips as she nodded. "Born, raised and educated in Westridge—from kindergarten to college."

"College?" He shook his head. "Don't tell me. Political science major, right?"

"Wrong." She laughed. It was a tentative sound but a laugh nonetheless. "Economics. I worked as a financial planner a few years ago," she found herself confessing. "And believe it or not, all in Westridge."

"I see." Matt chuckled. "No dreams of seeing the world and setting it on its ear after graduation?"

Her smile faded. She'd had the world at her fingertips already—or so she thought. What need had there been to search for more? "No," she answered quickly. "I...got married." She focused on her hands for a moment as her mind traveled fleetingly backward.

She and Evan had met on a warm, brilliant summer day much like today. Angie's studies had been too important for her to devote much time to the social aspects of college life. But Evan had changed that. He was a very masculine and attractive man, intelligent with a smooth, polished manner. He had given her glorious sun-filled days of laughter, moonlit nights of loving. It had been an irresistible combination. Evan was a man who had known what he wanted, and what he had wanted was Angie. They had married during their last year in college.

There was a hint of wistfulness in the soft lines of her face, a silent wish for what might have been. But her eyes were dark with sorrow. Life had been so full then, so promising. She had had everything in the world to look forward to. Her career, her future with the man she loved, the joys of motherhood. She felt a dull, familiar ache. How had it all gotten so...so twisted?

"Angie?"

With a start she realized Matt was speaking to her, and she snapped back to the present. "Yes?"

He smiled crookedly, and she noticed he had pulled over to the curb. "I lost Bill at that last turn. Where do we go from here?"

Angie forced a laugh. "You'd better be careful, Chief. We can't let it be known that the chief of police hasn't mastered the city's geography yet."

His eyes crinkled at the corners. For an instant, just for an instant, Angie let herself appreciate the genuine warmth she saw reflected there. "Offering to help me with my homework?" he asked. His smile widened when she shook her head and hastily averted her eyes. Matt made her feel nervous—damn nervous.

"Never mind," she muttered. "I'm sure it'll come in time."

In time. It would indeed, Matt thought as he listened to her voice guide him the rest of the way to the ballpark. He hadn't missed the half-wistful, half-sad expression on her face the moment before. In time he would know all of her, all that had shaped her into the complex woman she was. The resolution, as well as the strength of the conviction with which he made it, surprised him. Was it because he needed a friend?

He *did* want Angie Hall as a friend. But he also wanted more from her. He was aware that it wasn't just desire for an attractive woman that beckoned him. Why, Matt couldn't have said. He knew only that he felt it very strongly, and he was a man used to trusting his own feelings, his instincts. So many times they were all he had to rely on.

Most of the youngsters had already assembled at the park when they arrived. With Kim and Nancy in tow, Angie and Janice headed toward the rest of the team.

There was a small set of bleachers behind the first and third baselines, and it was there that Bill and Matt directed their steps. Bill carried the baby, and Matt was a little surprised when Casey skipped readily along beside him.

"Wait till you see these girls play," Bill said with a grin. "Funniest thing you've ever seen in your life. Nancy plays because Kim does, and those two are thicker than thieves. But Kim...well, Kim's pretty good."

Matt's eyes squinted thoughtfully against the bright glare of the afternoon sun, watching the pigtailed, ponytailed crew take their positions on the field. He'd been a baseball fan for as long as he could remember, and as always he found it hard not to get involved in the game. He bounded to his feet more than once, startling Casey the first time, but then she giggled when he shot a sheepish grin down at her. He groaned, he cheered, but as the game wore on, he discovered Bill was right. He found it harder and harder to contain his laughter.

In the batter's box one young girl continually swung her bat after the softball had been caught snugly in the catcher's mitt and tossed back to the pitcher's mound. Another chased a base hit halfway around the outfield before she finally scooped it up in her hands, only to drop it at least three times before she sent a determined lob that landed no more than three feet away.

Bill was also right about Kim. She hit a double and a home run, and made several good fielding plays at second base. As young as she was, she handled both ball and bat with a deftness that surprised Matt. After the game he went up to her.

"Good game, Kim," he congratulated her. Tilting his head, he peered at the number emblazoned on the royal-blue jersey. "Fourteen, huh? Just like Ernie Banks."

He'd been about to lay a hand on her shoulder, but the sudden stiffness in her small body stopped him. He smiled encouragingly instead. "Do you know who Ernie Banks is?"

She shook her head. The movement was barely perceptible.

"He played for the Chicago Cubs when I was, oh, not much older than you." He stopped, hoping she would say something. Instead, she just stared up at him, her hands still clutching her baseball glove. Something about her reticence reminded him of Angie, but at least she hadn't shied away from him as she had with another father who came up and clapped her on the shoulder.

"He was quite a home-run hitter, Ernie was." His smile widened. "Just like you."

A spark blazed in the wide brown eyes that stared up at him before a hint of wariness replaced it. "I better go back to my mom," she hedged, then ran off to where Angie was still surrounded by parents and children.

Angie had watched the incident from a distance. Kim looking a man straight in the eye was rare; in fact, she couldn't remember the last time it had happened. Usually she hung her head shyly. It surprised her that the child hadn't flown away like a trapped bird that had been set free. She was pleased at Kim's response, small though it was, yet it vaguely disturbed her that it had happened with Matt Richardson.

It wasn't like her to be so petty, and it occurred to her that she was trying very hard *not* to like Matt. She wasn't, she decided, being fair. She owed him a chance, that much at least. *Just don't let him get too close.*

"So what'd you think of our game?" Janice's cheerful voice came to her ears. Angie saw that Matt had walked up beside her, and it was him that Janice addressed. Most of the other parents and children had dispersed to their cars. The dusty field was almost deserted.

Matt raised his eyebrows, as if considering. "It was quite an experience," he finally told her smoothly. "One I'm sure I won't soon forget."

"A guy with tact!" Janice exclaimed. "All I ever hear from Bill is that the two of us should have been cheerleaders instead of coaches." She nudged Angie playfully. "Where'd you ever find this guy?"

It was on the tip of her tongue to retort that she hadn't found him at all; rather, it was the other way around. Only the glimmer of amusement in Matt's eyes stopped her. It irritated her that Janice seemed so intent on pairing her with Matt.

And Matt certainly wasn't helping matters any, she reiterated darkly an hour later. It had been his suggestion that all of them go for pizza afterward, and Janice and Bill had enthusiastically agreed.

The parlor, decorated in a Gay Nineties motif, was alive with the sounds of laughter and music from a player piano in the corner. Matt seemed perfectly at home with her friends, and both Janice and Bill were all ears as he talked about his days on the Chicago police force.

"What's the best excuse anyone ever gave you for speeding?" Bill asked.

Matt thought for a moment, then smiled. "A woman once told me she was in a hurry to get home so the ice cream she'd just bought wouldn't melt."

"Sounds good to me." Janice's eyes gleamed. "Did it work?"

A bushy eyebrow lifted. "Are you kidding? It was January, and the temperature had to be at least fifteen degrees below zero!"

Janice looked so forlorn that Angie hid a smile in her napkin. Ice cream was one of Janice's weaknesses. She was one of those people who perpetually claim to be on a diet, but late-night trips to the freezer were probably the main reason that she never lost the ten pounds she'd gained over the past few years.

To her amazement, Angie discovered that she enjoyed listening to Matt as he recounted several more humorous tales. But she was wise enough to realize that there were two sides to every coin. A man in his line of work would also be exposed to the seamier side of life, undoubtedly on a daily basis in a city as large as Chicago. The stress, the pressures, were nothing to scoff at, and she found herself thinking of him with new respect. She also wondered what was behind the decision to turn his back on his home and his career. Seventeen years of job security was not something to be taken lightly.

In fact, Angie could have relaxed completely if it hadn't been for the man sitting next to her. They'd had to crowd the chairs around the table to accommodate all of them, and again she found herself next to him. Wedged tightly between him and the girls, she couldn't ignore the slight pressure of his knee riding gently against her own. The contact was casual but unavoidable.

Angie breathed a sigh of relief when everyone rose to leave a short time later. Janice looked up at her as she bundled the baby into a sweater. "You sure you don't want a ride home with us, Angie?"

Her tone was bland, a little too innocent, but before Angie had a chance to open her mouth, Matt offered, "I'll take her and the girls home. It would be too crowded in your car." He patted his stomach and grinned. "Especially after that pizza."

It was all she could do not to strangle both Matt *and* Janice. Angie loved her friend dearly, but she could live without the matchmaking efforts. If she hadn't known for certain that the two of them hadn't met before today, she'd have suspected a little conspiracy between them.

"I hate to make you go out of your way," she told him.

"It's really no bother." Matt's tone was as warm as hers was cool. He opened the restaurant door for her. Angie brushed by him, flanked by her two small daughters. Her slender shoulders were held proudly.

The sky had darkened to a bluish-purple haze that heralded the coming of night. The sun was a vivid ball of orange as it prepared to plunge beneath the horizon.

Matt's eyes lingered on the western sky as he pulled the car door shut behind him. He sat for a moment, one hand draped carelessly over the steering wheel, absorbed by the sight. "You don't see sunsets like that at home," he remarked quietly.

In spite of herself Angie softened. "Home?" she echoed. "Is this your way of telling me you're resigning after all and going back to Chicago?" she asked teasingly.

Not a chance, Matt thought fervently. He shrugged, his expression rather sheepish. "Habit, I guess." There was a thoughtful pause. "It's hard to think of Westridge as home yet," he admitted. Starting the car, he pulled onto the street.

A few minutes later he pointed out a white frame house as his. Even through the darkness she could see that it was large, the fenced yard neatly cropped. "Looks like a big house for only one person," she commented. A half smile touched her lips as she remembered what he'd told her only that afternoon. "I had you pegged as a cliff dweller."

Matt grinned. "I asked for that, didn't I?" It occurred to him that they both seemed to harbor a few misconceptions about each other. But at least she wasn't without a sense of humor. He liked that. In fact, he was finding that there wasn't much about Angie that he *didn't* like.

They had pulled into her driveway by now. Matt cut the engine, then turned to Angie.

There was an intent look on his face that sent a prickly feeling up her spine. Angie glanced over her shoulder at Kim and Casey, huddled together in the back seat. Both were sound asleep.

"I'd better get the girls inside," she said quickly, fumbling for the door handle. "They've had a long day."

"Here, let me take Casey." A strong pair of arms reached in and lifted the child before Angie had even climbed out of the car. She woke Kim, then dug in her purse for her house key while Matt stood patiently on the porch.

Inside, she escorted a sleepy Kim up the stairs while Matt trailed along behind her. She couldn't suppress a faint twinge of annoyance at how Casey's small blond head nestled cozily against his broad shoulder before his gentle hands lowered the still-slumbering child to the double bed. Angie shooed Kim off to the bathroom with her toothbrush and nightgown.

Matt stepped into the hallway and tactfully closed the door. Angie heard his footsteps treading the stairs while she pulled Casey's shirt over her head. She roused slightly but was fast asleep once more by the time Angie tucked the blankets around her two daughters.

Matt rose from the chair he'd been sitting on when she entered the living room. "You're still here." She tried to sound surprised, hoping he would pick up on her cue. The presence of a man in her house was something she wasn't used to.

He smiled. "You won't get rid of me that easily."

A vaguely unsettling feeling came over her. Angie wasn't sure she wanted to put an interpretation on that statement. "I'm finding that out, aren't I?" she said smoothly.

"You're not still angry about this afternoon, are you?"

A slender brow arched. "Now why should I be angry?" A slight edge crept into her voice. "Just because you—"

"Horned in on your day."

Angie's mouth closed, and she studied him openly. He was

smiling, his eyes reflected only amusement, yet she sensed he was perfectly serious. "Well," she said grudgingly, "Janice did invite you." And hadn't there been a few times during the day when she hadn't really minded his being along? Though not, she reminded herself, when he was making her nervous—as he was right now.

"No," she said finally and realized she meant it. "I'm not angry."

"But you'd rather I stayed the hell out of your territory."

Her eyes narrowed at his mild tone. What was he after? "You're very blunt," she said slowly.

"I like to know where I stand, Angie." A small silence spun out between them. Matt didn't pretend to be a mind reader, though he had learned to read a great deal into a person's expression. But Angie... She didn't flinch from eye contact, and she betrayed little of her thoughts. She was tense, however; Matt could see it in the slight stiffening of her shoulders.

"We're not enemies, you know. In fact, I'd like to think we're on the same side."

His voice was disarmingly gentle, so much so that it caught her off guard for a moment. What manner of man was Matt Richardson—really? The worn, faded jeans that embraced the taut male thighs, the thin cotton shirt that hugged broad, muscular shoulders, the harshly carved features that gave him a tough, rugged look... The image sent an unexpected quiver of awareness through her stomach. But she knew so little about the man himself.

She made an attempt at lightness. To her dismay, she sounded breathless. "I suppose we are, as long as we're not discussing the city's budget."

Matt suppressed a smile. The budget? It was the last thing on his mind. "Can we talk for a minute?" He inclined his head toward the sofa, then held out his hand. "Though not," he added, "about the budget."

His eyes flickered over her, and there was both warmth and an undeniable male appreciation in those silver depths. The glance, as well as his words, should have served as a warning. Yet strangely, Angie wasn't obliged to listen. It occurred to her with a sudden flash of humor that, if she couldn't trust the chief of police, she couldn't trust anyone.

Shyly, rather hesitantly, she accepted the hand he offered. His skin was warm, the fingertips faintly callused. His hand fell away the moment they were seated on the sofa, and Angie wasn't sure if she was relieved or disappointed.

Matt was silent for a few seconds. "I have a confession to make, Angie." A smile tugged at the corner of his mouth. "When we first met, I told myself, Matt, there's a woman with everything. She's smart, savvy, dresses well, looks even better. *And* she drives a Mercedes."

Angie found herself falling in with his mood. "What happened to the part about being a cliff dweller?"

"That, too," he said smoothly.

Her ponytail had come loose hours ago, and a heavy wave of hair swung over her shoulder as she laughed, that carefree sound that never failed to stir him. The light from the nearby lamp transformed the long silken strands of her mane into silver and gold. Matt fought the urge to reach out and run his fingers through her hair, to see if it was as soft as it looked.

"Well?" She was looking at him expectantly. "What did you think of this woman who has everything?"

A hand came up to absently finger his jaw. For the first time he wondered what had possessed him to bring up the subject. "To tell you the truth, I thought you were just another wealthy snob who enjoyed looking down her nose at everyone else."

"Just another wealthy snob," she found herself teasing. "A species you're familiar with?"

"Thanks to my ex-wife, yes." The words were emphasized by a lift of his brows. "Not a species I particularly care for."

Oddly, Angie wasn't offended. Todd had told her much the same thing once. But the people she cared about and who cared about her knew differently. And it was somehow important that Matt know, too.

"I have a confession to make," she told him, her eyes sparkling humorously. "Contrary to popular opinion, I am *not* a wealthy woman. Comfortably well-off, I'll admit, thanks to a rather timely investment in oil futures—"

"Just as I thought. Bright. *Very* bright."

"Lucky," she put in dryly. Then the smile on her lips blossomed further. Her voice dropped to a conspiratorial whisper. "You won't tell anyone my Mercedes is ten years old, will you? And that I bought it used?"

"Scout's honor," he promised, and held up his hand.

"What Boy Scout troop did you belong to, Matt Richardson?" Dubiously she eyed the two fingers so proudly displayed.

Matt grinned and answered her question with one of his own. "Has anyone ever told you you'd make a great detective, Ms Mayor?" He dropped the hand he'd been holding up and settled it along the back of the couch. His gaze drifted over the soft curve of her cheek, the fragile line of her throat, then coasted up to settle on the loose waves that fell over her shoulder.

"I like your hair down," he said suddenly.

Her hand automatically reached for the curls that skimmed her collarbone. "Thank you," she returned breathlessly. She felt more like a self-conscious teenager than a thirty-two-year-old woman.

"It makes you look more relaxed. And I don't feel like you're about to bite my head off—" a slight smile lifted the corners of his mouth "—the way you did last Monday in your office. *And* last night," he added.

Her own smile was hesitant. "I...you put me on the spot Monday. And I think you were making a pass last night."

No, he countered silently. He was about to make one now.

"It wasn't a criminal transgression the last time I checked." He was teasing her, but this time she didn't respond. Instead, she lowered her eyes, pretending a fascinated interest in the knee patch on his jeans.

A gentle finger raised her chin. "I'm glad I was wrong about you, Angie." Eyes like beaten silver settled with disturbing accuracy on the curve of her mouth. "Because I'd like to get to know you. The *real* you." His voice dropped further. "The woman no one else sees—warm, vibrant and alive."

There was no denying the underlying seriousness of his words, whisper soft in the sudden stillness of the room, just as there was no denying his intent. He wanted to know her as a man knows a woman. Intimately. And hadn't she sensed all along that Matt Richardson was not a man who would be easily dissuaded?

Angie wished with all her soul that she could summon the icy disdain that he disliked so much. She couldn't risk letting him exchange their roles for anything that even resembled a male-female relationship. What he wanted was impossible. She felt suddenly inadequate. Wholly inadequate in a way she hadn't felt since Evan was alive.

She didn't realize she had risen and moved away from him until she felt the coolness of the windowpane beneath her fingertips.

Outside, the world was still and dark. The midnight canopy

high above displayed a brilliant cluster of stars. A night breeze sighed through the trees, then fell silent.

On the wall beside the rich wooden frame of the window, a shadow suddenly loomed. Every muscle in her body tightened, heightened to an almost painful awareness. Slowly she turned.

The impressive width of Matt's shoulders blocked out the light, and she could see nothing of his features, only a dark, menacing form. There was strength coiled in those lean, ridged muscles. He seemed so big; the nuance of power and force was suddenly frightening. She fought the surge of panic that clawed its way up into her throat when hands, large, strong and so very, very male, reached for her.

She shook her head and flinched when he would have touched her. "Don't, Matt. Don't!"

His hands immediately dropped to his sides. There was a heartbeat of silence while they stared at each other, one watching, the other waiting.

"Angie?" The voice was low, questioning. The utter calm of his tone had an inexplicably soothing effect on her.

"Matt, please." Hair like corn silk whispered over the fragile bones of her shoulders as Angie took a deep, steadying breath, a little ashamed of her reaction. "What you're asking...well, I'm—I'm just not—"

"I know. Not interested." He gave an odd little smile. His voice was almost unbearably gentle. The flicker of fear in her heart vanished as quickly as it had come. "I'm going to have to change that," he added softly, so softly she had to strain to hear.

She felt a wave of something that might have been regret. Even if she wanted to, she wasn't sure she could have accepted what he was offering. Once there was a time she'd had an unswerving faith in her womanhood. But Evan had managed to kill even that.

"Don't, Matt." She shook her head resignedly. Her smile was a little sad. "Please...don't even try."

"Can you give me one good reason why I shouldn't?"

Angie was silent, her mind filled with a yawning bleakness. She couldn't have given him many. Instead, she could think of only one. Evan.

"You sound very sure of yourself," he said into the silence.

She ignored the question in his tone. Her marriage had ended in a state that could only be called nightmarish. She would discuss it with no one. Least of all another man.

"I am," she said finally. There could be no mistaking the cold finality of those two simple words.

"Because of Todd?"

She straightened her shoulders. Matt had moved back a step. She no longer felt trapped. "Todd is the city manager," she told him clearly. "And we're friends, no more, no less."

Matt stared at her so long she began to grow uneasy once more. "Then Todd," he finally said very quietly, "is a fool."

"Matt, please." She gestured vaguely with one hand. "Let's just drop it."

"Not until I find out why I don't have more than a snowball's chance in hell with you."

Angie's lids closed wearily. Stubborn. Lord, but this man was stubborn!

"Is it because of your ex-husband?"

Angie's eyes snapped open. For one paralyzing second she was afraid she had given herself away with her stupid maidenly response to him earlier.

Matt had mistaken her silence for concurrence. He hesitated, not certain what he could say if she was still carrying a torch for her ex.

"I'm sorry," he began quietly. "I know how painful a divorce can be." He paused. "But there's no point in pining away for—"

Pining away! She had thanked God for the day that Evan had been removed from her life! And still she hated herself for it, even while she fought the irrationality of her feelings.

Drawing herself up to her full height, she lifted her chin and stared across at him. Her voice cut across his like the sudden crack of a bullet. "My husband is dead, Matt. I'm a widow."

CHAPTER SIX

THE SHOCK OF that statement still hadn't worn off when Matt let himself through the front door of his house less than fifteen minutes later.

For the second night in a row, he sat alone in the darkness. Only this time his thoughts lacked the self-satisfaction of the previous night. And this time there was a tall glass of amber liquid locked tightly in his hand.

He leaned his head back wearily. All along he had thought the worst of Angie. Even when his assumptions weren't borne out, he realized that deep inside he'd suspected she'd been milking an ex-husband for all he was worth. Her clothes, the Mercedes, the antiques...

His retreat had been hasty and clumsy. He didn't doubt that Angie was glad to see him leave. He'd had no idea what to say or what to do. And it didn't help that Angie had retreated into cool silence.

The mistake had been an understandable one, and Angie herself had done nothing that might have avoided it.

"Who are you kidding, old man?" he chided himself grimly. "She all but told you to mind your own business."

But if nothing else, he had learned several important things. It was hard to look at a woman as stunning as she was and not think of a word like seduction. Yet his attraction to her wasn't something fleeting; he wanted her more than he'd wanted anything in a long, long time. For a moment, a mere fraction of a second, he'd thought she was afraid of him. But it was gone so quickly that he decided it was only his imagination. Still, there was no arguing that she was a woman who was very—no, *extremely*—careful around the opposite sex.

Not the type of woman to allow a man many mistakes.

THE WEEKEND LEFT Angie feeling strangely restless. The usual peace she felt when enjoying herself with the girls had been diminished by a tall, gray-eyed man whose image she couldn't seem to banish from her mind, no matter how hard she tried. Sunday seemed to drag endlessly.

Angie wasn't normally a moody person, but she was unusually short with the girls on Monday morning and she snapped at Georgia for an oversight in marking her calendar for a luncheon Friday afternoon. The recommendations that the task force had put together on the fate of city hall were sitting on her desk, and after reading them through, she had to schedule a meeting with Matt sometime that day in order to prepare for that evening's city council meeting—not a move she relished any more than the council meeting itself.

Angie's moodiness did not go unnoticed by Georgia, however. It was almost eleven-thirty when her assistant breezed into the office, humming softly. Angie frowned. When was the last time she'd heard the woman humming to herself?

Georgia walked over and peered into her empty coffee cup. "Looks like you need another morning pick-me-up. Maybe it'll improve your mood."

"Obviously yours doesn't need improving," Angie muttered.

"Can't say that it does," the other woman agreed. She tossed the morning edition of the *Westridge Bulletin* onto Angie's desk. "Have you read that yet?"

"Are you kidding? It took me an hour to wade through that report on city hall!"

Her assistant laughed. "Why not do it now?" she suggested. "There's an item in there you might be interested in."

Angie nodded and began to automatically flip to the section containing area news. Georgia stopped her with a shake of her head. "Not there, boss lady. Check out the social tidbits instead."

"Social tidbits?" An eyebrow arched mockingly. "I can do without all the local gossip, thank you."

Georgia laughed. "I don't doubt it. But you might want to read Blair Andrews's column."

Angie's expression turned even more threatening. "Good Lord," she muttered. "I'm not sure I want to see this."

Her assistant laughed once more, a sound that might have been a giggle, coming from anyone else. "Sure you do. I got quite a kick out of it myself."

Giggling. Humming. Was Blair Andrews's story responsible?

It was strange. Very strange. Georgia normally had no more love for Blair than she did.

Angie had little time to wonder, however, as Georgia had reached for the newspaper once more. Folding it, she thrust it back onto Angie's desk and stabbed a finger at the bold dark print in one corner.

"Read," she commanded.

Feeling distinctly apprehensive, Angie picked up the newspaper. The article was part of a weekly column that touched on a variety of social items—birthday and anniversary parties, school proms and plays, who was off for his latest trip to Europe, and so forth. A people notebook of sorts.

Topping the list was last Friday night's get-together for Matt Richardson. Angie's eyes were immediately glued to the feature.

> Everyone who is anyone in our fair city was on hand to welcome Matthew Richardson, newly hired chief of police, at a reception in his honor last Friday night at the Sheraton. Particularly welcoming was Mayor Angela Hall. One can't help but wonder about the subject under discussion during their midnight tête-à-tête on the terrace. Could it be that our mayor, normally seen on the arm of City Manager Todd Austin, likes to keep things all in the family? Stay tuned for the latest on Ms Mayor and the Chief.

Angie's fingers tightened on the edges of the paper before her eyes flashed accusingly upward. "You think this is funny?" she asked Georgia in a gritty tone.

The answer was obvious in Georgia's delighted cackle. "All I want to know," she responded cheerfully, "is whether it's true or not."

"Oh, it's true, all right," chimed a masculine voice from the doorway. "Ask her fellow partner in crime."

Both women looked up at the same time to see Matt Richardson standing there, arms crossed over his chest as he leaned his shoulder against the doorjamb.

Georgia spoke first. "You mean you really—" she broke off and turned to Angie "—and you..." Her voice trailed off, and she looked at Matt once more.

The sight of unflappable Georgia gaping at Matt would have

amused Angie under any other circumstances. But she was too busy fuming at the room's other occupant to notice.

"Unfortunately," Matt added, his eyes never leaving Angie's face, "Miss Andrews has a rather vivid imagination. Her speculation is just that—speculation. Mayor Hall and I may have had a melding of minds that night, but certainly not a melding of hearts." *Yet,* he amended silently.

It wasn't, perhaps, the most prudent choice of words. Matt could tell by the way Angie glowered at him. He had a hard time holding back a smile and felt his spirits lift for the first time since Saturday. She wore a powder-blue suit that enhanced the translucent quality of her eyes. Would she have worn it, he wondered, if she knew how utterly feminine it made her look? But the glacial frost that radiated from across the room continued in full force.

This time he knew better, though. He'd already had a glimpse of the woman beneath the cool exterior, and she wasn't the cold, hard creature she appeared to be—no matter how hard she tried to convince him.

"Anybody home in there?"

The cheerful voice came from the outer office. Matt stepped aside to allow Georgia to pass through the doorway. Angie followed when she heard Georgia greet Sam Nelson.

"Why, Sam, how nice to see you!" Angie's voice was warm, her smile wide when she spotted Matt's predecessor near Georgia's desk. Seeing Matt looking on from the doorway, she quickly introduced the men. While the two exchanged pleasantries, she was very conscious of the dissimilarities between them. She'd always thought of Sam, with his ruddy cheeks, silver-streaked chestnut hair and rotund stomach, as being the teddy-bear type. Next to Matt's imposing height and build, the impression seemed more marked than ever.

"What brings you back, Sam?" she asked with a laugh. "After a week of retirement, did you decide the easy life wasn't for you after all?" She glanced covertly at Matt. "Don't tell me—you're here to get your job back."

Sam grinned. "Not much chance of that. No, retirement suits me just fine. Except it gets a little lonesome sometimes." He winked at Georgia. "That's why I came to carry this little lady off to lunch. You don't mind if I keep her out a few minutes late, do you?"

Angie's eyes widened, then settled on her assistant. "No. No, not at all." Her voice was faint. "Stay as long as you like."

Sam had already handed Georgia her sweater. For the first time she noticed Georgia's wine-colored dirndl skirt actually complemented the soft rose of her blouse. Georgia wearing clothes that didn't resemble something pulled off a scarecrow...Georgia humming...

Georgia had a beau, and from the way Sam was smiling at her and she was simpering back as they went out the door, it wasn't something that had sprung up overnight.

"Is this your usual reaction when someone spirits your secretary off for lunch?" Matt's voice was filled with humor.

Angie didn't realize her mouth had dropped open until she felt a lean finger beneath her chin urge it gently upward.

She was a little hurt that Georgia hadn't told her about Sam, but remembering the smile that wreathed Georgia's face at his attentions, she couldn't help but be glad for her, as well. But she was still too stunned by what had happened to be thinking clearly.

"It's just that Georgia...well, Georgia doesn't like men!" Angie blurted the words before she even realized it.

"Hmm. Must be something about this office."

She flushed at the unwelcome reminder. She realized she'd been nursing a half-hearted hope that seeing Matt in a business light, rather than a personal one, would quell the uneasy reaction he always managed to rouse in her. But it appeared that wasn't the case.

"You wanted to see me about something?" She strived for a polite note.

"I'm here at your summons. Remember?"

A sheepish expression flitted across Angie's face and she nodded, then turned to lead the way into her office.

"It *is* lunchtime." Matt's reminder came just as she sat down in her chair. "Shall we see to our stomachs first? We could go to that restaurant across the street."

"No." She shook her head quickly. "I...I really have a lot of work to do." Reaching out, she straightened a stack of papers, as if to lend credence to her words.

"I thought you might say that," he said dryly. "That's why I came prepared." He disappeared into the outer office. When he returned a few seconds later, he was carrying a small paper sack. "Voilà!" He held it up with a smile. "Lunch is served." Pulling out two plastic-wrapped sandwiches, he asked, "Ham or turkey?"

"Ham." She relented with a faint smile. She couldn't find it in herself to argue with him, especially since the sandwich he handed her looked rather good, and it tasted even better.

Matt pulled a chair up to her desk. "Well, here we are again," he commented lightly. "Alone at last. Shall we call Blair Andrews to take notes this time?"

"And ruin a perfectly good lunch? Please, show a little mercy!"

There it was again. That spark of humor that so entranced him. Matt shared in her amusement then grew more serious. "Did her column this morning really bother you that much?"

Angie sighed. "It did," she admitted, "but to tell you the truth...well, it doesn't anymore." She paused. "I guess I'm just a little on the sensitive side when it comes to publicity, especially when Blair Andrews is the author," she confided with a soft laugh.

Matt shrugged and carefully unwrapped the other half of his sandwich. Her statement was more telling than she knew, and he was just beginning to understand that Angie Hall was an intensely private person. Was it because her job sometimes placed her under scrutiny from the public? Somehow he didn't think so.

There was much that he wanted to discover about her, but he knew that he would have to take things slowly with her. Deliberately he changed the subject.

"What was it you wanted to see me about?" He pared a slice of tart green apple and offered it to her.

She took it, munching thoughtfully for a moment. "You're aware of the problem we're having regarding city hall? Whether to rebuild completely or renovate instead?"

"Rumors abound in these hallowed halls," he remarked dryly. "And I heard you mention it at your press conference last week."

Angie nodded. The press conference and the ensuing exchange in this very office with this very man weren't something she cared to rehash. She went on quickly, "The committee's recommendation is in, and they feel renovation is the better approach. I tend to agree."

Matt looked rather puzzled.

"It's not something that's wholly up to me. The council has to vote on it," she explained. "And while the cost differential between the two is certainly there, I've made a proposal regarding the expenditure of the excess funds."

"Oh, yes." Matt tipped his head to the side. "Some kind of social program, isn't it?"

"Partially. We'd also like to expand the transit system." Rising, Angie moved to look out at the small square of lawn below her window. "As for the other, that's where you come in, Matt." His name slipped so easily off her tongue. She went on, "Westridge has a city-operated center for senior citizens, and we cooperate with the county in coordinating programs for juvenile delinquents." Her next words came with far more difficulty. "I was thinking in terms of some type of women's center, something that offers temporary shelter to women who need it, with counseling perhaps for rape victims and..." She faltered and suddenly became aware that her skin was clammy, her hands gripped tightly together.

"And assault victims, battered wives, that type of thing?"

Angie's heart gave a betraying lurch, but she swallowed and tried for an even tone. She even managed to turn and face him. "What do you think, Matt? Is there a need in Westridge for something like that?"

"It's a crime that there isn't one already. We hear so much about victim's rights and restitution these days that I just assumed..." He looked up at her, his expression grim. "A lot of rapes and cases of abuse are never prosecuted because they're never reported. The ongoing support of a crisis center can sometimes change that." He shook his head disbelievingly. "I don't see how Westridge has managed without one for this long. It's not the type of problem that's confined solely to large metropolitan areas."

"The idea surfaced several years ago when I was a member of the city council, but nothing ever came of it, despite the fact that Sam Nelson was behind it all the way. Money was tight then, and neither one of us carried enough clout to get it approved." Her tone was somber. "Even now the response has been lukewarm. But if the endorsement for a new city hall comes through and funds are earmarked for that, I'm afraid money will once again be a problem."

For a moment she was torn between conflicting emotions. Granted, the existence of a women's shelter at the time of her marriage probably wouldn't have changed a thing. But it might have made life a little easier if only she'd had someone to talk to, someone who understood her confusion.

It was shame that held her back then, and it was shame that held her back now. She despised herself for being so cowardly.

Her thoughts grew bitter as her gaze dropped. She stared numbly down at her hands.

No, it could never be known that Angie Hall, solid citizen, respected mayor of Westridge, had been abused by her husband. She would probably be accused of a private crusade. But wasn't that what this was?

In a way it was, she acknowledged silently. But not completely. It was a community need, one that Matt recognized, as well.

Taking a deep breath, she took her place behind her desk once more. "So." Her tone was brisk, and she forced a smile. "You don't mind if I quote you on that, do you?"

"Not at all," he said firmly. "I think I can even manage to gather a few supporting facts and figures before tonight. I can have Margie bring them by later this afternoon."

When he stood up, the warmth in her smile and voice were genuine. "Thanks, Chief," she said softly. She gestured at the remains of their lunch stuffed back into the paper bag. "Next time lunch is on me."

"Bribery, Ms Mayor?" His voice feigned shock, but his eyes were dancing. "Don't worry. I won't tell if you won't."

Angie found she was still smiling after he left. Oddly enough, the tension between them seemed to have eased, although for the most part she suspected it had been rather one-sided in the first place.

Her good humor didn't last more than a few minutes after his departure, though. Todd knocked on the door, then stepped inside, shutting it behind him. He was impeccably dressed as usual in a three-piece camel-colored suit, starched white shirt and polished leather shoes. Fastidious to a fault, his brown hair lay neatly on his head, not a single strand out of place.

"Well, I certainly am popular today." Her welcoming smile faded as she caught sight of his handsome features drawn into a tight-lipped expression. "You just got back from vacation," she chided gently. "You're supposed to be all smiles and full of news about the fun you had—"

"News? I'm full of news, all right. About you and our new police chief." His tone, for all its quietness, held a bitter note. "He moves rather quickly, wouldn't you say?" He halted directly in front of her, placed his palms flat on her desktop and glared at her. "I think I deserve an explanation."

Angie felt her temper rise at his flat demand but kept her voice calm. "If Blair was anxious to start a fire, she certainly succeeded, didn't she?"

Todd's eyes narrowed. "Dammit, Angie, you know that you and I—"

"I know that you and I are friends, nothing more," she stressed tightly. "That's the way it's been, and that's the way it's going to stay."

"Because of our new police chief?"

"Matt Richardson has nothing to do with this, Todd. And even if he did, it wouldn't really be any of your business," she informed him coolly.

He stared at her for a long time, then straightened abruptly. "You know how I feel about you," he said in a low voice. "You and I—"

Angie shook her head wearily. "Please don't, Todd. We've gone over this before." The last time had been only a few weeks earlier. Todd had attempted to kiss her, something he'd done a few times in the past year, but she'd always managed to gently discourage him.

"I don't like the thought of you with another man."

Her eyes met his squarely. "I haven't been with another man, Todd. And despite what Blair Andrews seems to think, I'm really not interested in Matt Richardson." Her heart speeded up, as if to belie her words. She might not be interested in him, but she was certainly *aware* of him in a way that had nothing to do with either her job or his.

Some of Todd's tension seemed to ease, but his tone was still accusing. "You won't even give us a chance, Angie."

Angie was silent. Todd was nice. A pleasant companion. Good-looking, charming, intelligent. But even if her marriage hadn't been the disaster it was, she knew that he wouldn't have kindled an answering spark of feeling inside her—that special emotion she'd once felt with Evan.

"I value our friendship, Todd," she told him carefully. "But I'm happy with my life as it is...and I won't change my mind," she finished in a low voice.

He wasn't satisfied with her response. She could see it in his turbulent expression. But he must have sensed her conviction as he paced around the room. Finally he halted before the window, his hands thrust into the pockets of his trousers.

"What did you think of the task force's report on city hall?" he asked abruptly.

"I tend to agree with their findings, and I certainly respect their opinion." The task force included two of the council's eight members, plus an architect and an engineer. "This building may be old," she added, "but it's solidly constructed."

Todd's eyebrows lifted. "Let me guess," he said. "They don't build 'em like they used to, right?"

Angie regarded him quietly. "Whichever way we go, it's a publicly financed project. We can't afford not to be conservative."

"Meaning we're under the taxpayers' thumb."

"In a way, yes," she affirmed.

He shook his head, grimacing as he walked toward the door. "If you ask me, it's about time this city did something innovative for a change. It seems all we ever do is drag our heels."

In a way Todd was right, she reflected after he'd gone. The city's residents had always been on the conservative side and rather resistant to change. There were no sprawling shopping malls, no brand-new condominiums cropping up on the outskirts. In many of the neighborhoods, it was as if time had stood still. Cupolaed Victorian houses were the rule rather than the exception. In Angie's eyes it was all part of the city's pervasive appeal.

Yet that same reluctance to embrace new challenges and ways was also responsible for the lack of a women's shelter. It was altogether possible—no, probable—that she would have one heck of a battle on her hands. And tonight was the perfect opportunity to launch the offensive.

SHE'D BEEN RIGHT to think of the meeting as a battlefield. The task force recommendation that city hall be renovated roused both passionate praise and stinging criticism. Angie's patience was sorely tried at least a dozen times when the heated exchange between John Curtis and Anna Goodwin threatened to erupt into a shouting match.

John Curtis was young, in his mid-thirties, an attorney whose views were just a little too radical for Angie's tastes. Bold and brash, he made it no secret that he maintained a few political aspirations of his own.

On the other hand, Anna was a local businesswoman whose family had lived in Westridge for generations. Fair-minded and thorough, there could be no doubt that she had the city's best interests at heart.

If indeed the council was made up along party lines, these two were the leaders of the opposing factions.

By the time the three-hour meeting finally broke up, tempers were short and nerves were stretched to the breaking point. Todd, who was usually rather vocal in his support of Angie, was surprisingly quiet.

But perhaps it wasn't so surprising after all. He was polite but subdued. Angie guessed he was still angry about the scene in her office that afternoon. She meant to have a word with him after the meeting, but he left before she had the chance.

She was the last one to leave the council chambers, and it was after ten o'clock before she shoved a mountain of papers back into her satchel. Closing the door behind her, she sagged against it for a moment. Her lids fluttered shut as she let the blessed quiet of the darkened hallway seep into her senses.

"How'd it go?"

Her eyes flew open in time to see a dark form detach itself from the shadows a few feet away and come toward her. She relaxed as she belatedly recognized the voice as Matt's.

She blew a wispy strand of gold off her forehead and grimaced. "Sometimes I have the feeling all we ever do is agree to disagree."

"The city hall issue didn't go the way you hoped?"

Angie shook her head. "We thought it best to delay the vote a little longer. Maybe by then I'll be able to muster enough support for the renovation project to pass. As it stands right now, we're divided right down the middle." She added that her own vote was used only in the event of a split decision by the eight-member council, but that was something she tried to avoid.

Matt nodded. "What about the shelter?"

Her shoulders sagged. "Until the other issue is decided and we know the funds will be available, we really can't commit to it. I barely scratched the surface."

He reached for her satchel. "I think what you need is a shoulder to cry on."

"You've lightened my burden already." She was a little

amazed at how easily the gentle teasing sprang from her lips, especially after the past few hours. Her feet fell into line with his as they started down the hallway, their footsteps echoing hollowly on the cold marble floor.

The hazy light from a streetlamp shone down on the two figures that descended the broad stone steps. Once they were on the sidewalk, Angie stopped to look back at the building. Dozens of glittering stars lay scattered across the night-darkened sky, but her attention was captured by what lay below. Her eyes lingered on the dense green ivy trailing alongside her office window, the portico entrance that lent the structure a clock tower charm.

"I hate to think of bulldozers and wrecking cranes tearing this place apart." It filled her with a sense of sadness, but even as she spoke, a picture of yellowed ceiling tiles flashed into her mind. She even imagined she heard the radiator in her office hissing and clanking the way it had done nearly every day last winter.

Matt looked at her rather oddly. "You're really rather sentimental, aren't you?" There was a note of wonder in his voice.

"I guess I am, at that," she admitted. Her gaze shifted to his face. The silver light of the moon softened the starkly masculine planes and angles of his features. "Why are you so surprised?" she asked softly.

A sheepish smile lit his face. "I guess I shouldn't be. Not after seeing your house and all the antiques inside it."

Angie laughed and started toward her car. "That's something I come by naturally. My mother likes to drag my father off to garage sales and antique shops. He shouldn't complain, though. She's always the one who does all the stripping and refinishing."

"Your parents live here in Westridge?"

"Not anymore. They decided they'd had enough of rainy winters about three years ago and migrated to the Sunbelt. They live in Arizona now." They stopped some twenty feet from where her car was parked. Without quite being aware of it, she reached out and touched his arm. "Matt, I...I'd like to thank you for all the extra effort you put out today."

"Fruitless though it was."

"Fruitless though it was," she agreed with a rueful laugh. "Round two is coming up, though."

Matt's lips edged up a notch. "Does that mean you no longer want to fire me?"

She liked his slow smile. Strong white teeth were revealed, made whiter still by the contrast with his dark skin. A fine network of laugh lines radiated outward from his eyes. There was much to like about Matt Richardson, she told herself. Perhaps too much.

"I never did want to fire you, Matt." Her brows arched reprovingly.

"No," he said dryly. "You just didn't want to hire me. Besides, you heard Sam Nelson say just this afternoon that he wasn't about to come back."

Angie couldn't quite stop herself from trying to look stern. "I thought we had ceased hostilities. Frankly, I think it's an improvement."

Amen to that, Matt echoed in fervent silence. "Angie?"

Her delicate features etched in moonlight, she looked almost ethereal. Ethereal and untouchable.

"Yes?"

He shoved his hands in his pockets, feeling as awkward as a kid on his first date. "You, uh, you wouldn't want to grab a cup of coffee before you head home, would you?"

For a moment he thought she wasn't going to answer. And it irritated the hell out of him that she didn't look at him when she finally spoke.

A fleeting look of distress crossed her face, then she slowly shook her head. "I'm sorry, Matt. Maybe another time. The meeting lasted longer than I expected, and I really should be heading home."

The silence stretched out while she fumbled in her purse for her keys. When, he asked himself harshly, was he going to get the message? How many times did she have to tell him she wasn't interested?

"Sure," he muttered finally. Even to his own ears his voice sounded strained. He leaned against his car as he watched her walk the short distance to her car.

Suddenly he straightened with a frown. "Wait a minute. You're not going anywhere." His tone was grim as he pointed to her car. "Your tires have been slashed."

CHAPTER SEVEN

"YOU DON'T HAVE to do this, you know. I could have called Janice. Or Mrs. Johnson."

Matt sighed. Angie had just climbed into his car and now sat as close as possible to the other door. He'd sensed the invisible barrier she put up between them the minute he suggested coffee, a barrier that widened by miles when he offered her a ride home.

"Mrs. Johnson?" His tone was polite, but he felt like being anything *but* polite. Many women found him attractive, and it wasn't ego but fact that told him so. But Angie made him feel just a little like a toad spawned from the gates of hell.

"A neighbor," she supplied. "She's staying with the girls tonight."

Deliberately he pushed the key into the ignition, aware of the blue eyes trained intently on his every movement. *Women's lib!* he thought disgustedly. It struck a deep blow to a man prepared to offer some old-fashioned generosity.

"Then it would be a shame to drag the three of them out at this hour, wouldn't it?" He couldn't quite keep the sarcasm from his voice. "Especially when you already have a ride home."

There was a lengthy silence. He finally heard a stiffly muttered, "I suppose you're right."

Matt glanced at her from the corner of his eye. Was it his imagination, or had she pushed back even further against the door? She had no need to fear him. Didn't she know that? Yet suddenly he had the strangest sensation that it wasn't pride or anything remotely connected with it that triggered her reaction. The realization slammed a lid on the slow rise of his temper.

"You know you're not doing wonders for my male ego." He got no response; he really hadn't expected one. He paused, then asked quietly, "Are you afraid of me, of being alone with me?"

Angie couldn't prevent the sudden tensing of her fingers on the strap of her purse. She had to force herself to face him.

What she found there was oddly encouraging. His eyes were questioning, a little puzzled. His expression was incredibly gentle, and his roughly chiseled features seemed softer.

"No," she breathed slowly, then smiled as she realized it was true. Matt made her feel strange and fluttery inside, but she wasn't afraid of him.

"Good." Matt caught his breath at her radiant smile, and he found his own lips responding likewise.

He started the car, and this time when silence reigned, it was a far more comfortable one. It was Angie who finally broke it a few minutes later.

"Matt." Frowning, she reached up and tucked a swirl of gold behind her ear. "Who do you think could have slashed my tires?"

It had been a flagrant act of vandalism. All four had been neatly sliced and punctured. But before Matt had a chance to respond, she found herself speculating aloud. "Do you think it might have been—" Abruptly she checked herself, turning the idea over in her mind.

"Who?" He glanced over at her.

Angie hesitated. "We had a few fireworks at the meeting tonight, and I couldn't help but wonder..." She stopped, realizing how she must sound to him. Paranoid. That's exactly how she was acting.

"It was probably just a couple of kids hell-bent on a little destruction—at someone else's expense."

She considered his statement. "You're probably right," she said finally, then added glumly, "With the kind of day I've had, I should have expected something like this."

A short time later he angled the car into her drive. Angie fought against the sudden stiffening of her body when he switched off the engine and pulled the keys from the ignition. Would he want to come in? *Of course he will,* she chastised herself fiercely. He hadn't exactly bothered to hide his interest in her. Her mind groped for excuses. The girls. Mrs. Johnson. They both had to work tomorrow.

When she glanced over at him, she discovered his eyes upon her, dark and unreadable in the moonlight. "Thanks for the ride," she said, reaching for the door handle.

"I'll walk you to the door," he told her and dropped his keys into his pocket.

She flushed at the faint note of censure in his voice. Matt was right behind her as she stepped onto the sidewalk, and it occurred to her that despite their rocky beginning Matt had been nothing but a perfect gentleman.

In spite of the apprehensive tingle she felt in his presence, she realized her behavior had been petty and a little waspish. In fact, there were a few times she'd been rather rude. No, she definitely wasn't proud of herself.

The porch light had flashed on at the sound of the car doors slamming, and Mrs. Johnson now stood in the doorway.

"Hi," Angie greeted. "How were the girls?"

"Oh, just fine." A pair of bright eyes, startlingly blue beneath her snowy white hair, twinkled at Angie. "They've been in bed since eight-thirty."

Angie nodded and stepped inside. She turned toward Matt, still standing on the porch. She quickly introduced him to the elderly woman, then smiled tentatively at him. "Would you mind walking Mrs. Johnson home? Then, if you'd like, you can stop back in for coffee."

Mrs. Johnson waved aside her request and bundled her ample form into a sweater. "Oh, there's no need for that. I can see myself home."

"I wouldn't dream of it." The smile Matt directed at the older woman would have melted the polar ice cap. Mrs. Johnson, a widow for the past twenty years, seemed utterly susceptible. She was absolutely beaming as Matt offered her his arm.

Angie was still chuckling about it when she came down the stairs from checking on the girls a few minutes later. Hearing footsteps on the porch, she opened the front door. Matt stood on the threshold.

"Is your offer still open?" he asked. "Or was it just for Mrs. Johnson's benefit?" The mild amusement in his voice took the sting out of his words.

Angie opened the door wider, and he stepped inside. "Speaking of Mrs. Johnson," she commented dryly, "you seem to have added one more to the list."

"The list?" He looked totally blank as he followed her into the kitchen.

She pulled two stoneware mugs from a rack on the wall. "Mrs. Johnson. Janice. Georgia," she said over her shoulder. "Quite a fan club, I'd say."

"Georgia?" He sounded incredulous. "Your secretary, Georgia?"

"Believe it or not, one and the same." She filled a cup and

handed it to him. "She's not half as scary as she looks—and acts."

Matt was feeling rather pleased with himself. "Must be all that Chicago charm," he murmured. "Think there's a chance some of it might rub off on you?"

She was amused by the little-boy hopefulness in his eyes. It was far less threatening than the ruggedly male aura he possessed; so far tonight she'd done a commendable job of ignoring it. Mentally she crossed her fingers, the words echoing silently in her head. *So far...*

Her cup in one hand, she gestured to the living room. "Why don't we go in there?" she suggested.

She knew it was a mistake the minute they sat down. Not that Matt was sitting too close. She had the feeling he deliberately chose the far end of the sofa, and oddly, it set her nerves aflutter. And with the lamp glowing dimly in the corner, the house silent around them, the clock on the mantel ticking peacefully away, it was a potent—and unwelcome—reminder that the two of them were alone together in what might be considered a rather intimate setting.

Angie couldn't help it. She switched on the lamp sitting on the end table nearest her. Their eyes met briefly, and she knew for certain that he was aware of her sudden unease.

A moment later, however, his voice betrayed nothing. "Do you need a ride in to work tomorrow morning?"

She shook her head quickly, but not before Matt glimpsed a flash of pride in her eyes. "I'll have to take care of getting my tires replaced first thing in the morning, so I don't know what time I'll be in."

He took a sip of his coffee, his gaze never leaving hers. "You're a very independent woman, aren't you, Angie Hall?"

Instinctively she felt her defenses rise, but when she saw that he meant no offense, she relaxed—somewhat. "I've had to be," she returned quietly.

Matt leaned back against the cushions and regarded her. "You've been alone—" he frowned "—how long now?"

Her fingers tightened around her cup. A faint bitterness crept into her thoughts as her mind delved backward. Evan had been lost to her months before his death, but she knew what Matt meant.

"Two years," she answered, not looking at him.

The silence spun out between them. There was a faint rustle as

Matt reached out to set his cup on the coffee table. "It just occurred to me," he said slowly, "that the other night...well, I never said I was sorry about your husband."

It was an awkward apology, and as he saw her face shut down all expression, he cursed himself for a fool. It was obvious the subject of her husband's death was a painful one. He heard her utter a toneless thank you, then walk to the window where she stared solemnly out at the dark night.

Her lovely profile was hidden in shadow, but there was something abominably pitiful about the slender lines of her back and shoulders set in proud but rigid lines. It was a sight that sent some nameless emotion stabbing into his heart. She seemed so vulnerable. So alone despite the determination and ability to stand on her own two feet.

Matt was a man who understood pride. He was also a man who understood pain, and he felt a strange kind of empathy stir deep inside himself.

He moved toward her, responding only to the loneliness he glimpsed beneath her facade of control. Perhaps it was borne of the desire to comfort, for there had been many times in his own life that he would have welcomed comfort from the arms of another.

He laid his hands on her shoulders, a featherlight touch, nothing that would frighten her. "Angie..."

Exactly what he might have said, he would never know. The muscles of her shoulders stiffened beneath his fingers, and he saw her drop her head. "No more questions, Matt." She moistened her lips. "Please."

It seemed a simple request, and yet it was far from simple. Angie was not a woman who would easily bare both heart and soul, and he sensed that there was much she held deep inside herself, perhaps too much. What would it take for her to confide in him, to trust as he wanted her to trust? Time? He had time, all that he needed. And patience? He *had* to be patient, for he suspected Angie would give him no choice.

Ever so slowly he turned her around to face him, then let his hands drop back to his sides. Her eyes, those gorgeous blue eyes framed with feathery black lashes, were dark and shadowed. Her tension radiated from her like a shield of armor, but it was a barrier he was determined to tear down. Little by little, if necessary.

"Do you dislike me, Angie?"

The mildness of his tone, as much as the question itself, startled her. "I—no." She took a deep breath to combat the erratic beat of her pulse. He was close, so close she could see the individual lines that fanned out from his eyes, the faint darkening of his beard-roughened jawline that proclaimed he was a man prone to five o'clock shadow. "No, I don't dislike you."

"But you're not comfortable with me, either."

Her thoughts were vague and a little disjointed. A part of her realized she'd been right to be wary of him. Nothing escaped his notice, nothing.

She wanted to look away, yet she couldn't. Her eyes traveled with unerring accuracy to the face that hovered just above her own, a face whose harshly masculine beauty she couldn't deny. They lingered for long, uninterrupted seconds on his mouth, a mouth that looked strangely inviting with its sensuously curved lower lip.

"No," she confessed. "No, I'm not comfortable with you!" She was suddenly upset with him for riling her like this and angry at herself for letting him get to her. She would have stepped away, but his hands on her shoulders wouldn't let her. Those same hands coasted down her arms, sending a prickle of sensation over her skin. To her dismay, it wasn't unpleasant. Indeed, it was entirely too pleasant for her own good.

"Why?" he asked very quietly.

"Why, what?" She deliberately chose to misunderstand.

"Why aren't you comfortable with me?" Just as deliberately he fitted their hands together, palm to palm, finger to finger.

His skin was warm, not at all soft like her own. She was acutely conscious of the way his large hands dwarfed her own.

"Because of this?"

This was an undeniable feeling of heat and awareness flowing between them, hotter than fire, charged with the sizzling energy of a lightning bolt.

Angie jerked her hands away as if she had been burned. "Why are you doing this?" she asked in a low voice, fighting the impulse to back away.

Maybe it was to prove to himself that she wasn't as unaware of him as she pretended—or perhaps that was what he was trying to prove to her. It was, he decided, a little of both.

"I'm very attracted to you, Angie. And I think if you're honest with yourself, you'll admit you feel the same."

She looked away, feeling suddenly ill equipped to deal with

such candor. She had the uneasy feeling that he saw right through her, that he was aware of every nuance of emotion she was trying to hide. He made her feel exposed. And never again would she allow a man to do that to her. Never.

"The only logical thing to do is see where that attraction takes us," he added.

"Then I'd suggest you find yourself another taker!" she retorted. She'd struggled a long time to rebuild even a measure of the confidence she'd lost at Evan's hands. She wouldn't stand by and let another man tear down what little she had regained!

Matt hid a smile. Her eyes were huge in her pale face. She reminded him of a frightened rabbit, but she had the tongue of a spitting tiger. He knew what she was trying to do, but he wasn't buying it.

"The only one I'm interested in is you," he said in a voice as wispy soft as cotton.

Angie shook her head, as if to negate his words. His gentle manner, the sensitivity that he didn't bother to hide, made his masculinity all the more overpowering. Still, both seemed almost at odds in such a hard-featured man. Yet all she had to do was look into his eyes to know that he wasn't as hard or tough as he appeared at first sight. The knowledge confused and unsettled her.

Her eyes slid away, but in the fraction of a second she allotted him, Matt was taken aback at the depth of emotion he saw reflected there, a kind of vulnerability that was quickly replaced by something that might have been despair.

"Matt..." Somehow she didn't even question that her voice was tainted with regret. "I really think you should find someone else."

"Janice is already spoken for. So is Georgia. And Mrs. Johnson...well, I think she's a little old for me."

His grin was so utterly disarming that she felt her heart turn over. She knew he was trying to lighten the suddenly intense atmosphere, but it made her all the more determined to say what she had to. "I think you should find someone who has more to give than I do," she told him quietly.

His grin evaporated. She felt as if he had penetrated clear to her soul, and his next words seemed to prove it. "You have two daughters who obviously aren't suffering from a shortage of anything—especially love."

Angie chose her words carefully. "The love between a parent and child is different. The other kind, the kind between a man and a woman..." She faltered uncertainly. How could she say what she felt without revealing too much of herself? Even now after all this time, when she looked in the mirror, she saw only a shell of the intensely passionate woman she had once been.

For just an instant she experienced a burning sense of betrayal. Her looks were something she had always taken for granted, but Evan had made her feel unattractive. Worthless. He had stripped her of her pride in her sex, the most precious gift a woman could give to a man.

Was it any wonder she had avoided men in all but the most impersonal of relationships since Evan's death? Todd was the only one she had let get even remotely close, and she had set boundaries he didn't dare impose upon. She was right. She had nothing left to give.

She took a deep, unsteady breath, angry with Matt for putting her through this. "Let's just say it's not for me," she finished in a low voice.

For his part, Matt was trying to decipher the fleeting emotions that flitted across her face, not the least of which was fear. What did she have to be afraid of? "You're saying you're not capable of that kind of love anymore?" He couldn't quite keep the skepticism from his voice.

"I'm not," she agreed quickly—a little too quickly, she soon realized. She started to avert her eyes, but a lean finger laid on her jawline prevented her.

"You're wrong, Angie."

The quiet conviction in his voice frightened her as nothing else had. Matt Richardson was a threat, a threat to the carefully constructed life she had built for herself. It was enough that her life revolved around herself and her daughters...for now.

For now. The phrase caused a feeling of dread to gather in her stomach. She couldn't stop her mind from jumping forward. What about tomorrow? Next year? What about forever? That was something she didn't dare let herself think about.

Her gaze focused somewhere in the vicinity of his shirt collar. It was the only way she could say what she had to. "I'm not ready for a man in my life again," she said in a voice so low he had to strain to hear.

"How do you know if you haven't tried? And you haven't, have you?" he mused aloud. "Not even with Todd."

"Todd is a friend," she asserted stiffly.

"So you've said." He watched her closely. "What about me, Angie? Am I a friend?"

"You tell me!" What was his point? she wondered irritably.

"I'd like to be." The admission came freely, as Angie had expected. She had already discovered he was not a man to mince words. "I'd also like to see our relationship go beyond friendship." His eyes echoed the sentiment as they made a leisurely tour of her body. He made no attempt to hide either his desire or his approval.

"If I wanted a man in my life again, which I don't," she reiterated stiffly, "it certainly wouldn't be you!"

The slow smile that spread across his face set her teeth on edge even further. "You'd rather have a nice, safe man who makes no demands, right?" He paused, hoping he wasn't going about this the wrong way. "I've no doubt that losing your husband was hard on you. But that was two years ago, not yesterday. And it doesn't change the fact that you're a beautiful woman, a beautiful, *unattached* woman. Like it or not, that makes you fair game." He paused, then added softly, "The sooner you let go of the past, the easier it will be."

"And all the more convenient for *you,* I suppose." She squared her shoulders proudly. "What makes you such an authority, anyway?"

The slight hardening of his eyes was the only sign of his anger, but in spite of everything, he felt a familiar, though long-forgotten pain twist through his gut. Marriage to Linda hadn't been the easiest thing in the world to cope with, but it hadn't stopped him from feeling he'd lost everything when she divorced him.

"I know," he said evenly, "because I've been there. It's not easy to pick up the pieces after someone you love is gone, but sooner or later it has to be done."

To her horror, she felt herself on the verge of tears. What he said sounded perfectly logical, but true to human nature, emotions weren't always logical.

"You don't understand," she whispered. "My husband..." A hollow emptiness welled up inside her, and she closed her eyes against it. How could she tell him of her secret shame, the humiliation Evan had put her through?

It wasn't until she felt the roughness of Matt's palm against her own that she realized she had thrust out her hand. Her eyes flew open to find it blanketed firmly within both of his. Slowly, giving her time to pull away if she wanted to, he lifted it between their bodies, twining his fingers with her own.

Angie found she couldn't look away as his lips found the sensitive skin on the back of her hand. The touch was so fleeting, so featherlight, that she might have convinced herself it was purely her imagination—if it wasn't for the ripple of sensation that shot down clear to her toes.

Then he settled her hand firmly on the muscled landscape of his chest, still holding it lightly beneath his own. Beneath her fingertips Angie could feel the hardness of muscle sheathed in smooth skin, the faint rasp of hair below the fine linen of his shirt and the slow, steady beat of his heart.

Her body trembled.

Matt felt it, too. "You said you weren't afraid of me," he reminded her quietly.

"I...I'm not." Her voice was whisper thin as she fought a silent battle within herself. She knew what he was doing, and all her self-protective instincts cried out against it. "I'm not ready for this," she heard herself say.

He shook his head and wedged his hand more lightly over hers, as if to deny her words.

She felt his heartbeat accelerate.

"You see?" His smile was almost sad as he saw her eyes widen. "I think it's too late." Once more his lips caressed the back of her hand. "It'll be okay." His whisper was a sound that carried the night-dark intimacy found only between lovers. "Nothing's changed—not really. Things can be just as good, maybe even better, the second time around."

Then he was gone, and she was left alone. Alone in the silence of an empty room...and an empty heart.

She had a vague unsettling feeling that Matt was wrong, and nothing would ever be the same again.

CHAPTER EIGHT

HER IMAGE TAUNTED MATT all through the long hours of the night. He dreamed of a woman with eyes the color of a cloudless sky and shimmering golden hair that danced around her shoulders, reminding him of sunlight in its purest form. Every nuance of her femininity intrigued him—her slim, delicate gracefulness, her subdued elegance, her polish and poise, her lilting, carefree, laughter. Laughter he hadn't heard nearly as often as he would have liked.

The woman who had everything. The thought mocked him, a blatant reminder of his human frailties. He'd branded Angie callous and cold without knowing anything at all about her. And now? Now he still had much to learn about her, but at least he knew better than to label her insensitive.

Grimacing, he rose from the kitchen table, dumped his cold coffee into the sink and poured himself another cup. The naked vulnerability in her eyes last night had shocked him. It roused protective instincts inside him he hadn't even known he possessed. He wanted to reach out and shield her in his arms, put himself between her and anyone or anything that might hurt her.

What stopped him was the certain knowledge that she would not have welcomed his touch. A wry smile touched his lips. If Angie had been so inclined, he wouldn't put it past her to get her message across to him loud and clear, through physical means or otherwise.

Yet he felt a thrill of elation as he recalled the feel of her small hand trapped in the heat and hardness of his own. No matter how slight the gesture had been, however minor or inconsequential it might have seemed to someone else, he *had* touched her, both inside and out, this woman who did not like to be touched.

Angie. Linda. He couldn't stop himself from making one last comparison. Both fair, both fragile and ethereal-looking, both possessing a remoteness that issued a silent challenge to covetous male eyes. But there, and once again Matt flinched, the similarities ended.

Angie was intelligent, financially solvent, and in spite of her claim to the contrary, he knew her capacity for love and tenderness hadn't yet reached its limit. He suspected she didn't even realize how sensual she really was; he had the feeling she saw it as something to be hidden deep inside.

Angie was strong while Linda had been headstrong, cold and uncaring. Angie had struggled through a rocky period in her life and emerged victorious, though not without a few battle scars, he reminded himself grimly. But Linda had found it far too easy to rely on others, with no thought about how or why someone else might be hurt. Matt knew there was no way on earth that Linda could have gotten through it on her own.

Still, it disturbed Matt that Angie still carried a torch for her dead husband. The torment in her eyes cut him to the quick, yet it only deepened his desire for her. For Matt, thoughts of Linda no longer dredged up old ghosts, but it was obvious that didn't hold true for Angie.

Fighting the shadowy hold of her husband wasn't going to be an easy hill for her to climb, and he sensed she wasn't going to make it any easier for either one of them.

But she was strong. Strong on the outside, fragile and so very vulnerable inside, and so determined not to show it. That was his Angie.

His Angie. He grinned, caught up his jacket from the closet and locked the front door. She wasn't his yet, and if last night was any indication, she certainly wasn't going to fall into his arms like a ripe plum.

Angie needed him, he thought fiercely, as much as he needed her. She just hadn't discovered it yet.

LATE THAT NIGHT Angie sat behind the huge rolltop desk in her den. A late evening breeze brushed a swirl of leaves against the windowpane. Kim and Casey were tucked snugly into bed. Only minutes before the clock on the living room mantel had chimed nine o'clock. It was a scene steeped in contentment, in peace and tranquility.

But there was no peace in Angie's heart. Shadowy memories of Evan were back with a vengeance because of Matt Richardson. He'd kissed her hand. *She'd wanted him to kiss her mouth.*

With a groan Angie threw down her pencil and pushed herself
away from her desk. For three days her thoughts had displayed a
rather irritating tendency to veer off in *his* direction whenever she
let her mind slip. Much as she hated to admit it, it was because
she was so acutely aware of him as a man, a very attractive man.

But thinking of Matt in that way reminded her of Evan, and at
the end making love with Evan had been an ordeal. Though they
had once shared a satisfying, active sex life, she hadn't been able
to respond as she once had.

"Angel...my sweet Angel," he'd whispered so many times
while holding her tenderly in his arms. How she had loved the
sound of that tender endearment coming from his lips, loved it
and flourished in the headiness of his desire.

Later there were no warm, breathless words of love, only cruel,
ruthless taunts. He'd called her frigid and other ugly, dirty names.

It was a vicious circle, one that Angie hoped would end soon.
Was it any wonder that she would have liked to forget what happened with Matt the other night?

Unfortunately, Matt wouldn't let her.

Spooky suddenly appeared in the doorway of her den and
rubbed against her legs, then looked up at her. Angie laughed and
settled the fat furry length of silver stripes onto her lap.

"What would you do if some pesky old tomcat kept hounding
you?" She ruffled the cat's silky fur. Spooky responded by gently
nudging her nose under Angie's hand for more. "I guess that's
a silly question to ask you," she teasingly accused. Spooky had
borne three litters of kittens before Angie took her off for a nice
little visit to the veterinarian.

Besides, Matt wasn't hounding her—precisely. But he certainly
wasn't backing off, either.

The phone perched on one corner of her wide mahogany desk
chose that moment to give a strident peal of summons. Spooky
slid off her lap and onto the floor. At the doorway she cast a
leisurely look back at her mistress as if to say, "I'll leave you
two alone now," before strolling from the room.

Angie cast a jaundiced eye at the phone. It rang two more
times. Sighing, she reached for the phone, then spoke a cautious
hello into the mouthpiece.

"Will you have dinner with me tomorrow night?" a voice
asked without preamble.

Against her will Angie smiled. It had become Matt's standard
greeting the last four nights. She glanced at her watch and saw

that it was nine-thirty. "You're half an hour late," she told him nonchalantly. Before he had called precisely at nine.

"And you haven't answered my question."

She could tell he was smiling. "I don't think you want to hear it," she teased back.

"I think I do."

Angie hesitated. It was getting harder and harder to turn him down. "No," she said finally.

She knew he must have detected her indecision when he laughed. "You know you still owe me a lunch. I could collect on that." There was a slight pause. "I don't suppose you'd care to make a little wager instead?"

"The chief of police a gambling man?" She pretended to be shocked. "What would people think if they knew?"

"Just don't tell my boss," he pleaded. "Okay?"

Angie chuckled and switched the phone to her other ear. "What is this infamous bet you're so anxious to make?"

"That you *will* have a meal with me within the next week."

"Hmm," she mused thoughtfully. "I think I should warn you I don't like to lose."

"Typical statement, coming from a politician."

She couldn't seem to stop smiling. It was odd how that always happened during these nightly phone conversations with Matt. "That reminds me—what will I be winning?"

"Me," he replied without hesitation.

Her breath caught in her throat. Her laugh sounded rather strangled. "Matt..." she began.

"Oh, all right." He relented good-naturedly. "If you win, you don't have to take me to lunch. I'll buy yours instead. And if I win—" his voice dropped to a low, husky pitch "—I'll settle for a kiss, freely given, even more freely accepted."

Angie's heart stood still. A feeling of warmth stole through her, spawned by an image of a dark-haired, impossibly handsome man from Chicago.

It took a moment before she could breathe again. It was only a game, she told herself. A game that children indulged in. *A game between lovers.*

But there was no denying that Matt was proving what she already knew. She liked him. She liked him far too much for her own good.

"I hope you're not a sore loser," she heard herself say lightly.

"The way I see it, I can't lose either way."

It didn't occur to her until after she'd hung up an hour later, but that was exactly how she felt, too.

THERE WAS A familiar-looking BMW parked at the baseball field the next morning when Angie and the girls piled out of the Crawfords' station wagon.

Bill spied it at the same time. "Say, Angie." He winked at Janice, then grinned. "Isn't that Matt Richardson?"

Angie nodded, her eyes on the figure lounging against the shiny black hood of the BMW. It was Matt, all right. Taut, trim, powerful-looking. A brown-and-gold-striped knit shirt stretched across shoulders that seemed impossibly wide, especially in comparison to the narrow hips hugged tightly by a pair of worn jeans.

Somehow she wasn't surprised to see him. He had offhandedly asked last night if Kim had a game today, and she had half-suspected—or was it hoped?—that he would show up.

Bill cupped his hands and shouted to Matt, whose lean legs carried him fluidly across the grass. His dark hair was attractively feathered across his forehead by the breeze. Angie's heart knocked wildly as he approached.

His hello and smile encompassed the three adults, but his eyes lingered on Angie before he reached out to ruffle Casey's curls. "Hi, there, squirt," he teased. Casey giggled, her eyes bright and sparkling.

"Hi, Nancy." He smiled at the youngster, then looked at Kim. "Hi, Kim. All set for the game?"

Solemn brown eyes surveyed him before the child slowly nodded. Matt noticed how she edged closer to her mother, her thin hand slipping into Angie's. He wondered a little about her insecurity and made a note to ask Angie about it.

"Speaking of the game, we'd better get out there." Angie nodded to where the rest of the team had started to gather on the opposite side of the field.

"You know why he's here, don't you?" Janice asked smugly as she fell into step beside Angie.

Angie rolled her eyes. "It's not very hard to figure out, especially after the way you practically knocked our heads together last week."

"I know, I know. Cease and desist. You already made that very clear." Janice grimaced, then glanced back to where Matt and Bill stood together talking, Casey and Eric nearby. "But I'd say the fact that he's here, without any outside interference from me, speaks for itself. And I don't see you complaining," she added almost challengingly. They stopped in front of the team's low-slung wooden bench. "Do I get to be your matron of honor this time?"

Angie shook her head, but she was smiling as the crowd of young girls began to gather around them. It was just like Janice to be so optimistic and hopeful; sometimes she wished she were just a little more like her. As for Matt...well, when he wasn't eyeing her in that disturbingly male way he had, she could relax and enjoy his company.

The game resulted in a victory for Kim's team, their first win of the season. Caught up in the chattering excitement around her, Angie found herself responding to Matt's delighted expression as he came toward them. She'd heard Matt cheering Kim whenever she made a good play, and while it might only be motherly pride, she felt a warm glow when he approached Kim.

"Beating the opposition eighteen to fifteen calls for a celebration. You like ice cream, Kim?" Kim's eyes lit up, and she nodded tentatively. Encouraged, he turned to Angie. "How about it, Coach? Is there any place close we could go to grab an ice-cream cone?"

Angie checked her watch. It was nearly noon. "I don't know," she began doubtfully, glancing at the two children. "It might spoil their lunch—"

"Oh, Mommy!" Casey groaned.

"Uh-oh." Matt flashed a lopsided grin. "Sorry about that. I didn't even think about lunch."

She felt a small tug on her hand. "Can we go, Mom? Please?"

Soulful brown eyes looked pleadingly up at her. Kim rarely asked for anything, so she hated to say no because of something as trifling as a late meal. The three imploring faces awaited her response. She couldn't refuse.

"All right," she relented, then glanced at Matt, a twinkle in her blue eyes. "But only if Mom gets to have a banana split."

"Done," Matt said in satisfaction. He asked Bill and Janice if they would like to come along, but they declined, saying they were due at Bill's parents' for the afternoon.

They had nearly reached Matt's car when Angie heard a voice hailing her from behind. She turned to see Todd Austin striding toward her.

"Hi, Angie. I stopped by your house, but when you weren't

there I thought I might find you here." Todd wore a pair of crisply pleated slacks and a pale yellow golf shirt. "Hello, Kim. Casey." He nodded politely at the two girls, one on each side of her. Was it her imagination or had Kim's fingers tightened on hers?

"Hello, Todd." Her mind more on Kim's reaction than on Todd, she began to ask what had brought him here, but Casey's voice overrode hers as she looked up at Matt.

"Can I have orange sugar ice cream?"

Matt looked at Angie blankly. "Orange sugar?" he mimicked silently.

"Orange sherbet," she explained, glancing at Todd. From the corner of her eye, she saw Matt grin down at Casey. "You can have anything you want, hon," he told her.

Todd looked past Angie to where Matt now stood behind her. "I'm sorry," he apologized rather stiffly. "I didn't mean to interrupt."

It wasn't until Matt stepped forward and extended his hand that Angie realized she had been remiss in not introducing the two. Todd had been on vacation when Matt started his job.

"You must be Todd Austin," he said easily. "I'm Matt Richardson."

"Oh, yes. Our new chief of police." Todd was polite, but his tone was distant as his eyes moved assessingly over the foursome.

His expression was faintly accusing when he looked at Angie again. That, combined with the coolness in his voice and his possessiveness earlier that week, made her just the slightest bit edgy. Still, considering how closely she had to work with Todd, she didn't like such tension existing between them.

"Was there something you wanted to see me about, Todd?" she asked with a faint smile. "Matt was just about to take us out for ice cream. Kim's team won their first game of the year."

For just a moment he looked angry, then he seemed to relax. "I thought you might want to review the rest of the budget material this weekend. Parks and recreation just came through this morning."

Angie groaned. Ratification of several departmental budgets was on the agenda for Monday's council meeting. "Don't tell me. More changes?"

Todd nodded, his expression rueful. "This is the last, I hope. I've got everything with me if you want to go ahead and take it now."

"That'll be fine." She walked with him to his car, parked about ten spaces over from Matt's. He handed over a leather-bound bundle, then stared at her for a moment.

She sensed what was on his mind. "Todd, I don't want any hard feelings between us," she said quietly.

He was silent. "Because of him?" he finally asked, indicating Matt with a slight incline of his head.

He looked so disappointed her heart went out to him. But there was no point in encouraging him needlessly. "No," she said very gently. "To tell you the truth, I'm not really sure how I feel about Matt," she admitted. "And where you're concerned, I can't pretend to feelings that aren't there, either. I like you, Todd—very much. But only as a friend. Do you understand?"

"Yeah," he muttered. "Can't get much plainer than that." He looked down and shifted his feet, then finally looked back up at her. "I guess I made a fool of myself, huh?"

She shook her head, relieved to note that he was smiling.

"Everything okay?" Matt glanced over at her quizzically when she got into his car a few minutes later. Casey and Kim were already sitting in the back seat.

"It is now," she answered.

"Can I ask you something?" he asked presently.

"Ask away," she said lightly.

"Am I competing with someone else? Todd, for instance? I know you said there was nothing going on between you two, but the way he looks at you..." His voice trailed off.

It would have been the perfect way out, Angie realized. She didn't want Matt Richardson or Todd Austin or any other man in her life. Yet here he was, here *they* were together. And she really didn't mind.

She couldn't lie to him, any more than she could lie to herself. "No. There's no one. Todd would like to change that, but..." She hesitated.

"You wouldn't."

She nodded.

"I see." The makings of a smile appeared on his lips. "Does that apply to me, as well?"

Angie stared down at her hands. Now there was a question—a very good question indeed.

Her silence reached all the way to Matt's heart. Damned if cool, competent Angie wasn't just the slightest bit shy. He took her silence as encouragement. Granted, it wasn't much to go on, but he would take what he could get.

A blond head suddenly bobbed between them. "I thought we were gonna get ice cream!" Casey complained.

Matt sighed. This was one discussion he'd have liked to continue. Instead, it crossed his mind he was quickly learning that patience, especially as it pertained to Angie Hall, was indeed a golden word. But he could wait. It would make the reward all the more precious.

An hour later both Casey and Kim had devoured hamburgers and French fries, as well as half of their ice-cream cones. Angie watched as the waitress walked toward their table with a tray in her hands.

"I'll probably regret this tomorrow," she laughed as the dish containing triple scoops of ice cream covered with thick, rich toppings and a fluffy mound of whipped cream were placed before her. "My over-thirty figure can't handle very many of these." Her eyes glinted teasingly. "Banana splits are my one weakness."

And you are mine, he added silently, wishing he could be honest, totally honest, with her. Sitting across from her in the booth, his eyes took in the slim bare arms resting on the tabletop. He'd already committed her body to memory—full, round breasts that he fairly ached to fit into his palm, legs that were long and slim, topped by that delightfully curved derriere....

"Your over-thirty figure couldn't get any better," he finally told her, his eyes as warm as his voice. Smiling, he gently pushed the dish closer to her.

Angie picked up her spoon. Her face flushed with unexpected pleasure at his compliment. "Sure you don't want some?"

He nodded. "Better eat it while you can," he added with a chuckle. Kim and Casey, seated on either side of her, had turned covetous eyes to their mother's treat. His smile deepened as Angie took her first bite, then closed her eyes. It tasted disgracefully rich, almost sinfully delicious.

It wasn't until she was nearly finished that she looked up and caught Matt's expression. His smile was gone, but his eyes were fairly dancing with merriment that reflected a boyish charm.

He leaned toward her, his words meant for her ears alone. "You lose," he said very softly.

Angie couldn't help it. Her mouth curved with unwilling amusement. Until that moment she had completely forgotten about the silly bet he had insisted on several nights ago—that within the week they would share a meal. And now, it seemed, she owed him a kiss. What was it he'd said? Freely given, freely accepted. Oddly, the prospect filled her with a strange tingle of excitement, a feeling of feminine warmth and anticipation. It had been so long that she almost didn't recognize it. Almost—but not quite.

"Are you copping out on me already?" His voice was laced with devilry.

Her palms grew suddenly damp. *Not yet anyway,* she answered silently. Wordlessly she shook her head.

"Later, then?" She heard him voice the question, saw an even deeper question in his eyes.

She glanced around the crowded restaurant, needing a moment to compose herself. Matt wouldn't force her into anything. She didn't know how she knew it—she just did.

And somehow that gave her the courage to smile shyly across at him. "Later," she echoed huskily. Later...

CHAPTER NINE

ON THE WAY HOME, it struck Angie how different Matt was from Todd. Todd was tense sometimes. A worrier, not always particularly patient.

But the easy way Matt acted with the girls, especially, impressed Angie. He didn't seem to find Casey's nonstop questions at all annoying, though several times Angie saw him trying hard not to laugh. He even tried to engage quiet Kim in conversation. Kim responded shyly, but Angie marveled that she even responded at all. Her usual reaction when a man spoke to her was to drop her eyes and look away, pretending she hadn't heard.

Yes, Matt was different. He was kind and sensitive. The very fact that he hadn't pressured her into something she wasn't sure she even wanted, much less something she wasn't ready for, was proof positive. Many men would have already sought greener pastures. As virile-looking a man as he was, he would have no trouble attracting his share of female attention.

Angie had shied away from men ever since Evan died. Matt Richardson, however, was the kind of man she could care about, really care about. But did she dare? It was a question she didn't yet have an answer to.

With a start she realized that Matt had pulled into her driveway. She smiled a little self-consciously when she felt his eyes on her profile. "This is starting to become a habit," she murmured. "You dropping me off at home."

He followed the movement of her slender hand as it tucked a wispy strand of gold behind her ear. The rest of her hair lay in a single fat braid down her back. The simple hairstyle, along with the fact that she wore little makeup, made her appear very young.

He suddenly remembered the dark anguish in her eyes when she spoke of her husband. Was it selfish of him to wonder how to ease her pain and replace it with a golden glow of love for him? Perhaps. But it didn't stop him from wanting to try.

"I'm not complaining, but I may start charging you mileage," he teased.

Casey was bouncing impatiently on the back seat. Matt got out and eased the seat forward allowing the two girls to get out. "Wait," he called as they began to run toward the house. "I almost forgot. I have something for each of you." He went around to the rear of the car, opened the trunk and brought out two small, gaily wrapped packages. The square one he handed to Casey, the other to Kim.

Casey wasted no time in ripping the paper away. "Look, Mommy!" she cried delightedly. "Care Bear stickers. And a book to put them in!"

"Just what you've been wanting." Angie smiled at her daughter's excitement, then turned her attention to Kim. She was peeling away the paper much more slowly and carefully. From the circular shape Angie guessed it was a ball of some sort, but she was a little surprised when Kim held up a rather battered-looking league ball.

Matt dropped down to one knee beside her. "Remember I told you about Ernie Banks last week, Kim?"

The child nodded. "He played for the—" she hesitated, her small brow furrowed in concentration before she announced "—the Chicago Cubs!"

Angie wasn't surprised that she remembered. As young as she was, Kim was fairly familiar with the major league teams. But her own pleasure was echoed in Matt's face as he flashed a smile.

"Ernie hit a home run with this ball," he told her, then rotated the ball slightly and pointed to a place that had been hidden by Kim's palm. "See that? That's Ernie's autograph."

Kim's eyes lit up like hundred-watt lightbulbs. "He really signed this?"

"Sure did."

"Gee," the little girl breathed, then frowned once more. "How did you get it?"

He laughed. "I was about fourteen at the time and I spent most Saturday afternoons at Wrigley Field. I got my head knocked around a few times, but when Ernie blasted that ball into the center field bleachers, I scrambled around until I found it. Then I waited outside at the end of the game. When Ernie came out of the locker room, I asked him to sign it for me. He was my hero in those days."

"You were really there when he hit a home run?" Kim's voice was filled with excitement. "A grand slam?"

"It wasn't a grand slam, but I was really there." His eyes twinkled. "And now it's yours, Kim. You'll take good care of it, won't you?"

"You bet I will!" It was such an enthusiastic avowal that Angie was startled. She was even more startled at the gentle expression that softened Matt's harshly carved features as Kim looked up at him. "Thanks, Mr. Richardson," she said with a trace of her customary shyness. Then a wide grin appeared. "Thanks a lot!"

Angie's throat was poignantly tight. It had been a long time since she'd seen her daughter's face exhibit such radiance—far too long. She hadn't seen Kim this happy since before Evan's death.

"That was really sweet of you, Matt." She paused, her head angled as she watched him rise lithely to his feet. "The baseball...it must have meant a lot to you if you've kept it all these years."

Angie's voice was warmer than he'd ever heard it, at least when she'd spoken to him.

He shrugged, just a little embarrassed. His eyes followed the two girls as they went around the side of the house. "It did for a long time," he admitted, turning his attention back to Angie. He'd had so little as a child. There were no train sets proudly set up by a doting father at Christmastime. He'd never even had his own bike. But Angie was right. The baseball he'd given Kim was something he'd always treasured.

"Kids aren't hard to please," he said, voicing his thoughts. "And Kim...well, Bill told me how crazy she is about baseball. I thought she might like it."

"Like it?" Her laughter sounded like bells tinkling in a spring breeze. He'd never heard anything so sweet. "She loves it. And speaking of heroes, I think she may have a new one—by the name of Matt Richardson."

A look of pleasure appeared in his eyes. "How does her mother feel about that?"

There was something boyishly appealing in the way he stood there grinning lopsidedly at her, with his hands stuffed into the front pockets of his jeans. Yet there was nothing even remotely boyish in the sheer physical presence of the man, the impression of strength and power reflected in both mind and body.

He had pushed up the sleeves of his shirt against the warmth of the afternoon, revealing strong, muscular forearms covered with a dense layer of silky dark hair. Angie's heart executed what felt like a triple somersault.

"Her mother," she heard herself say lightly, "thinks she couldn't have made a better choice." Was she flirting? It certainly sounded like it!

Their eyes met. His were bold, bright, a tentative question in their depths. Hers weren't quite so direct; Matt thought he detected a hint of uncertainty.

He took an involuntary step toward her. "Angie," he began.

The sudden pitter-patter of footsteps on the sidewalk drowned out the sound of his voice. Matt heard a gate slam and looked around to find Kim and Casey tearing around the side of the house. "Mommy! Mommy, something's been in our yard!" Wearing a fearful expression, Kim latched on to her mother's hand.

Angie and Matt started toward the rear of the house. A moment later Angie's jaw dropped at what she saw there.

The yard was a shambles. The neatly designed borders of flowers and shrubbery that edged the house had been uprooted. Fragile blossoms, tiny branches and clumps of dirt had been strewn across the grass. The picnic table beneath the towering elm tree had been upended. The delicate white wicker lawn furniture was smashed into bits and pieces as if it had been stomped upon and carelessly kicked aside. To top it off the pristine white boards on one corner of the house had been defaced with a dark red spray paint.

"Good Lord," she muttered numbly. "Something *has* been—"

"Not something," Matt said grimly. "Some*one*." A tight-lipped expression on his face, he asked, "Any idea who could be responsible?"

"None." Her eyes were puzzled as they swept around the ravaged yard. "Why on earth would someone do this?" From somewhere she dredged up a weak smile, remembering what he'd said when they'd found her tires slashed. "A couple of kids hell-bent on a little destruction?"

It was possible, Matt admitted silently. But somehow he didn't think so. He had the feeling this was intentionally aimed at Angie. "Any rowdies in the neighborhood who might vandalize?" he asked instead.

"Not that I know of."

"Has anything else like this happened lately?"

"No," she responded quietly. "This is a relatively quiet area of town. There have been a few burglaries from time to time, but that's all."

Matt walked across the yard and peered over the tall fence to the narrow alleyway that ran the entire length of the block. He glanced over at the thick, seven-foot hedge of arborvitae that separated Angie's property from Mrs. Johnson's. "Whoever did it probably climbed over the fence from the alley and didn't even have to worry about being seen. But it won't hurt to check with some of the neighbors and see if anyone saw or heard anything." He turned and started back toward the gate.

As it happened, no one had, and Angie was fully involved in cleaning up by the time Matt returned. He noticed the wheelbarrow sitting on the patio, already heaped full of withered plant life. "You should have waited for me," he admonished gently.

Angie bent over and picked up a handful of what had once been a bright yellow spray of marigold blossoms. In the few minutes that he had been gone, her surprise had given way to anger and now to a feeling of tired resignation. "Don't tell me you're going to offer to help with this, too," she said as she straightened up.

Matt crossed his arms over his chest. "Is there any reason why I shouldn't?" he countered.

Angie sighed. "There's really no need. It won't take that long—"

"Aren't you forgetting you have budget material to go over?"

She grimaced and waved a hand. "No, but that doesn't mean you have to..." Her voice trailed off as he walked over and took the rake she still held in one hand. Without a word he turned and began raking up clumps of dirt. Angie stared at his broad back, thinking that he was the most persistent man she had ever met in her life.

She perched her hands on her slender hips, trying very hard to feel offended, but somehow the feeling just wouldn't come. "Is this a habit of yours? Coming in and taking over someone else's life?"

"Is that what I'm doing?" he asked mildly, glancing back at her over his shoulder. "I thought it was called helping a friend. Although that friend does owe me something—" his smile was unrepentant as his eyes dropped meaningfully to her mouth "—and hasn't yet paid up."

Angie was the first to look away. "I suppose you want to make it two now."

"One will do, Angie. One will do very nicely...for now."

The playful edge to his words didn't lessen the suddenly erratic fluttering of her pulse. To cover her reaction she turned her back to him, bent from the waist and grabbed another handful of azalea branches. "I still think you must have better things to do with your time than spend it cleaning up someone else's yard," she muttered, not really caring if he overheard.

Matt leaned on his rake, pausing to savor the enticing picture she presented. At the moment Matt couldn't think of *anything* better.

SEVERAL HOURS LATER Angie was repainting the corner of the house. It was just as she finished the last sweeping stroke with her brush that she sensed she was being watched.

She jerked her gaze upward and saw that Matt's eyes were trained intently on her face. They were so dark and cloudy that she had the strangest sensation he was looking right through her, that it was someone else he was seeing.

The sun had warmed the afternoon temperature to the mid-eighties, and Matt had peeled off his shirt against the heat. His body was lean, and dense swirls of dark hair carpeted the whole of his chest and abdomen before dipping down beneath the waist-band of his jeans. She wondered if those midnight curls were as soft as they looked.

"Matt?" The sight of his bare torso caused an unevenness in her voice. "Is something wrong?"

He shook his head. "I was just thinking..." He paused, then took the shovel he was holding and propped it against the wheelbarrow. "I was just thinking how different you are from Linda," he finished quietly.

Linda. She felt a prickly sensation trail down her spine. Jealousy? No. It couldn't be. "Your ex-wife?" she asked.

"Yes."

Angie bent and replaced the lid on the can of paint. Watching her, Matt's smile ebbed. "She wouldn't have been caught dead with paint on her hands."

"Or dirt under her nails?" she guessed, displaying her own as a prime example. At his nod she found herself asking, "What was she like?"

"Spoiled. Rich. Vain," he said without hesitation. He picked up his shirt and pulled it over his head, then walked over and sat down at the picnic table before he spoke again. "She looks a little like you," he admitted with a sheepish half smile. "Blond, fair skin." The smile widened. "Never saw her with a sunburned nose, though. Guess it's just one more reason I like you so much."

Angie laughed and wrinkled her nose. She had no intention of becoming seriously involved with Matt, but she admitted to a certain curiosity about the woman who had once been his wife. "Oh, come on," she protested, sitting down across from him. "She must have had something you liked, or you wouldn't have married her. Was she pretty?"

He was silent for a moment. "No," he said finally. "She wasn't pretty. She was beautiful. Absolutely gorgeous."

At his words Angie felt an unexpected pang. She glanced down at the faded blue shorts and T-shirt she wore, now splattered with white paint, and realized she must look anything but alluring. "Is that why you moved away from Chicago?" she asked softly. "To get away from the memories?"

Matt sent her a wry look. "I've been divorced for six years, Angie. Fool that I was for marrying her, I'd be an even bigger fool if I mooned that long over a woman like Linda."

Angie frowned. It was the last thing she expected him to say. "Didn't you love her?" It was none of her business, she knew, but the question was out before she even realized it.

He was immersed in thought for so long she didn't think he'd heard her. "I loved her," he said at last. "But after a while it just wasn't enough."

Angie's heart caught painfully. She knew the feeling only too well. At the end that was exactly how she'd felt with Evan.

"We weren't the people we thought we were," Matt went on. "Linda came from a very old, wealthy Chicago family. Her father was a judge, her grandfather an Illinois supreme court justice. We met when her father received a threat from a man he'd once sentenced to a twenty-year term for manslaughter." He seemed to hesitate. "In a way she was everything I always thought I'd wanted but could never even hope to have. To her, I think I was like the forbidden fruit—a tough-talking detective from the wrong side of town."

Oddly, Angie understood completely. There was something

very raw, almost primitive, to Matt's earthy good looks—something that kindled a certain fascination for the unknown.

Like it or not, Angie finally admitted to herself how much she was attracted to him. But it wasn't just his aura of elemental strength that drew her to him. He was gentle, sensitive, emotionally warm and giving in the way only a man who was supremely confident of his masculinity could be.

Had Evan ever been like that?

"How long were you married?" she asked, trying to vanquish the disturbing thought.

"Three years. Three very long years. Oh, it started out okay." He ran his hand along the back of his head as he searched for the right words. "Linda thrived on constant adoration—the perfect social butterfly. She wasn't happy unless she was going to a party or we were giving one...." The sigh he gave expressed his feelings more clearly than words.

"Is that why you don't like parties?" she asked, smiling faintly.

Matt nodded. "I didn't mind at first, but it got tiresome, fast—real fast. We lived in a high rise her father owned, but it wasn't long before she wasn't satisfied living on my salary. If I didn't approve of something she wanted—trips to New York, clothes, jewelry—she went behind my back to dear old Dad."

"So you divorced her," she murmured.

He shook his head. Angie found it rather disconcerting that he looked away from her and focused instead on the two children playing on the swing set in the opposite corner of the yard.

"No," he said after a lengthy silence. "She divorced me." He half turned to her, a self-deprecating smile on his lips. "It was rather odd, really. For so long I'd thought of our marriage as a match made in hell, but what I went through after Linda divorced me was even worse. Because much as I hated to admit it, I still cared. And my life didn't get any better until I finally accepted that our relationship was over."

This time it was Angie who looked away. She knew what he was trying to say, that she needed to get on with her life and forget about Evan. *I have,* she wanted to cry, *in all but this one thing.*

"The burnt child dreads the fire," Matt quoted softly. "Isn't there a saying like that?"

She nodded stiffly. "I don't see what that has to do with me, though."

"Don't you?" he asked quietly.

Angie said nothing. She only continued to stare in silent fascination at the redwood-planked tabletop.

"I know it hurts to lose someone you love so much, but that doesn't mean you should be afraid to risk it again."

So he thought she was afraid of love? She swallowed the bittersweet laugh that rose in her throat. If she was, it wasn't for the reasons he thought. For a moment she almost hated herself for her deceit, yet it was easier to let him think devotion to Evan was holding her back.

Pride had driven a wedge between Matt and his wife. And it was pride that had come between herself and Evan. He had come to resent her usurping his role as the major wage earner of the family.

Angie had seen enough of male pride to last a lifetime.

"Look at me, Angie."

A faint tremor ran through her at his soft demand. Slowly, unwillingly, her mouth parted, her gaze lifted to his. They were gentle, those antique-silver eyes, gentle and compassionate, warm with understanding and sympathy. Eyes to be trusted.

Love and trust were fragile and precious. It was a lesson she had learned the most painful way possible.

"I'm trying to make this easy on you, Angie. Why are you determined to make it so hard? Am I really that hard to talk to?"

Her breath emerged in a long sigh. "No," she admitted quietly. "You're very easy to talk to—"

"As long as we're not talking about you."

He seemed so genuinely puzzled that she truly wished they could be friends, without the complication of being attracted to each other. If only Matt didn't want more than she was prepared to offer....

"Angie, what am I going to do with you?"

The hint of humor in his tone caught her by surprise, but she found herself relaxing. "Nothing?" she responded hopefully.

"You'd like that, wouldn't you?" he countered dryly, rising to his feet. Extending his hands, he helped her up.

A rush of warmth shot through her at the touch of his hands on hers. Dismayed by her involuntary reaction, she attempted to pull away, but Matt wouldn't let her. Angie felt his fingers tighten around hers as he smiled at her reassuringly.

Matt wondered why he sensed an element of fear inside her whenever they touched.

He dropped one hand to his side. With the other he laced their fingers together loosely. "Come on," he told her. "You can walk me to my car."

She fell into step beside him, but as they passed through the gate she spied Mrs. Johnson hurrying toward them. One hand held a napkin-covered platter, the other a lattice-topped cherry pie.

Angie sighed, but there was a fond gleam in her eyes. "Mrs. Johnson," she began, "you really shouldn't have—"

"Nonsense," the elderly woman chided. "When Chief Richardson stopped by earlier and told me what had happened in your backyard, I decided a little supper was the least I could do. These old bones aren't good for much, but at least I can still whip up a batch of Southern fried chicken and a pie."

With that she handed the platter to Matt, the golden-brown pie to Angie. "She's so modest." Angie shook her head and glanced at Matt. "Her fried chicken is probably the best on *both* sides of the Mississippi. In fact, I've been telling her for years she ought to be giving the Colonel a little competition. And her pie..." She rolled her eyes expressively.

Mrs. Johnson beamed. "The secret's in the crust—ice water and a little vinegar, just enough so that the flour and shortening hold together." If the older woman was capable of slyness, it was a sly glance indeed she sent Matt. "Plenty for all of you." She turned and started to walk away.

"But you'll stay, too, won't you?" Angie called after her.

"I've already eaten, dear," came the reply over her shoulder. "Send the girls over later. I've got another little treat for them."

Angie stood speechless, still holding the pie.

Matt wasn't sure which was funnier—Mrs. Johnson's obvious ploy or Angie's reaction to it. "Not that I'm complaining," he said, barely containing his laughter, "but we seem to be the object of quite a few matchmaking efforts."

"You noticed?" Angie commented tartly, but her eyes were sparkling. "Come on, let's take this inside."

After they had deposited the food in the kitchen, she turned and smiled at Matt rather shyly. "Mrs. Johnson was right, you know. If we add a salad and some rolls, there'll be plenty for all of us." For a second she seemed to hesitate. "You're welcome to stay for dinner," she finally said. "It's the least I can do after everything you've done for me this afternoon."

It was an offer made on the spur of the moment, an offer she suddenly wanted him to accept even though she wasn't sure she knew what she was getting into.

Matt studied her for a moment. "I don't think so," he said slowly, then smiled. "I don't want to wear out my welcome, you see."

She shook her head. "You haven't, Matt. At least not yet." When he again declined, she insisted, "Then take something home. The kids and I will never eat all of this." She pulled a plate from the cupboard and filled it with several crisp pieces of chicken and a generous wedge of pie.

The merest hint of a smile played on his lips as he took the plate she offered. "You know what this means, don't you? Prince Charming will have to make another visit—this time to return a plate instead of a shoe."

"I...I know." There was a strange breathless catch in her voice.

Moving carefully, Matt set the plate aside and reached out to tuck a shining strand of gold back behind her ear. She tensed but didn't retreat as he half expected. When he felt her relax, he extended his fingers and slid them beneath the long braid that fell down her back.

"That reminds me." His voice was whisper soft, the touch of his fingers almost caressing as he stroked the baby-fine hair that grew on her nape. "There's a small matter of a bet we made several days ago...."

There was no need for him to go on. Angie felt herself flush, but the spark of humor she encountered in his warm, gray eyes reassured her.

They were standing only inches apart, bound by fingers that seemed strangely reluctant to part. Slowly she moved to him directly. Charcoal lashes drifted closed as she wordlessly offered her lips.

A low masculine laugh was the last thing on earth she expected.

"You're supposed to kiss me," Matt reminded her when her eyes flew open.

"Oh," she said in a small voice, then smiled.

Matt caught his breath at the brilliance of that unexpected smile, a smile that seemed to make the afternoon sun burn brighter still.

"Freely given, even more freely accepted, wasn't it?" she asked.

This time it was he who nodded wordlessly.

Angie's hand, so tenderly imprisoned within his, gently withdrew to join its mate on the broad landscape of his chest. Through the fabric of his shirt, the faint rasp of wiry hair teased her fingertips. Against her legs she could feel the hardness of his denim-clad thighs. Her heart began to thunder in her chest, and her senses were awash in a tingle of expectation. She slowly levered herself upward.

His lips were hard but yielding, soft yet firm. She kissed them lightly, hesitantly, a touch like the wings of a butterfly. Yet even at the featherlight contact, she knew a moment of sublime pleasure. Her body stirred to life with feelings long denied...but not forgotten.

Matt felt her draw back as if she'd been burned. But not before he saw the expression of confused wonder on her face.

He had to fight the urge to pull her back into his arms and capture her mouth with his once more, to give in to the pent-up longing that burned inside. The brief taste she'd given him was tempting, so tempting. But he wanted her willing, and he wanted her trust. And he knew he had to have *both* before she would come to him.

He could hardly believe how quickly this feeling inside had happened. The feeling was part pleasure yet part pain because Angie was still fighting it. He could only call it love.

A lean finger at her chin tipped her face back to his. "One of these days," he said softly, "you're going to take a big step forward."

"And?" Angie was mesmerized. She felt as if her deepest secrets were no longer her own...but his.

"And I intend to be here when you do." His thumb discovered the tender curve of her mouth. "Because together we're going to get through this—whatever it is that's holding you back."

To Angie, his words sounded very much like a promise.

CHAPTER TEN

TOGETHER. It was a word Angie hadn't used in a long, long time. So long it felt alien to hear it on her lips, hear it still echoing in her mind on Monday night as she prepared for bed. Even a long soak in the bathtub hadn't cleared her thoughts.

It was a word that frightened her. For in his own unique way, with his quiet insight, his gentleness, his warmth and his caring, Matt was the most frightening man she had ever known.

Evan had betrayed her. He had violated their love. She couldn't willingly let any man have that kind of power over her again or open herself up for that kind of heartache. No, she wasn't ready for involvement with Matt. She couldn't afford to let herself grow close to him in any way.

She couldn't stop herself, either.

Gently. Oh, so gently, but with a thoroughness that alarmed her, he was invading every corner of her life. Her mind, her thoughts...her heart?

And there wasn't a thing she could do about it because she was lonely—especially at night. She missed the closeness, the sharing, the comfort and security of a warm male body lying next to her.

Angie couldn't fool herself any longer. She was a woman with a woman's needs, and her body was telling her that it had been too long since those needs had been met. It was as if that one brief kiss she'd shared with Matt had opened up a Pandora's box. Coaxing. Luring. Drawing out her most secret feminine desires.

She had once been an intensely passionate woman, a woman who took immense pleasure in the physical intimacies of marriage. The secret fire of her womanhood had been dormant inside her for two years...but no more.

She wanted Matt. She couldn't look at him, she couldn't talk to him, she couldn't even say his name without wondering how it would feel to lie naked next to him, with nothing between them, his hands touching her all over.

Moaning softly, she tore off the towel wrapped around her head and sat down at the dressing table. "What am I going to do?" she thought half angrily, half desperately. Snatching up her brush, she began to work through the tangles in her still-damp hair, wincing as, in her frustration, she yanked her hair a little too hard.

Matt knew something wasn't right when he called that night. She sounded tense, irritable, when she answered the phone.

"Is something wrong?"

The calm question only seemed to irritate her further. *You know very well what's wrong,* she wanted to cry. *Why can't you leave me alone? I was coping so well until you came along.* Instead, she snapped, "Nothing's wrong."

Silence crackled over the wire. "Are you sure?" he asked after a long moment.

There was such concern, such tender consideration in his voice that Angie closed her eyes. "I'm sorry, Matt," she apologized in a low voice. "I'm fine. Really. It's just that...well, it's been a very long day. The council had a special meeting tonight."

"On the city hall issue?"

"Yes." Laying the hairbrush on the night table, she sat on the edge of the bed and began to massage the slight ache in the middle of her forehead. "Would you believe John Curtis brought in sketches of a new building? You should see it!" she said disgustedly. "It's all concrete and clutter. It would be as out of place in Westridge as the Empire State Building."

Matt had trouble holding back a laugh. Sentimental Angie. Still, he knew how much this meant to her. "How did the vote go?"

"Exactly the way I expected," she said glumly. "Split right down the middle. Fireworks before and after—and naturally Blair Andrews was there with her photographer in tow."

"Something tells me I'll be in for a treat when I see the morning newspaper."

"Undoubtedly." She echoed his dry tone. "I expect to be featured on the front page, nose-to-nose with John Curtis. Damn that man," she continued hotly. "He certainly isn't looking for a taste of humble pie, that much I do know!" She had expressed the same sentiment to Todd right after the meeting.

"Really pushing for a new building, isn't he?" Matt murmured.

"I'll say. I'm beginning to think this entire issue will still be unresolved by the time the next mayor takes office." She leaned against the headboard wearily, absently running her finger down the lapel of her robe. "I'm sorry, Matt. I really didn't mean to unload on you like this, but Anna Goodwin and I have talked till we're blue in the face trying to get Steve Jackson and Mike Matthews to see our point of view. And so far it hasn't done any good. If we end up with a new building instead of renovating, we'll never get a women's shelter. It's so...so frustrating!"

Frustrating. It was a word he was rather familiar with himself, but he didn't say so. He knew he wasn't the only one who felt the invisible bond growing between them, yet she still held so much of herself apart from him.

Hell! Who was he trying to kid? It was Angie's husband that still stood between them, and for the life of him, Matt didn't know what to do about it. Their relationship was in limbo, and he wasn't sure he dared trespass the perimeter that she had silently drawn. He sensed they were at a crucial point, but he was afraid if he pushed too hard, he would lose her.

Yet he couldn't deny that she was far more comfortable with him than she'd been at first. They talked freely, easily, about everything except two things—their relationship and her husband. Angie clammed up whenever he attempted to veer in either direction.

Maybe she wasn't living in the past, but she was holding on to the memory of her husband. She'd been married for ten years, he reminded himself grimly, and the marriage had produced two children. He couldn't expect her to forget about a man she'd loved all that time as if he were no more than a casual acquaintance. But he didn't expect it to take forever, either.

With a mental sigh he picked up the threads of their conversation once more. "If things don't turn out the way you'd like, you might consider private funding to start a women's shelter," he said slowly. "A lot of them are funded by private donations."

"And what happens when the donations stop coming in?" She shook her head. "No, I'd rather see a city-funded center. Then at least there would be some measure of stability." She mulled a second longer. "Though if worse comes to worst, that may be the only solution. It would be better than what we have now, or maybe I should say what we *don't* have."

"That reminds me," Matt said thoughtfully. "Have you ever been in one?"

Angie's heart lurched. Surely he didn't know! "N-no," she replied cautiously.

"Would you like to visit one? I could probably arrange it. Sam was telling me just yesterday about a shelter near Seattle. In fact, I was thinking about asking you and the girls to a Mariners' home game on Saturday. Maybe the Crawfords would like to come, too. If you think Kim and Casey wouldn't mind going with me, you could tour the shelter and see how it operates while we're at the game. Unless you'd rather I came along, too?"

"No. There's no need," she said quickly, perhaps too quickly. But when Matt said nothing, her heartbeat returned to normal. "That's a great idea," she murmured thoughtfully, then smiled. "Kim's never been to a major league game. I think she'd love it." It suddenly occurred to her that Kim might not feel comfortable being alone with Matt, but if Janice and Nancy were along, as well... "How about if I let you know tomorrow?"

A warm feeling was flowing through Angie as she hung up the phone a few minutes later. But when she crawled into bed, the too-familiar feeling of loneliness assailed her. She closed her eyes against the yearning ache in her belly, an ache borne of images in the dark—sharp, sensual images of strong male hands lingering over her body, a long, muscled body poised above hers.

Turning over, she clutched her pillow tightly against her breasts, her entire body now seized with a near-painful heat. A silent litany played over and over in her mind before she finally fell asleep a long time later. Together.

If only she could believe...

"ARE WE THERE YET?"

It must have been the tenth time Kim had posed the question in the last hour. Angie's worries had been for nothing. Kim had expressed only the slightest reticence at going with Matt to the baseball stadium, but by this morning it was gone. She had been awake since six-thirty, anxiously waiting for Matt to pick them up shortly before lunch.

"Almost," Angie assured her. Bill and Janice trailed several cars behind, and the freeway ribboned on ahead of them. She half turned in her seat to point out a large sign at the side of the road. "See? We're only ten miles from Seattle."

"We were lucky to get such good seats," Matt remarked. When he'd called the stadium earlier in the week, a group of seven had exchanged their seats that day for a game later in the month. "At Wrigley Field box seats are usually impossible to get unless you buy them weeks ahead."

"Box seats!" Casey sounded horrified. "I don't want to sit on boxes!"

"You don't sit on a box, silly." Kim frowned at her little sister. "Box seats are closer to the field. Right, Matt?"

"Right, Kim." Matt's lips quirked at Kim's self-important tone. Glancing over at Angie, he saw her fighting to hold back a smile, as well. She was wearing a lacy blouse with a high Victorian collar tucked into pleated slate-gray slacks. Her hair had been pulled back into its usual austere twist, and she appeared as calm and collected as ever. She kept toying with the strap of her purse, though, and he wondered if she was a little nervous about visiting the shelter.

"By the way," he said casually in an attempt to get her mind off whatever was bothering her, "I saw Sam pick up Georgia after work last night. They seem to have something hot and heavy going. Any wedding bells in the offing?"

"Not that I know of. Although I must admit the whole thing between those two came as something of a surprise. To tell you the truth, Sam is the first man she's gone out with in the four years I've known her."

Matt raised an eyebrow. "Maybe she has and you just haven't known about it—" He stopped when Angie emphatically shook her head. "Don't tell me," he surmised dryly. "She's the spinsterish schoolteacher type."

"Not exactly," she admitted. "Georgia—" She hesitated. "Georgia just hasn't had much use for men in her life."

"I see." Matt's tone was grave, but his eyes held a faint light. "Condition of employment, was it?"

She knew he was thinking of the night she'd told him she didn't want another man in her life, and she smiled self-consciously. "Georgia's mother died when she was very young," she began to explain. "She had to raise several younger brothers and sisters."

"Where was her father?"

Angie checked to make sure the two girls in the back seat weren't listening before she spoke again. "Her father left when she wasn't much older than ten. He simply went to work one day and never came back."

Matt's fingers tightened around the steering wheel. It was the only visible sign that her words affected him. "So that's why she decided to steer clear of men?" he asked finally.

"That might be part of it, but that's not all."

"That's not all?" His surprise seemed genuine.

"Unfortunately, no. Georgia had always wanted to go to college, but she didn't have the money. She's smart though, and she was able to get a good job with an accounting firm." Angie took a deep breath. She felt a bit uncomfortable telling Matt this. "It was the first time she'd ever really been out on her own, and she was relatively inexperienced when it came to men. And then—"

"She fell in love with her boss," he guessed astutely.

"Her *married* boss," she confirmed grimly. "She didn't know until it was too late. And even then he continued to string her along, promising that he would divorce his wife."

"But he never did."

"That's right."

Matt shook his head. "So Georgia is a woman with a past," he mused dryly. "I'd never have guessed it." He chuckled as her eyes began to widen. "Oh, don't worry. I won't tell a soul. I can keep a secret as well as the next person."

Angie detected no reproach, no reproof in his tone, but it did betray a hint of disappointment, and that affected her far more strongly. Angie's throat tightened oddly. Matt had paved the way for her to talk about Evan many times this past week. She knew, deep inside, that he would understand, yet she couldn't remember Evan without feeling hurt, and degraded, and ashamed. How could she ever bear to talk about it openly and honestly when it was so sordid and ugly? she thought on a panicky note. She had never even been able to tell Janice or Georgia of Evan's abuse.

Her thoughts couldn't have chosen a worse path to follow. They had exited the freeway and were driving along a tree-lined boulevard. Matt turned off onto a side street and stopped the car. For a few seconds Angie stared at the two-story stone building before her, demons from the past chasing through her mind.

"I won't go in with you." Matt spoke in a low voice and inclined his head toward the two children in the back seat.

Angie took a deep breath and forced her mind back to the present. "Marilyn Winters, right?"

He nodded, his eyes focused sharply on her face for a second. "We'll pick you up after the game," he said, then turned to the girls. "Say goodbye to your mom, kids."

Summoning a smile that was as much for her own benefit as

that of Matt and the girls, she leaned back for hugs and kisses. Then she stepped out onto the sidewalk and closed the door. Kim and Casey turned around and waved as the car moved away from the curb. Angie stared after it for a long moment before she finally squared her shoulders and headed toward the doorway.

Inside, a tall woman with a cap of jet-black curls was seated behind a desk. Angie placed her age at somewhere near her own. "Hi, there. Can I help you?" the woman asked in greeting.

She glanced around the sparsely furnished room before her gaze returned to the woman. A tentative smile creased her mouth. "I'm Angie Hall," she began. "I'm here to see Marilyn—"

She got no further. The woman had already rounded the desk and clasped her hand in a firm handshake. "I'm Marilyn, and you must be the mayor of Westridge." Sparkling dark eyes looked her up and down. "You're not exactly what I expected."

She suspected this woman had a talent for making one feel warm and welcome, and, as Marilyn led her through the shelter, she soon discovered she was right.

The first floor consisted mainly of a small reception area, which doubled as an office, a supply area, a small kitchen, a living room and a counseling area. The upstairs had been turned into bedrooms.

Angie shivered in spite of the day's warmth when they returned downstairs. The center was sparsely furnished with only the bare essentials. Only the fact that the worn furniture looked comfortable kept the atmosphere from being downright spartan. Even the box of toys in the corner of the living room looked as if it had seen better days.

"Not the best home away from home, is it?" Marilyn sounded grim as she watched Angie scan the room. She handed her a cup of coffee, then sat down behind the desk again. "Most of what we have here has been donated. We do what we can, though, and hope it's enough."

Angie curled her fingers around the cup, absorbing some of the warmth from the hot liquid. "How long have you been in operation?"

"Three years now." Marilyn grimaced. "Give or take a few months that we shut down because of lack of funds."

"Most of your staff are volunteers?"

Marilyn nodded. "A lot of our budget goes for paying the psychologist who consults with the counselors. Some of the rape and abuse cases we've had have been pretty traumatic, and sessions have lasted for months.'' She shook her head. ''Like I said, it's not much, but it beats having nowhere else to go.''

Something in her quiet tone brought Angie's eyes to hers in a flash. The other woman's face reflected a great deal of compassion and silent understanding. A disquieting thought sped through Angie's mind—if Marilyn knew, did Matt? The finger that traced a path around the cracked edge of the cup wasn't entirely steady.

''I didn't realize it was that obvious,'' she said in a low voice.

''It isn't.'' Marilyn paused. ''Except maybe to someone who's been through it.''

Angie stared at her. Marilyn Winters seemed so vibrant, so alive. For a moment she had trouble reconciling the woman before her with a woman who had been battered and bruised. There was a frown on her face as her gaze dropped to the shining gold band on Marilyn's left hand.

Marilyn smiled when she saw the direction of Angie's eyes. ''Put there by a man who cared enough to see me through some bad times.'' The smile broadened. ''A very persistent man!''

Persistent. Matt's dark face immediately swam before her, and her lips twitched unwillingly. ''Is there any other kind?'' she murmured dryly.

They both laughed, and Angie felt some of her tension ease. Marilyn's expression grew more serious, though, when she rose and came around to perch a slender hip against the side of the desk. ''I always tell the women who pass through here that the important thing to remember is you're not alone.'' The words were accompanied by a gentle squeeze of Angie's shoulder. ''And no one should be afraid to ask for help.''

Angie's tentative smile froze at the sound of the door opening. A policeman came inside, followed by a young woman who held a baby in her arms. Fear stood out starkly on her face; a nasty-looking bruise darkened her cheekbone. Angie closed her eyes. A frigid cold seemed to permeate every part of her body.

She heard the words ''family fight'' pass between Marilyn and the officer. Then he turned to the woman he'd introduced as Bonnie. ''You'll be able to stay here until your husband calms down,'' he reassured her. Angie didn't hear the rest of the low-voiced conversation.

It wasn't until the door closed behind him that she saw the child standing behind his mother's legs, clutching a blanket and a bedraggled stuffed animal. She realized he was no older than

Casey. She nearly cried out as his uncertain gaze trickled around
the room before finally coming to rest on her.

She was on her knees in front of him before she even realized
it. "It's okay," she whispered past the lump in her throat. Her
smile was tremulous. "Everything will be okay, you'll see." She
opened her arms, and the little boy walked into them without a
word.

Marilyn was right, she thought after the trio had been settled
into a bedroom. It was good that the shelter was here for women
like Bonnie.

But no woman should have to go through such hell in the first
place.

THE CLEAR DAY had vanished with the onset of night. The star-
studded sky of the past few weeks was hidden behind a curtain
of dense gray clouds. As Angie stared straight ahead, a lone silver
streak of lightning zigzagged across the sky.

There was a definite threat of rain in the air by the time Matt
pulled into her driveway at nine that evening. An hour earlier
Casey had crawled onto Angie's lap and had proceeded to fall
fast asleep. Her head sagged limply against Angie's breast, and
one small hand lay curled on her shoulder.

Glancing back, she saw that Kim had sprawled out on the back
seat as much as she could wearing a seat belt. Neither one roused
when the car rolled to a halt.

Matt's smile encompassed both sleeping children. "Too much
excitement," he said. "I'll give you a hand getting them inside."
Strong arms reached for Kim and he followed her into the house.

"Upstairs," she whispered, juggling Casey against her shoulder. A floorboard creaked as she headed toward the stairs.

A low chuckle sounded behind her. "We've been through this
before. Remember?"

How could she forget the Saturday he'd gone with them to
Kim's game? Angie flushed, but the feeling of resentment she'd
felt that night when the two of them had executed this same ritual
was absent tonight. In fact, she was rather glad of his help.

Kim opened her eyes just as Angie was about to leave the
room. "Mommy?" she whispered.

Angie sat on the edge of the bed. Lowering her voice to a
whisper, she asked, "Did you have a good time today?"

Kim nodded and smiled, a wide smile that Angie had seen all

too little the past few years. "The umpires were all dressed the same, and they wore funny little hats." She giggled. "When they came out on the field, Casey asked Matt why all the priests were there."

Angie's laughter joined her daughter's, though Matt had already told her of the incident. Pushing the soft brown curls off Kim's forehead, she paused. "Do you like Matt, Kim?"

"I didn't think I would at first." Kim hesitated, then smiled. "But I do now. He's really nice."

"And of course the fact that he gave you an autographed baseball doesn't have anything to do with it." Angie's eyes were twinkling as she gazed down at her daughter.

"Well—" Kim bit her lip, her eyes sparkling impishly "—that was when I decided he was okay after all." She added rather shyly, "He told me he'd help me work on my batting and my pitching. Then maybe next year I can pitch instead of play second base." She stopped and looked up pleadingly at Angie. "Is it all right, Mommy? If Matt helps me?"

Even if she'd wanted to, Angie couldn't have refused. "Of course it is, sweetie." As she spoke, she felt a curious tightening in her chest. It was at times like this that she prayed the lack of a father figure in the girls' lives didn't affect them adversely, either now or when they were older.

Keeping Evan's memory alive in the minds of his two daughters hadn't been easy for Angie. Regardless of her own feelings about Evan, she felt it wouldn't have been fair to Kim and Casey to shut him out of their lives completely.

"You miss your father, don't you, hon?" The words came with difficulty, though she tried not to show it. It was always that way when she spoke of Evan to the children.

The spark immediately faded from Kim's eyes. Angie felt as if her heart were being torn in two as the seconds marched silently by. Finally Kim turned over on her side and tucked a hand beneath her cheek. "I think I'd like to go to sleep now," she whispered in a small voice.

Angie sighed, seized by a feeling of inadequacy. "Sure, baby," she murmured. "Sure." She kissed her good-night, then went downstairs, her heart weighing heavily in her chest.

She found Matt in the kitchen, and he handed her a steaming mug of coffee.

"Thanks," she murmured gratefully, sinking down onto the

nearest chair. She felt tired, but she knew it was because the day had drained her emotionally.

Matt sat down next to her, studying her as he raised his cup to his lips. Her deep blue eyes were shadowed, and though her complexion looked as fresh and dewy as it had this morning, he thought she seemed a little pale.

"You okay?" he asked gently.

"I'm fine."

The smile she flashed was bright, a little too bright, he thought. "You didn't eat much when we stopped for dinner," he pointed out, then smiled crookedly. "And you can't plead too many hot dogs and peanuts like the girls and me."

Angie was silent. The memory of Bonnie still fresh in her mind, she had been too shaken to eat. Even now, hours later, the idea of food held little appeal.

"I'm sorry," she said feebly, not knowing what else to say. A part of her wanted to tell him what had happened, and yet the woman's bruised face, two small children—it simply struck too close to home.

She could feel his probing gaze on her face. She saw him frown, and aware that some of her feelings must have shown in her expression, she jumped up. "Spooky," she muttered. "I'd better let her inside. She wasn't in the yard when we left this morning and she's probably starving."

She flipped on the back porch light and stepped outside to call the cat. Wrapping her arms around herself to ward off the night's coolness, she happened to glance back at the door just as Matt was coming through. It was then that she saw something twisted around the door handle, the faintest sparkle in the darkness. An eerie chillness inched up her spine.

Puzzled at the odd expression on her face, Matt followed the direction of her eyes. They both realized what it was at the same time. Spooky's collar.

Angie moved closer, watching as Matt struggled to free the collar from the door. It had been twisted and knotted over and over again—the work of a human hand. When at last it was free, Angie stared down at the mangled bit of leather and rhinestone that lay in Matt's hand.

His eyes met hers. "Someone," he said very quietly, "took this collar from Spooky and deliberately—"

"No," she muttered disbelievingly. "No!" She rushed from the patio and frantically began to call Spooky.

"Angie!" Matt's voice was sharp as he pulled her around to face him. "You won't find her—"

She refused to let him finish. "No!" She yanked her arm free of his grip, unwilling to let herself give in to a sickening feeling of dread. "She's around here somewhere," she cried. "She has to be! She's a house cat, Matt. The farthest she roams is the Crawford's. She's never outside much longer than an hour or so, especially when she's hungry, and she wouldn't have run away!"

Her eyes were dark with anguish as she stared up at him through the moonlit darkness, and he sensed a kind of wild desperation in her. "I'll go have a look around and see if she's wandered off somewhere," he told her quickly, then followed it up with a firm order. "You go inside, sit down and relax. If Spooky is anywhere near here, I'll find her."

But he didn't, and a muffled oath hovered on his lips when he saw Angie huddled on the top step half an hour later. She looked so forlorn, though, he just didn't have the heart to tell her the cat was probably dead.

"You didn't find Spooky, did you?" She tried not to sound too glum, but when he shook his head, she couldn't stop her shoulders from slumping. "I suppose someone could have seen her and taken her in for the night," she murmured, allowing him to pull her to her feet.

Matt placed a hand on her shoulder but didn't respond until he had guided her to the living room. She flopped down on the sofa and dropped her head back, too tired and bemused to notice Matt's preoccupied expression as he paced restlessly around the room.

Finally he halted in front of the fireplace, his hands thrust into the pockets of his jeans. "I don't think you'll find her, Angie," he said quietly. "Finding Spooky's collar like that...it wasn't a prank. You realize that, don't you?"

She shook her head slightly, her lips pressed together. "Maybe someone saw her and decided to steal her. Maybe she wandered off and someone took her in for the night...."

She was grasping at straws, and they both knew it. "This was deliberate," he countered bluntly. "To get at *you* somehow. Spooky might well be dead—at the very least kidnapped—and I don't think you'll ever get her back."

"Come on, Matt," she started to protest. "I think you're reading too much into it."

"Am I?" His voice was harsh. "First your tires were slashed. Then the vandalism in your yard, and now Spooky."

"You mean you think the three are connected?" If she sounded rather skeptical, she couldn't help it.

"Then who put the collar on the door?"

She faltered at the demand in his voice. "I...I don't know." The thought of someone in her backyard again filled her with a feeling of unease. She bit her lip, not quite meeting his eyes. "Still, I wouldn't call it anything but a run of bad luck."

"You can call it whatever you want," he told her grimly, "but what I'd like to know is why."

"If you're right, it's because someone's decided I'm public enemy number one." The halfhearted attempt at humor fell miserably short. "Don't glare at me," she muttered in response to his withering look. His mouth only tightened further, and she retorted, "If I'm on someone's hit list, then it's up to you to find out, isn't it?"

"Exactly," he said grimly.

At that she straightened abruptly. "Matt!" she cried. "I was being sarcastic. You don't have to take this so seriously."

"It's time someone did because *you* obviously aren't going to."

His tone dared her to argue, and for a moment there was a standoff. Suddenly Angie's shoulders slumped. The hours at the shelter, Spooky disappearing...it was all too much.

"Matt, please." She sighed wearily. "Can't this wait until some other time?" She tried to smile, but she found her mouth was trembling at the corners.

She knew Matt had heard the curious catch in her voice. There was an unaccustomed ache in her throat as she watched his expression change from challenging to one of the utmost gentleness.

She was beginning to fear that gentleness. Matt was a man who had known bitterness and loneliness, too. And still he was unafraid to show the soft side of his nature.

"I'm sorry, Angie," he said quietly. She felt the cushions beside her give beneath his weight. "I didn't know Spooky meant that much to you."

Again she tried to smile. The attempt was even more pitiful than before. She was so damn vulnerable, Matt thought to himself half angrily, and she was just as determined not to show it. But he capped the lid on the spurt of temper and reached out a hand to touch her shoulder.

Every muscle in her body tightened against him, but deliberately he kept his hand where it was, spanning the width between her shoulder blades. He was tired of these games, but at the same time he realized he didn't dare move too fast for her. Still, he couldn't help being a little hurt by her reaction.

"Just relax." He spoke without realizing he did so. "I won't hurt you."

Surprisingly, she did relax, almost as soon as his hand began a soothing motion with his fingertips, running lightly across the nape of her neck.

"God, you're tense," he murmured with a frown. "Turn around, okay?"

Reluctantly she complied. His left hand joined its mate at the base of her neck, and his thumbs began to slowly ease the tension from her muscles.

"It's not only Spooky bothering you, is it?"

Perhaps it was his quiet voice, the kneading motion of his fingers that made her feel oddly secure. Or perhaps it was the fact that there was nothing sexual in his touch, only a desire to ease her pain. Had Evan ever exhibited such tender concern? she wondered poignantly.

Whatever the reason, she found herself responding. "No," she admitted. "It's not just Spooky, although the girls will be heartbroken if we don't find her."

The gentle assault on her muscles stopped for a moment, then resumed. "It's the shelter, then, isn't it?" It was more a statement than a question.

Again she grew rigid beneath his hands, and he thought she would draw away. Then he felt her take a deep breath and he sensed the sudden turmoil inside her.

"It was awful, Matt." Her voice, no more than a whisper, held a depth of emotion he'd never heard before. "Awful," she repeated again, then shuddered.

Strong arms immediately closed around her from behind. For once Angie didn't question the move as her back connected with the solid strength of a warm male body. Held tightly against Matt's chest, his arms wrapped securely around her waist, his heartbeat echoing steadily beneath her shoulder, she only knew that she felt safe and warm and sheltered. And surely it wouldn't hurt to lean on someone else's shoulder...just for a while.

"What happened?" he asked softly.

Haltingly Bonnie's story emerged. But it wasn't only Bonnie's story. It was Angie's, Angie's and countless others'. Matt offered no solutions; he offered no advice. He was simply there, and that was enough.

There was no question the incident had affected Angie profoundly. Matt was stunned at the raw emotion in her voice. When she had finished, time had slipped quietly by.

"If I had known how much this was going to upset you, I wouldn't have arranged for you to go." There was an edge of self-disgust in his voice. "I'm sorry, Angie."

"Matt!" She twisted around so that she could see him. Without realizing it, she laid her fingers along his jawline, wanting only to ease the tight lines around his mouth. "Don't be sorry," she pleaded urgently. "If anything, it's only made me that much more determined to establish a shelter here in Westridge."

His eyes held hers for an endless moment, then a slow smile claimed his mouth. "And if ever a woman could take on city hall and win, it's you."

"Let's hope so." She found herself teasing back. He looked so different when he smiled, she marveled silently, so unlike the harsh stranger who had walked into her office only a few short weeks ago—and turned her life upside down.

Slowly, suddenly, she became aware of the position that they were in. Matt was tucked into a corner of the sofa, and she was wedged between his hard thighs, her hip nestled intimately against the most masculine part of him.

Her breath came jerkily. Her hand began to fall away from his face, only to be stopped by Matt midway.

"Don't," he whispered. "Don't be afraid to touch me. And don't be afraid to let me touch you."

Did his voice tremble? That Matt might be vulnerable, too, had never really occurred to her. Yet when it did, she felt something come undone inside her. If it wasn't for that vulnerability, she could have resisted.

But she couldn't. Dear God, she couldn't. She could only watch in wonder and fear as he slowly lifted her hand and replaced it on his cheek.

"Touch me, Angie. Touch me..."

She was helpless against such gentle encouragement. Her eyes drifted closed, and with a tiny moan her fingers moved. Tentatively, slowly, she discovered the chiseled hardness of his cheekbone, the lean hollow below, the tiny lines that faded outward from his eyes. The abrasive feel of his night-shadowed beard sent a cramping feeling of excitement racing through her.

Her lids snapped open. She stared directly into eyes that burned with a warm silver glow, a glow that beckoned, enticed.

Her lips parted. His name emerged as a husky sigh. "Matt..." It was a plea, but whether it was for him to stop or continue this strange spell of awareness he had cast over her, she didn't know.

But Matt did. He only prayed that this was the right thing to do...and the right time to do it.

He felt her tense when his lips settled over hers. He didn't draw away, he just continued to graze his mouth lightly against hers, the contact so featherlight it was almost nonexistent. Soon the hands that had knotted into fists at his shoulders slowly uncurled. He hesitated, then savored her breath misting warmly, intimately with his, before deepening the kiss.

A heady sensation engulfed Angie when his lips fully encompassed her own, trapping her mouth under his with tender temperance. In some distant part of her mind, she sensed that she and Matt had been heading inevitably toward this moment since the night he'd driven her home.

It seemed just as inevitable that her body was responding with a wild, sweet will of its own. A thousand tingly sensations rained over her as his tongue dipped sensually into the moist warmth of her mouth, sweetly tempting with a delicious artistry that stole her breath away.

Her hands, no longer content to lie passively against his shoulders, slid around to explore the tautened muscles of his back. She yearned to feel his bare skin and paused only a moment before slipping her hands under his shirt.

His skin was smooth and hard. She thrilled to the feel of muscle and bone beneath her questing fingertips. Her hands wavered between shy and bold as she discovered the supple length of his back. Then, as if savoring the exquisite sensation of warm skin and sinewed muscle, she slowly traced a lingering pathway downward, stopping only when she encountered the waistband of his jeans.

Her breasts ached where they rested against his shirt. Her nipples, already beaded with desire, grew harder still. Suddenly she longed to thread her fingers through the mat of hair on his chest and discover for herself whether it was as soft as it looked.

Her fingers began to trace an outward line along his belt, delighting in the lean strength of his body. It wasn't until her fingers encountered an alien hardness, the cold smoothness of metal, that a numbing realization set in.

Matt was wearing a gun.

CHAPTER ELEVEN

MATT WASN'T PREPARED for her withdrawal. The depth of her response took him by surprise, but pleasure at her reaction soon overrode all else. He had dreamed of this, of her body soft and pliable against his, her hands running wild over his skin. He'd longed for it so much it almost seemed too good to be true. And it was.

One moment she was warm and willing, the next, still and unresponsive in his arms. His mind still spinning with the most potent desire he had ever experienced, it took a few seconds before he realized something was wrong. She was trembling, but not in pleasure or anticipation.

"Angie?" Slowly he lifted his head to stare down at her questioningly. He kept her firmly within the circle of his arms. "Did I hurt you?"

Angie wet her lips. The feel of smooth, deadly metal still lingered against her skin. It had been cold...so cold.

Matt felt her quiver. He let her go, his eyes puzzled as she wrapped her arms around herself as if to ward off a chill. She was staring straight at him, yet he had the unnerving sensation it wasn't him she was seeing at all but someone else. Watching her stare at him, her lovely blue eyes filled with anguish and pain, kindled that fierce protectiveness that she alone evoked in him. Yet he sensed he didn't dare touch her.

"Angie?" he repeated. His voice was calm, but there was an edge of authority in it.

She started at the sound. She swallowed deeply, and her eyes seemed to refocus on his face. "You...you're wearing a gun." Her voice, thin as it was, carried the ring of accusation.

"I always do," he returned quietly. Up until that moment he'd forgotten the small caliber weapon tucked into a holster at his hip.

He realized she must have felt it. But there was more to her

reaction than just being startled. Much more. At the same time
he was aware once again that there was a lot he didn't know
about Angie. No. No, that wasn't right. There was a great deal
that she refused to share with him.

Their knees still touched where she sat huddled beside him; he
had only to reach out a hand to touch the softness of her cheek.
But at this moment he felt as if they were aeons apart.

"Does it scare you?" he asked. "My wearing a gun?"

The words fell into a hollow silence. Angie closed her eyes
and leaned back against the cushions. It was apparent that she
was fighting some silent inner battle.

"It doesn't scare me exactly," she finally admitted, then gestured vaguely. "It just..." She stopped, gnawing at her lower lip
with her teeth.

"Bothers you?" he supplied. "It's not unusual for cops to wear
off-duty weapons, you know."

"No, I don't suppose it is." She paused. "I just never really
thought about your wearing one, though," she added in a low
voice.

"I try not to advertise it." He deliberately reached out to tuck
a wayward strand of hair behind her ear. She didn't flinch or move
away. Encouraged, he asked softly, "Why are you so afraid of
guns?"

"I'm not," she said quickly. Angie realized by Matt's knowing
half smile that he would challenge her denial. Angie sighed dispir-
itedly. Matt wouldn't be satisfied with anything less than the truth.
And what did it matter if he knew?

She didn't look at him as she said tonelessly, "Evan was killed
by a rifle. He was on a hunting trip, and it went off one night
when he was cleaning it."

For the longest time Matt didn't say anything. Angie began to
wonder if he'd even heard her. Then she felt his touch, so tender,
so achingly sweet, it made her throat swell with emotion.

A lone forefinger turned her face to his. At the same time he
reached for her hand, threading their fingers together, his thumb
stroking a reassuring pattern on her flesh.

"Evan was your husband?" he asked quietly.

She nodded wordlessly.

"Do you know," he said very softly, his lips hovering a mere
breath away from hers, "that's the first time you've ever said his
name to me? No, don't pull away." His fingers exerted the nec-

essary pressure to keep her hand where it was. He seemed to hesitate. "Does it really hurt so much after all this time?"

She almost hated herself for the flicker of pain she heard in his voice. Matt believed she still loved Evan. She regretted deceiving him like this, but it was easier. So much easier.

"Please, Matt." Her eyes pleaded with him. "I don't want to talk about him. Please."

Matt was tempted to hold her tight and never let her go, to demand that she talk to him once and for all. Instead, he dropped her hand and got to his feet, his expression both grim and regretful.

"We've been tap-dancing around your husband's ghost too long already," he said quietly. "Dammit, Angie, anyone can see you're holding too much inside. I think you *need* to talk about him."

Long, tension-filled seconds reigned as he confronted her. Her delicately sculpted features were almost colorless. The dark anguish in her eyes was like a dagger to his heart. He despised himself for the torment he was putting her through, but at the same time he felt she left him with no other choice.

Angie shook her head helplessly. It was one thing to talk about a marriage gone sour, but quite another to divulge the hell Evan had put her through. There were some truths far too painful to reveal.

"I can't, Matt. I just can't." Her voice caught raggedly.

A minute slipped quietly by. Then another.

"Is it always going to be like this with us?" His voice cut through the tense, waiting silence. "One step forward, two steps back?"

She couldn't face his demanding, accusatory stare. Her gaze dropped to her hands, clasped tightly in her lap to still their trembling. Why couldn't he just let her go? she wondered despairingly. Couldn't he see what this was doing to her?

Conversely, she realized he meant well. Because he cared. And so did she. But she didn't want to feel this way about Matt, or any man. She had suffered a betrayal of the worst kind, and while the sane, sensible part of her said it wasn't logical that her feelings should carry over to another man, another part of her wasn't listening.

"I told you once I wasn't ready for this."

When she finally looked up at him, her smile was so sad, so bittersweet, he felt a gnawing ache begin deep inside his chest.

"And I told you we can get through this." His chest expanded with a deep, unsteady breath. "We, Angie. Not just you. And not just me, but *us*."

Together, he meant. The word resounded in her mind. "I wish I could believe that." Her voice was almost whimsical, but her deep blue eyes seemed haunted.

Matt stood and advanced toward the door. There he turned. "I want you, Angie, and I'm prepared to wait," he said very quietly. "Because someday there won't be any secrets between us." His eyes found hers across the width of the room. "Someday soon."

The door closed softly behind him.

That day would never come, she thought sadly, her heart filled with an inexplicable emptiness. She had let Matt come far too close already. Even though she had seen the gentle, caring side of him, she knew he could be as strong and forceful as Evan had been, and that made her wary of him. Matt was so determined. But so was she.

No, that day would never come. She would see to it. Somehow...

Spirits at the Hall household on Sunday, although not at an all-time low, certainly could have been improved upon. Angie had tossed and turned the night before and woke bleary-eyed with a nagging headache. The girls reacted to the news of Spooky's disappearance exactly the way she'd said they would. They were crushed. As for her own blue mood, she refused to examine the source, though she told herself firmly it had nothing to do with Matt Richardson! The three of them moped around the house, and even a trip to McDonald's that evening failed to cheer up the two youngsters.

More from a sense of duty than any real hope, on Monday she placed an ad in the lost and found column of the newspaper, just in case Spooky turned up. Then she spent the day buried under a mountain of paperwork, though one reprieve came when the council ratified the city's budget that evening. By Wednesday, what with trying to muster support for the city hall renovations and the women's shelter, she felt as if she'd stepped onto a merry-go-round.

Her work had always served as a way of getting her mind off any personal problems she faced, allowing her to put things in perspective. But as the week wore on, she felt the tight rein she usually kept on her emotions slipping further and further from her grasp.

She heard nothing from Matt. During Thursday's staff meeting he was polite, courteous but, above all, so damn businesslike she could have screamed with frustration. The moments she'd spent in his arms, his lips coaxing a warm response from hers, might never have happened.

Perhaps he'd finally decided to take her at her word. She'd said she wasn't ready for a man in her life, and, at long last, he must have realized she meant it.

In the cold light of day, she told herself that was what she wanted. She couldn't risk any kind of relationship with Matt, and if she'd let him believe otherwise, she'd have been guilty of leading him on. But in the dark hours of the night, when loneliness ran high and her defenses ebbed low, she missed him. She missed his late-night phone calls, his smile that eased the harshness of his features, the oddly tender light in his eyes, his gentle humor....

Matt, on the other hand, was feeling just as uncertain. He was at a total loss over how to proceed with her. Already he felt as if he'd been dragging his feet forever. Patience and understanding had gotten him nowhere, but at the same time he knew a woman like Angie would rebel just as fiercely if he decided to come on strong and determined. In fact, he thought grimly, nothing would send her running in the opposite direction more quickly than a few caveman tactics. If it hadn't been for the times he glimpsed a certain wistfulness in her eyes when she thought he wasn't looking, he might indeed have given up on her.

By Friday Matt was miserable, and Angie wasn't any closer to understanding what was in her heart.

Even Todd, showing an unusual sensitivity, noticed her blue mood. "Is something bothering you?" he asked point-blank in her office early that afternoon.

Other than the fact that my life has been turned upside down lately, not a thing. She bit back the uncharacteristic sarcasm and forced herself to lean back in her chair. "Not a thing," she said briefly. Todd hadn't made any more overtures toward her, but the friendly companionship they had once shared was gone. They had even disagreed over some city-related matters, something that had rarely happened before.

"Is it that incident with your cat?" he asked suddenly. "Or the vandalism in your yard?" He shrugged. "I wouldn't worry

about it if I were you. Probably just some rowdy kid in the neighborhood.''

"Matt Richardson thinks the incidents are connected." The
words were no sooner out than she was annoyed with herself once
more. He had already dominated her thoughts to the nth degree,
and here she was talking about him!

Todd's smile was skeptical. "Coming from Chicago, he probably thinks there's a mugger lurking around every corner, too."

Angie said nothing. Not only did she have no desire to discuss
either the two incidents or Matt, but she had the vague feeling
that Todd disliked Matt.

The next second her hand was on the intercom. "Georgia,
would you see if Steve Jackson is free for lunch next Monday?"

"Sure thing, boss," came the disembodied reply.

Todd lifted an eyebrow. "Still trying to woo him over to your
side of the fence on the city hall issue?"

For some reason his tone rankled. "Something wrong with
that?" she asked coolly.

There was a thoughtful expression on his face. "Steve seems
pretty adamant in his support of a new building—"

"And so are John Curtis and Mike Matthews." She gave him
a long, hard look. "It isn't going to stop me from trying."

"I don't know, Angie," he said with a shrug. "The money's
there. A lot of people think a new building is the way to go."
He smiled and added mildly, "Since it's not an election year, you
don't have to be overly concerned about the voters rallying
against you."

Angie couldn't believe what she was hearing. "That doesn't
even enter into it, and you know it! We've had public feedback
that proves there are just as many people who think a new building is a frivolous expense," she countered hotly. "And there are
other services that will go up in smoke unless we renovate and
use the excess monies elsewhere. It's a question of priorities,
Todd!"

He frowned across at her. "Don't be so defensive, Angie. I'm
on your side, you know."

"It doesn't sound like it," she retorted. He had the grace to
look a little sheepish, and she found her anger dwindling. She
pushed herself to her feet and rose to stare pensively out the
window. The bright blue sky was cloudless, providing a colorful
background for the lush green forests carpeting the ridges of the
foothills to the east. The quiet serenity of the scene before her

reminded her only too clearly of the tumultuous state of her emotions lately.

"I'm sorry, Todd," she said after a moment. "I haven't been in the best of moods all week." She turned slightly and offered a weary smile. "Maybe I've been cooped up inside too long. Summertime blues, I suppose."

"Maybe what you need is a day off," he suggested warmly. "Or better yet, a night out."

Angie began to shake her head, but suddenly the door burst open and Georgia rushed in.

"Will you look at this!" she announced. "Of all the nerve! Why, if I knew who did this I'd..."

The rest of her threat was lost on Angie as she walked over to pick up the piece of paper Georgia had flung down on her desk. She quickly scanned the typewritten message.

If you know what's good for you, Mayor Hall, you'll change your mind on the city hall issue. If you don't stop fighting those of us who want the new building, your cat disappearing will be the least of your worries. I'll be watching, Mayor, and waiting. Don't disappoint me, or you'll be sorry. Because next time it might not be your car, or your yard, or your cat...

An acrid taste rose in her throat. "Spooky," she whispered, turning pale. Matt was right. Spooky had been snatched deliberately.

A low whistle sounded behind her. Todd had come up and was reading the note over her shoulder. "You think this is a joke?" he asked quietly. He took it from her hand, his eyes moving over it once more.

Angie thought of Spooky's body, lying limp and cold. She closed her eyes and shook her head. "No," she said tonelessly. "No joke." Her legs felt like rubber as she eased herself into her chair.

The room was deathly quiet. At any other time the sight of Georgia wringing her hands fretfully might have made Angie laugh. But laughter was the furthest thing from her mind.

The sudden rap on the door made her jump. She looked up to see Sam Nelson poke his head inside the door. "There you are," he boomed at Georgia. "Can't seem to stay away from this place, so I thought I'd..." His voice faded when he saw the somber faces of the three occupants.

Angie managed a halfhearted smile and waved him to a chair. "Just like old times, Sam. Seems we have a minor crisis on our hands."

"Minor!" Georgia gave her a withering look and hastened toward Sam, the letter in her hand. "Take a gander at this, Sam!"

Sam ran a hand over his chin when he'd finished reading it and looked across at Angie. "Considering all that's happened lately, I don't think I'd take this too lightly if I were you."

"Why do you think he says losing her cat will be the least of her worries?" Georgia asked him anxiously, standing at his side.

"It's obvious," Todd interjected bluntly. "It's a threat. Support the new building or else."

"A threat?" At that, a hot tide of anger suddenly surged through Angie. "Dammit, I'm not letting someone push me around over something as important as this!"

Todd shook his head slowly. "I don't know, Angie. I think Sam may be right. Whoever wrote this means business." His eyes met hers. "You'd better be careful."

The need for caution was the only thing the four of them could agree upon. When Todd left for an appointment fifteen minutes later, Georgia wasted no time in picking up the phone on Angie's desk.

"Who are you calling?" Angie asked suspiciously. She didn't like the utterly determined look on her assistant's face.

"Who do you think?" Georgia pushed her glasses up on her head. "Georgia Hendricks for Chief Richardson, please," she said crisply into the receiver.

Angie's arm shot out to break the connection, but Georgia snatched the phone up against her ample bosom and smiled smugly.

Angie didn't bother to listen to the brief conversation between her assistant and Matt. She was too busy fuming. "There's no need to bring Matt Richardson into this," she said angrily when Georgia hung up. "Is there, Sam?"

Sam didn't have the chance to get a word in edgewise.

"No need!" Georgia's eyes fairly sparkled. "I suppose if you got a bomb threat you'd sit back and do nothing, too! Sam, tell her this is serious!''

"Seems to me you're doing a pretty good job of it yourself." Sam patted her hand and smiled encouraging up at her.

Smitten! The man was utterly smitten! It was clear to Angie she would get no help from his direction. "This is hardly as serious as a bomb threat," Angie tried to reason with Georgia.

Georgia propped her hands on her hips and gazed down her nose at Angie. "You and Matt Richardson may have had a lovers' tiff, but that doesn't change the fact that this is a matter for the police."

Lovers' tiff! Angie glanced at Sam, her cheeks reddening guilt-ily. "That's not the case at all," she muttered stiffly. "First of all, there's nothing at all going on between Matt Richardson and me."

Georgia's snort spoke far more eloquently than words. Sam cleared his throat and looked away.

Angie glared at her. "Second of all," she added firmly, "this letter is probably just—"

It was this scene that Matt walked into. "What's up?" he asked casually. "Georgia said it was urgent." He noticed Sam and nod-ded to him.

"Damn right it's urgent!" Georgia thrust the letter at him. "Feast your eyes on that!"

The letter in his hands, Matt eased himself onto a corner of Angie's desk. Only an arm's length away, Angie's heart began to do double duty. She'd put the moments spent in his arms firmly out of her mind, or so she thought until suddenly the memories came rushing back.

She couldn't stop her eyes from roving over him. He'd appar-ently come straight from his office and hadn't bothered to don his suit jacket. His tie was loosened, and at the sight of the springy dark hairs nestled at the base of his throat, she felt the urge to explore further inside his crisp white shirt. He'd rolled his shirt-sleeves up to his elbows, and his muscular forearms, liberally covered with the same dark hair, only enhanced his masculinity.

When her gaze moved reluctantly upward, the hard expression on his face put a halt to any further meandering of her mind.

"How and when did this arrive?" His eyes flashed among the three other occupants of the office.

It was Georgia who responded. "About half an hour ago. With the rest of the day's mail."

"Do you still have the envelope it came in?"

Georgia nodded and disappeared into the outer office. Returning, she told him, "It's postmarked yesterday. From here in town."

Matt nodded. He asked for a large manila envelope and slipped both the letter and its original envelope inside.

"Are you going to check for fingerprints?" Georgia cast an I-told-you-so look at Angie.

"We can try," Matt replied. "But the only way we can come up with anything is if we can get a good clear print *and* if it belongs to someone with an arrest record." He rubbed his jaw thoughtfully. "That might not be the case here."

"Oh." Georgia's face fell. "I thought you could tell just about anyone's."

"This is real life, not Hollywood," Sam injected dryly.

Matt echoed the sentiment. "Did anyone touch the letter besides the two of you?"

"Just Todd," Georgia replied.

"Todd Austin? The city manager?"

Angie nodded. "He was here when it arrived."

"We'll have to have the four of you stop by the lab then so we can differentiate between the prints."

Silence settled over the room for a moment, then Georgia anxiously questioned Matt and Sam. "What do you two think? Is Angie in any danger?"

The two men glanced at each other. It was Sam who responded first. "There's always a danger when you don't know who or what you're dealing with. This could be a crackpot, or it could be someone whose intent is deadly serious."

Matt nodded. "What happened to Angie's car and home certainly proves this person isn't entirely harmless. We can't afford to take any chances."

Both sounded anything but reassuring. "Hey," she protested in a rather feeble attempt at humor. "Are you guys trying to make me feel better or worse?"

Crossing his arms over his chest, Matt turned his head slightly to look at her. "I don't believe in sugar-coating the pill."

Her smile was weak. "In other words, better safe than sorry."

"My point exactly." Steadfast gray eyes gazed unerringly into hers. "That's why you can plan on having a shadow until we find out who's behind this whole thing."

His tone was so casual it took a few seconds before she grasped his full import. "Don't tell me," she said slowly, tapping a pencil on her desk. A faint note of disdain colored her voice. "You plan on posting someone outside my office. Something like that, I suppose."

That dainty little nose tilting pertly toward the ceiling reminded him of the first day he'd been in this office with her. He grinned at the memory. "Something like that," he agreed mildly. One lean hip swiveled neatly on her desktop so that he faced her directly. "It won't do any harm to have someone hanging around your office. Nothing too conspicuous, of course."

Angie tried very hard to ignore the muscled stretch of his thigh poised next to her. To make matters worse, Matt looked very self-satisfied. And she didn't like that look—at all.

"Sam," she implored, "this really isn't necessary, is it? I mean, if you were still chief..."

"But I'm not," Sam replied grimly. "Sorry, Angie, but if I were in Matt's place, I'd be doing exactly the same thing."

Angie sighed. She was beginning to feel as if a conspiracy was being mounted against her. "Next you'll want someone outside my house, too," she muttered irritably.

Matt's smile widened. "Not exactly," he admitted, then paused. "More like *inside* the house."

"*Inside* the house!" She shot to her feet. "Dammit, Matt, I value my privacy too much to let a perfect stranger—regardless of the fact he might be one of your officers—inside my house. I...I'd feel like I was under house arrest!"

And well he knew it. She guarded her privacy, her person, her feelings, like a fortress made of steel. His smile vanished.

Georgia's head swiveled from Angie to Matt. Matt had risen by now and towered over Angie. Nonetheless, knowing her boss as she did, she wouldn't have cared to place bets on the outcome of this discussion. "Excuse me, I think I'd better get back to my desk," she muttered. "Sam?" Sam wasted no time in rising and accompanying her.

The door closed silently behind them. Neither Angie nor Matt seemed to notice the pair had left.

"We're not talking about a perfect stranger *or* one of my officers," he emphasized quietly. "We're talking about me." He waited silently for the explosion he knew was coming.

It came soon enough, in exactly the form he expected. Surprise flashed for a fraction of a second in her eyes. Then they began to blaze. "All right," she flung at him flatly. "You were right. You were right about everything—my tires, the vandalism in the yard and Spooky. Is that what you want to hear? I have absolute faith in your ability to do your job. You don't have to prove anything to me!"

"Is that what you think I'm doing?" he demanded.

She opened her mouth to deliver a vehement yes, but something in his expression made her reconsider. Matt's face was carved in harshly rigid lines, revealing the tough, hard side of him she'd always known lurked beneath the smooth exterior. A muscle worked tensely in his cheek, but she could have sworn there was a flash of hurt in his eyes.

She walked around her desk, feeling she needed to put some distance between them so that she could think straight. She turned to face him when she reached the other side.

"Maybe not," she admitted reluctantly. She hesitated, groping for the right words. "But aren't you letting your personal feelings enter into this? If some other city official received a threatening letter, I don't think the long arm of the law, especially the police chief's arm, would extend all the way into his home."

"Probably not," he agreed. "But we're not talking about some other city official. We're talking about *you,* and I intend to make certain nothing else happens until we find out who's behind this." His gaze captured hers, and the intense warmth reflected there sent her senses clamoring wildly.

She turned aside before he could see the effect he had on her. There would be no arguing with him. Angie could see he was steadfastly determined, but thinking of the two of them together under one roof caused a flicker of unease to trace her spine. Matt had made no bones about his intentions, and it would be that much harder to keep him at arm's length—and that much easier to say yes to something she wasn't sure she could handle yet.

Still, she trusted Matt—at least as much as it was possible for her to trust any man. He wouldn't push her.

She hoped.

used her to keep him at arm's length, and that didn't change. Even up to the day she wasn't sure she would handle well, she blamed Matt—at least as much as it was possible for her to blame a man. He wouldn't push her.

She hoped.

CHAPTER TWELVE

THE EVENING WASN'T quite the ordeal Angie had expected. Not wanting to alarm Kim and Casey, she decided against telling them about the note she'd received. But she did have to come up with a reason for Matt staying with them, so she finally said he was having some remodeling done on his house.

"I hope you don't mind," she told him in a low voice after the girls had left the dinner table. "I didn't want to upset them." She hesitated. "Kim is...well, she's rather sensitive. I hate to rock the boat too often where she's concerned."

He nodded his agreement. "There's no point in scaring them." He pensively watched Kim run upstairs. "She's not overly fond of men, is she?"

A grim smile touched her lips. "You've noticed?"

"It's hard not to." His response was dry, but his eyes were filled with compassion.

Angie instinctively found herself softening. "Kim likes you, though," she admitted.

"I'm glad." There was such warmth in his voice that Angie felt a painful twist in the region of her heart. Matt could be so good for them—for all of them. Kim, Casey and herself. But knowing that didn't erase the twinge of fear in her heart, the fear of letting someone that close again.

"Losing her father was hard on Kim, wasn't it?"

Angie's fingers tensed on her napkin before she nodded and dropped the wadded ball onto her plate. "Casey was only two when Evan died, so she doesn't really remember him," she said quietly. "But Kim was older, and she and Evan were very close. He was at home with her for well over a year."

His brows lifted. "A house husband?"

Angie slowly placed the dishes on the counter. "In a way," she admitted, then dropped her eyes before he could see the bitterness she was sure would be reflected there. In a minimum of words, she told him how Evan had lost his job at the bank, then briskly she began to gather the plates and cups.

Matt followed her to the kitchen, a soiled casserole dish in one hand, a salad bowl in the other. He placed them on the counter, another question about Evan poised on his lips. At the sight of Angie's closed expression, he knew the discussion was over—before it had even really begun. Silently he cursed. Dammit, did she trust him so little that she could share nothing of herself with him? She had no need to protect herself from him.

Protect. The thought was jarring. It was an odd word to use for a woman who had loved her husband so much. It was obvious her reluctance to become involved with him had something to do with Evan—she'd told him so, in fact—yet some sixth sense told him she was also afraid. He wanted to demand that she talk to him, tell him what was behind her fear. And he would have, if it hadn't been for that damn threatening letter. No, now was not the time to press her. Better to wait.

But he'd been waiting all his life for a woman like Angie, so long he'd begun to wonder if she even existed. He'd loved Linda, yes, but not like this, *nothing* like this. Each time he saw Angie, he felt something new, something different from any emotion he'd ever experienced. There was the strong Angie, strong in her weakness, so determined not to show him her vulnerability. That made her all the more vulnerable, all the more dear to his heart. And there was the woman Angie, all soft, tempting curves and pliant feminine warmth. He ached for her so much he woke up shaking in the night, his body taut and demanding, longing for the time he could express that love in the way God intended.

What hurt was knowing that she was capable of the very same powerful emotions that stirred his soul. It hurt even more to acknowledge that she wouldn't allow herself the slightest of intimacies with him. She wouldn't *let* herself care.

He heaved a frustrated sigh, his thoughts faintly colored by cynicism. For his whole life nothing had ever come easy. He'd hoped Angie might be the exception. But that was not to be.

"Matt?" He felt a tentative tug on his sleeve and looked down into Kim's narrow, upturned face. "Matt, will you play baseball with me?"

He glanced at Angie. "I really should help your mom with the dishes, Kim. Can you wait just a few minutes?"

Angie was a little surprised by his generosity. Evan had never been a man to offer assistance with the housework. Catching him with a dishcloth, dustcloth or vacuum in his hand had been a rare occurrence, even while he'd been unemployed. Most times he'd left meal preparation and cleanup for her.

She waved away his offer and busied herself at the sink. "The dishwasher can handle the dishes, Matt. There's no need for you to stay inside and help." Belatedly it occurred to her she'd taken it for granted that he wouldn't mind playing with the girls. "Unless you've got something else you'd rather do," she added quickly over her shoulder.

He seemed to read her mind. "I like being with the kids, Angie." One dark brow quirked humorously. "And it isn't a way of trying to earn my way into their mother's good graces, either."

She swiped at the counter with the dishcloth, then turned to face him. "I know that," she told him softly, an even softer smile hinting at the corners of her mouth. Matt was not a man to pretend to emotions he didn't genuinely feel, emotions that came straight from the heart.

Yet the thought dismayed her as much as it filled her with a reluctant pleasure. Slowly but surely, Matt was tearing down all the barriers. Soon there would be nothing between them. Soon... In spite of the day's warmth, a sudden chill came over her. How would she feel when that day came?

AN HOUR LATER Matt called a halt to the horseplay going on in the backyard. Casey howled indignantly as he gave her a last push on the swing set. Kim frowned disappointedly and dropped her ball into her glove, but she didn't say anything.

Matt glanced between the two youngsters and pleaded, "Come on, ladies. Have a little mercy on a poor, crippled old man like me."

"Ladies?" Kim giggled.

Casey slid off the swing and ran up behind him. "How old are you?" she asked curiously.

Matt grinned, having no doubt about her reaction. "Thirty-eight."

"Thirty-eight!" she echoed. "Even Mommy's not *that* old," she mused with childlike candor. Then she boasted, "I'm gonna be five pretty soon."

"You are?" Matt smothered a laugh as her small chest puffed out proudly. "When?"

"On my birthday!" The child looked at him as if he'd suddenly lost his mind before skipping into the house. *Ask a stupid question,* he thought to himself wryly.

"Her birthday's in September," Kim offered. "Mine's in April."

"Is it? So is mine." His eyes softened as he looked down at Kim. Casey had her mother's coloring, but Kim's poignant air of vulnerability reminded him so damn much of Angie and her re-action to him—and it tugged at his heartstrings almost as much. "We'll have to celebrate together next year, won't we?"

She responded with a timid smile, then bit her lip and hung her head. She looked so pitifully uncertain that Matt dropped down on one knee beside her. "What is it, Kim?" he encouraged gently. "What's wrong?"

The tip of one sneaker toed the ground repeatedly before she finally looked up hesitantly. "Do you like my mommy?"

Both the question and the solemnly intent expression on Kim's face took him by surprise. He was on the verge of frowning when he realized she might take it the wrong way. *Like* her? Good Lord, he loved her.

His voice was curiously unsteady. "Yes, Kim. I like her...I like her *very* much." There was a brief pause while he took one small hand in his. He half expected Kim to draw away, but she didn't. "Do you mind?" he asked quietly.

She shook her head. "I...I like you, too," she confessed shyly. "Lots better than Todd." She smiled timidly, but a troubled look appeared in her eyes once more. "You won't hurt my mommy, will you?"

His answering smile faded as he felt her fingers tremble in his. Her anxious whisper tore into his heart, even while he wondered why on earth a child of eight would ask such a question. Yet somehow he sensed that his answer was somehow vitally important to Kim.

"No," he said firmly. He gave her fingers a gentle but reas-suring squeeze. "I would never hurt your mother. *Never,*" he emphasized.

"Promise?" Her eyes demanded that he do so.

"I promise," he echoed solemnly, then grinned at her. "Cross my heart and hope to die." The words were accompanied by the proper gesture, and Kim's face brightened as she giggled.

He was still pondering Kim's unexpected questions when the two of them entered the house a moment later. He caught a glimpse of Angie sleeping on the sofa. Pressing a finger to his lips, he made a game of tiptoeing the girls up the stairs for a bath. Regardless of how much she pretended otherwise, the day had been filled with a great deal of mental strain, and he hated to spoil this brief reprieve for her.

He felt rather proud of himself, especially in light of his bachelor status, because, by the time nine o'clock rolled around, Kim and Casey were bathed and snugly tucked in bed.

Angie was still asleep in the living room. Flaxen ribbons of gold had come loose from her topknot and trailed across the small throw pillow her head rested on. One hand was tucked loosely under the rose-tinted smoothness of her cheek. Her pale peach dress draped loosely over her breasts and hips, hinting at the supple curves beneath. She had kicked off her shoes, and they lay carelessly tipped on their sides under the coffee table.

The now-familiar wave of protectiveness swept over him. Oddly, it was the sight of her bare feet that triggered the reaction. Matt dropped into a chair across from her, smiling as he savored the feeling.

"What's so funny?" Angie lifted her arm away from her eyes and stretched before sitting up.

Matt's eyes lingered on her bare feet, now resting firmly on the floor. "Just trying to decide who you really are, Cinderella or Sleeping Beauty."

Angie smiled without restraint at Matt's rhetorical comment. She hadn't meant to fall asleep, but she was glad that she had. The short nap had eased some of the tension that had marked the day.

"Are the girls upstairs?" Her hands reached up to pin back into place the stray hairs that tickled her cheek.

"Upstairs, tucked in tight as a drum and clean as a whistle."

"You gave them a bath? And they're in bed already?" She halted in the midst of slipping on her shoes and stared across at him.

Matt chuckled at the stark surprise registered on her face and in her voice. "Don't worry, I didn't peek. Besides, Kim really needed a bath." He shook his head. "Maybe I shouldn't have taken her to the Mariners' game after all. We didn't get much batting practice in because she kept rubbing dirt on her hands and swinging the bat around. Just like the pros," he added dryly.

Angie's lips twitched. She had no trouble envisioning Kim doing exactly that. "Let's just hope she doesn't start spitting when she comes up in the batter's box."

"Uh, it might be a little late for that." Somehow Matt didn't look the least bit repentant as he laced his fingers across his stomach and stretched his long legs out in front of him.

"She didn't!" Angie gasped.

He laughed at Angie's horrified expression. "She did," he confirmed, feeling for all the world like a proud, doting papa. "Didn't you know it's the trademark of a true baseball player?"

"Oh, Lord," Angie muttered, but the humor of the situation suddenly struck her, and she found her laughter joining Matt's. "I wish I'd seen her," she reproved without heat. "You should have woke me."

"I thought you were busy," he admitted. "I didn't know you were asleep until we came inside. Besides, you needed the rest." He studied her quietly for a moment, his face pensive. "They're great kids, Angie. You should be proud of them."

His words made her feel warm and glowing inside. "You're really good with them," she told him unselfconsciously. The next second, though, a faint line was etched between her brows. "You and Linda, Matt." She broached the subject hesitantly. "You never had any children?"

Unknowingly she had hit a nerve. The pain reflected in his eyes dazed her for an instant, and she was taken totally aback. "You're so good with Kim and Casey," she told him quickly, speaking before she even realized it. "I just thought...I mean, you'd make such a wonderful father."

"It's something I always wanted," he admitted quietly. "In fact, I wanted the whole shot—a station wagon, a house in the suburbs, along with a houseful of kids." His mouth twisted in a bittersweet smile. "A baby would have ruined her figure. Linda wanted glamour and action. I knew that when I married her, but I thought I could change her." He stared into space as he spoke. "In the end I felt cheated. The only kind of family ties Linda really understood was a hand in her father's wallet."

Cheated. That was exactly how she'd felt when her marriage began to unravel. Why was it, she mused sadly, that when a person discovered a lifetime of happiness was just within reach, fate cruelly snatched it away? It had happened to her. And it had also happened to Matt.

It was but one more reason why she didn't dare risk any involvement with this man, didn't dare risk falling in love with him, a tiny voice whispered. Yet there was such longing written on his face that Angie's throat clogged with some nameless, twisting emotion that cried "liar" to that debilitating voice in her mind.

She wanted him so much, yet she was afraid of the tumultuous way he made her feel inside. She wanted to run and hide and never look back. But she also wanted to reach out and stroke away the lines of pain etched beside his mouth.

Angie did neither. Instead, she sat very still, her head lowered, her hands clasped tightly in her lap before she finally got up, murmuring that she wanted to check on Casey and Kim.

A pair of disturbed gray eyes followed her retreat from the living room. Matt eased up from the chair, tiredly rubbing the back of his neck and wishing he'd had sense enough to keep quiet. He must have said something to bring back unwelcome memories. Why was it that, every time he felt they were growing closer, something sent her running in the opposite direction, when all he wanted was for her to run straight into his arms?

Angie was composed but subdued when she returned down-stairs a few minutes later. Matt was on the phone in the kitchen, and she couldn't help but notice his intent expression as he listened to whoever was on the other end of the line. She gathered from his brief comments that the subject under discussion was the note she had received earlier that day, and she felt a sudden chill.

She pulled a quart of milk from the refrigerator and cocoa from the cupboard. She started to take two cups down from the rack on the wall, then glanced quizzically over her shoulder at Matt. He nodded in response to her unspoken question.

Busying herself at the stove, she stirred the milk, cocoa and sugar into a saucepan. The bright lights and homey familiarity of her kitchen were reassuring, and she tried to ignore Matt's sharp eyes watching her steadily.

She brought the cups to the table just as he hung up the phone. "Find out anything?" She tried not to sound overly anxious.

He shook his head and sat down next to her. "We could only get a couple of clear prints—yours and Todd's."

"Damn," she murmured. "I was hoping the fingerprints might turn up something." Thinking of what he'd told Georgia earlier, she summoned a wan smile. "Too bad this isn't Hollywood."

Matt's face was grave as he curled his fingers around the cup. "We don't have much to go on, Angie. You realize that, don't you?"

"I know," she agreed, sighing wearily. She started to lift her cup to her lips, then lowered it before it was halfway there. "It just now occurred to me," she said slowly, her brow knit in concentration, "that if someone is trying to influence my stand on the city hall issue, maybe some of the other city council members have also been threaten—"

Matt's firm shake of his head cut her off. "We've already checked. You're the only one." His tone was light, but his eyes were perfectly serious as they rested on her. "Any idea who might be on the warpath? Someone holding a grudge against you, perhaps?"

"Enemies, you mean," she stated unequivocally, then paused to consider who they might be.

"What about that newspaper reporter?"

"Blair Andrews?" She grimaced. "She doesn't like me, that much I know."

"Because her uncle lost the election to you?"

"Right." She was a little surprised that he remembered. "But slashing tires and kidnapping cats—somehow I can't see Blair stooping that low." Her smile was cynical. "She'd much rather hack me to bits in one of her columns."

Matt neither agreed nor disagreed. "What about her uncle?"

"He did resort to some rather dirty politics during the campaign," she recalled.

He crossed his forearms on the table and leaned forward. "Something like this?"

"Not exactly." She related in a low voice how Bob Andrews had tried to make an issue of the fact that before his death Evan had lost his job at the bank.

"Anyone else?" he asked when she had finished.

Angie thought for a moment, feeling a little like a tattletale in the third grade. It wasn't something she was entirely comfortable with.

"John Curtis is really pushing for a new city hall," she said slowly, then frowned. "In fact, I've been trying to figure out all day why someone would go to such lengths to get me to support the new building instead of renovating."

"What else?" Matt questioned skeptically. "Money."

"But how?" She looked at him in puzzlement. "Until the issue is decided, we can't even begin to take bids or anything like that."

Matt rapped his fingers against the table, momentarily lost in thought. "We don't know what or how high the stakes are, and we probably won't until we find out who's behind this." Angie got up to empty her cup into the sink, and he realized the action was a signal for him to stop. "Are you okay?" he asked.

She made a pretense of carefully rinsing the sink before turning to face him. Facing a known enemy was one thing, but facing the unknown was quite another. And although she'd been telling herself all day that Matt's insistence on staying with her was more self-motivated than anything else, as she absorbed the genuine concern in his eyes, she realized she'd done him a great disservice.

Silently she nodded in affirmation.

"You don't look okay." He watched her closely. "I could use a bit more convincing."

"I'm fine. Really," she insisted, though her smile was a little wobbly. "See?" She held out her hands. "Steady as she goes."

His eyes never wavered from hers as he rose and closed the distance between them. Lifting her hands in his, he turned each one over and lightly kissed first one palm and then the other. A ribbon of sensation shot through her veins at the touch of his lips on her skin. He loosely linked their hands together, then tested her grip.

"You're right," he murmured. "Steady as she goes." When he realized Angie couldn't meet his eyes directly, he added, "No one is going to think any less of you if you admit you're scared."

Time marched silently on. Angie marveled that he knew her so well. Certainly Evan never had, in spite of all the years they'd spent together. Yet where Matt was concerned, the knowledge both pleased and disturbed her. Still, that very contrariness was typical of her feelings toward him.

"Even you?" she asked finally.

She felt a gentle pressure on her hands. "Especially me." There was a strangely husky quality to his voice she'd never heard before.

"Do you ever feel that way? Scared, I mean?" She posed the question hesitantly.

"We all do, at some time or other."

Golden wisps of hair caressed her cheeks as she shook her head. "It's hard to think of you as being scared," she whispered. "You're so...so strong."

His grip tightened on hers for an instant. Angie was revealing more of herself than she ever had before, and he fought the need to envelop her in his arms and never let her go.

"You're wrong." His voice stole softly through the silence.

''Where you're concerned, I'm not strong at all.'' His hands withdrew from hers, only to frame her face so that he could stare directly into her eyes. ''Because it's getting harder and harder to keep from doing...this.''

He kissed her then, a kiss that spoke of need, of tenderness, of promises unfulfilled and promises yet to be made. It was a soothing touch, a yearning caress that sought to heal her hidden wounds, vanquish her secret fears and show her a world where yesterday was forgotten and tomorrow was a golden beacon of laughter and love.

Angie's lips trembled like the wings of a butterfly as his mouth teased and tempted. Their flesh melded, their breath mingled. The sensual magic of his lips on hers filtered through her like a warm ray of sunshine, affording her a tantalizing glimpse of paradise. Nothing on earth could have prevented her mouth from opening to welcome the tender invasion, the infinitely exciting thrust and parry of his tongue skirmishing boldly with hers.

Matt's restraint fell away like glistening beads of dew before the blazing heat of a morning sun. She was so sweet, so warm, and she was his—his to claim, his to love. He heard her sudden intake of breath as his hands slipped from her face to her waist, urging her body forward.

She melted against him, her hands slid up to test the tautened muscles of his shoulders before burying themselves in his hair. She felt his fingers steal upward to gauge the ripe fullness of her breast. Little tingles of excitement shot through her as his thumb feathered over the straining peak, the touch so light she almost thought she imagined it.

It came again—this time more firmly, a tender manipulation that seemed to last forever and ended much too soon. Sharp needles of exquisitely delicious sensations burst to life within her. *Again,* she prayed silently, her nipples swelling tautly against his hand. *Again...*

The low moan pulled from within her body echoed in his mouth. He knew a split second of ecstasy as his arms wrapped around her and drew her full and tight against him. The feel of her body, so sweetly cradled against the part of him that swelled with near-painful intensity, made him ache with the need to join with her, to share himself with her and show her his love once and for all. Matt felt rich as he'd never felt before.

Angie tensed. But she didn't draw away.

It was Matt who finally pulled back, trying hard not to let his shoulders slump with resignation.

Angie stared at him. One moment she was safe and warm and sheltered as she hadn't been in such a long, long time. The next she was cold and alone and chilled with an icy numbness that seemed to penetrate clear to her soul. She wanted him so much that it hurt inside, but she was ashamed of that wanting.

The raw pain that flashed across his face hurt her even more. "Matt..." His name emerged as a muffled cry. Her trembling lips opened, but no further sound came out.

He sensed she wanted to explain the conflicting emotions warring inside her. The tears that sprang to her eyes made his heart ache, but until she found it in herself to trust him with whatever it was that held her back, he could do nothing to help her.

It was the hardest thing he had ever done, but somehow he forced himself to rise and move to the doorway. There he looked back at her, his face carved into harsh, unreadable lines. "Good night, Angie," he said quietly.

She heard his footsteps on the stairs and the soft click of his bedroom door closing.

It seemed like hours, but in reality it was only minutes later that she climbed into bed, her mind still on the scene that had unfolded downstairs.

She dreaded these next few days with Matt. Tonight only proved what she had known almost from the start. Her body was willing, her spirit was weakening...and her heart was torn in two.

CHAPTER THIRTEEN

"Is SHE AWAKE?"

The whisper was hushed. It sounded as if it were muffled behind a small hand.

Angie groaned and squeezed her eyes more tightly. It was Saturday, Kim didn't have a game, so why couldn't the girls let her sleep in just a few minutes longer? She buried her face in the pillow, hoping they would tiptoe quietly out.

There was a giggle and the sound of footsteps shuffling along the floor.

"She's *still* asleep." Angie recognized Casey's disappointed singsong. "Can't we wake her up, Matt?"

"No," she muttered, still caught halfway in a world between sleep and wakefulness. "Let her sleep just a minute longer, Ma—"

Matt! Her eyes flew open. Her fingers clutched the bed sheet and pulled it frantically upward from her waist to her chin.

"*Now* she's awake," Matt commented dryly, grinning at two small faces, one on either side of him. He was standing at the side of the bed, wearing an old faded pair of jeans that tightly hugged the muscles of his legs. Bronzed, hairy arms peeked out from the rolled-up sleeves of his pale-blue-and-white-striped shirt, their sheen matching that of the wiry curls at the base of his throat. His strong jawline was dark with a shadowy growth of beard. But even though he hadn't yet shaved, he looked damnably good to her. In his hands was a fully laden tray, complete with coffee, juice and a single red rose.

"Sit up and eat, Mommy. We fixed you breakfast in bed." Casey beamed proudly.

"*You* didn't fix it." Kim frowned at her younger sister. "Matt did. And it was his idea, too."

Casey stuck out her tongue. "Well, I helped," she pouted.

"Did not!" Kim's eyes began to flash before Matt interrupted.

"Ladies, please! Let your mother eat before everything gets cold."

Miraculously, that seemed to settle the argument. Angie peeped out from beneath the sheet at the three sets of eyes fastened on her.

"Come on, Mommy," Kim prompted. "We did this specially for you."

"Yes, Mommy," Matt echoed mildly. "Sit up and eat."

It was hard to remain dignified with a sheer lacy nightgown and a sheet as her only protection against a knowingly amused pair of gray eyes. Angie didn't even try. Slowly, nervously, she sat up, pushing tousled blond waves back over her shoulders.

Holding the tray in his other hand, Matt handed her the robe from the foot of the bed. But not before his eyes had feasted on the tantalizing glimpse of honey-gold flesh beneath the sheer white nylon.

Angie felt the heat of that scorching gaze in every part of her body. She gave a silent prayer of thanks for the protection of her robe, scanty though it was, as her nipples responded with an involuntary pout. A tiny smile creased her lips as Matt carefully placed the tray on her lap.

"This was really very thoughtful of you," she murmured. Glancing at the clock, she noticed it was later than she'd thought—nearly ten. Knowing that Matt was asleep in the very next room, she'd lain awake half the night.

The side of the bed sagged beneath Matt's weight as he seated himself. "I can't take all the credit. Kim went outside and picked the rose, and she helped me find everything in the kitchen." The little girl beamed at his praise. "But it would be nice to know that the effort wasn't wasted." His eyes dropped meaningfully toward the plate she hadn't yet touched.

Angie automatically picked up her fork and lifted a bite of perfectly cooked scrambled eggs to her mouth. Matt chuckled at the look of surprise that darted across her face.

"Don't tell me I've lost my touch," he said lightly. "Too much cottage cheese?"

Her eyes widened. "Cottage cheese? You put cottage cheese in these eggs?"

"Family secret. Passed down from mother to son." He eased back slightly to watch her, enjoying the morning flush that tinted her cheeks, the unblemished perfection of her skin. "Overdone?" he asked solicitously as she lifted the fork a second time.

"They're perfect and you know it." Harboring a smile, she began to spread thick raspberry jam on a slice of toast. "You never told me you could cook. Do you have any other hidden talents I don't know about?"

A lengthy silence followed. She bit into the toast and glanced at him curiously. There was an extremely suggestive smile on his face. His eyes were filled with amusement, and the slightest hint of devilry.

"Let me guess." Even she was a little amazed that she was teasing him. "Is this where you tell me how great you are with your hands?"

"It's a thought," Matt murmured. "If nothing else, I certainly have a very willing pair of hands."

Angie opened her mouth, but the retort poised on the tip of her tongue never came. Kim and Casey had been exploring the contents of her dressing table, but now Casey had returned to the bedside. She and Matt noticed at the same time that Casey was studying his profile intently. There was a look of utter consternation on her face.

"Matt," she began worriedly, "how did you get all those slivers in your chin?"

The startled look on his face was too precious for words. Angie laughed until tears rolled down her cheeks. It wasn't until her hand wiped away the last watery trail that she found herself on the receiving end of an intent gaze.

"What is it?" she asked. "What's wrong?"

Matt's eyes suddenly shone with pleasure. "Do you know," he said softly, "that I've never heard you laugh like that before?"

Her heart turned over at the warmth reflected on his lean face. "I can't remember the last time I did," she admitted. "It...it feels good."

"I'll bet it does." His eyes roved tenderly over her face. After last night he had promised himself he would wait to kiss her, wait until she was more certain of her feelings for him. But she was smiling rather shyly at him, an alluring combination of innocence and sensuality that sent his control scattering to the winds. Unable to resist, he placed one hand flat on the bed and leaned forward to kiss her, unmindful of the interested eyes that watched nearby.

It was a sweetly gentle kiss, over almost before it had begun, but it was enough to make Angie's senses swim dizzily. Matt inwardly rejoiced at her dazed expression, then stood and lifted Casey high off the floor.

"Come on, squirt." He grinned at her. "Let's go get rid of those slivers, huh?"

Moments later Angie heard an electric razor in the bathroom. The sounds of mingled laughter reached her ears—Matt's, Kim's and Casey's—and she was filled with a poignant yearning.

At times like this she could almost believe that Matt was right, that with his help, she could learn to open up her heart once more.

Almost, but not quite.

AFTER ANGIE SHOWERED and dressed, she went downstairs. It was in the back of her mind that although Matt might be far more at home in the kitchen than most men, cleaning up was probably a different matter entirely.

The kitchen was spotless. The table had been cleared, the dishes stowed neatly in the dishwasher. Even the stove had been cleaned.

What was he trying to do? she thought to herself, not sure if she was pleased or annoyed. Prove himself indispensable?

She began to wonder if that was *exactly* what he had in mind when she saw him emerge from the garage, pulling the lawn mower along behind him. A second later the motor roared to life.

But there were some advantages to having another adult in the house, she conceded as she headed for the den. Most weekends were spent catching up on various household chores, both inside and out. When she was able to work on the speech she was to give at Tuesday's Downtown Merchants Association luncheon without a single interruption from the girls, it seemed almost a luxury.

Later that afternoon Matt asked that she come along while they did some shopping.

"But we don't need anything," she told him, puzzled at his insistence she join them.

He glanced up the stairway, where the two youngsters were playing in their room, before his eyes slid back to her. "How do you feel about a new addition to the family?"

Her heart gave a betraying lurch, as she thought of the previously unoccupied room next to hers—the room Matt had slept in last night.

Angie raised a slender eyebrow suspiciously as a rakish grin edged Matt's mouth. "I'm not sure I want to hear this," she muttered.

Matt laughed. "Don't look at me like that. Much as I'd like

to, I'm not about to haul you off to the nearest den of iniquity. In fact, for what I have in mind, we'll have not one but *two* chaperons.''

His eyes made a slow and leisurely reconnaissance of her slender body as he spoke. Angie was aware of a rush of warmth filtering through her. Feminine vanity? For so long now she'd thought Evan had destroyed that, too.

She couldn't have been more wrong. The smoldering look in Matt's eyes made her feel surrounded, possessed. It wasn't an unpleasant feeling; indeed, it made her feel as if there was a smile in her heart.

Perversely, it bothered her that she didn't mind him looking at her that way. Not nearly as much as it should have.

''You still haven't told me what we'll be shopping for,'' she reminded him. ''Or *where* we'll be shopping.''

''Uh, the pet store. As long as you don't mind, of course,'' he added rather sheepishly. ''I thought it might be a nice surprise for the kids. I know how much they miss Spooky, and I thought...well, maybe they'd like another cat. Or a dog.''

At first she looked startled, so startled he thought she might refuse. Then she smiled, that brilliant, entrancing smile that made him nearly forget to breathe.

''What are we waiting for, then?'' she asked, a playful lilt to her voice. ''You get the car, and I'll get the girls.'' Not bothering to hide her excitement, she collected her purse from the closet and off they went.

To Kim's and Casey's delight, there was one more passenger in the back seat of Matt's car for the return trip—a small pure black cocker spaniel puppy.

AFTER A LIGHT DINNER later that evening, Matt and Angie sat beneath the shade of the huge old elm tree that stood sentinel near the side of the house. Frothy clouds floated across the sky, reflecting pastel shades of purple and pink from the waning summer sun. It seemed a haven of peace and serenity from the disturbing events of the preceding day. Matt had ordered extra patrols in the area, and even the occasional glimpse of a police cruiser didn't bother her as much as when she'd first seen one that morning.

Worn out from chasing the puppy across the yard, the two girls dropped beside them. ''You know you two still haven't decided on a name for her," Angie told them. "If you call her puppy much longer, she'll think that's her name."

Apparently sensing she was the topic of discussion, the puppy draped both small paws over one of Angie's outstretched legs and gazed up at her with sorrowful brown eyes. Angie laughed and ruffled the silky hair around the dog's drooping ears.

"Any suggestions, Chief Richardson?" she asked Matt. He was lying on his back nearby, his feet crossed casually at the ankles. "After all," she reminded him, "*you* bought her."

He looked both lazy and relaxed, and at her question he opened one eye and squinted up at her. "Not for me. For the three of you."

She wrinkled her nose at him. "The least you can do, then, is help us come up with a name for this poor pooch."

Tucking his arms under his head, he opened his other eye and offered, "Whiskers?"

Neither Kim nor Casey looked thrilled. "Try again," she told him.

"Duke?"

"That's no name for a girl!" Kim looked disgusted. Matt chuckled and rattled off several more names, each one more ridiculous than the last. Finally Casey piped up, "How about Patches?"

This time it was Matt and Angie who looked at each other. The pup's fur was coal-black, unmarked by even a single patch of any other color. Fighting to suppress a smile, Angie started to point that out to Casey, but by now Kim had spoke up as well. "Yeah," she said excitedly. "Let's call her Patches!"

Angie promptly closed her mouth. With the two girls in agreement for once, she wasn't about to make any more waves. "Patches it is, then," she confirmed. Even the pup seemed to like it, jumping up and yapping excitedly.

Once again the girls ran around the yard, with the pup chasing them. Matt even joined in the game, but oddly enough, Patches tired out before the rest of them. The girls went into the house then and took the dog with them.

Angie raised an eyebrow when Matt dropped beside her once more. "Who did you *really* buy the puppy for?" she asked knowingly. "You or the girls?"

He grinned. "Come to think of it, I always did want a cocker spaniel when I was a kid."

"And that's why her bed is in my utility room?"

"I'd like to see you try to get that dog away from those kids." He looked rather smug.

"I couldn't and you know it." She frowned goodnaturedly. "And I think you knew that when you steered us away from the kittens and parakeets toward this little pooch."

He pillowed his hands behind his head. "Guilty as charged."

A comfortable silence settled between them. Angie leaned back against the tree trunk, her eyes drawn to Matt as if by some force she couldn't control. A faint breeze feathered his dark hair across his forehead. His eyes were closed, bristly lashes fanning out against the high sweep of his cheekbones. Her fingertips began to tingle. She wished she had the courage to lean over, to trace the arresting configuration of his features—across the tanned lines of his forehead to the stubborn angle of his jaw, along the jutting blade of his nose to that beautifully curved masculine mouth.

She wasn't prepared for the tide of feelings that rose inside her. She was attracted to Matt. There was little point in denying it. But this painfully sweet emotion that tugged at her heart was more than sexual attraction—much more.

"Angie?"

She realized he had opened his eyes and was staring at her. His mouth looked both hard and soft, readily inviting. He didn't bother to hide the spark of desire in his eyes, but it was tempered, restrained, an effort she knew he made solely on her behalf. Yet it was his voice—that quietly tender voice she was already so familiar with—that shook her to her very core. She tore her eyes away. She didn't want to remember his gentleness.

"It just occurred to me—" even to her own ears, her voice sounded high-pitched and strained "—that you've never talked much about yourself." She took a deep breath and stared straight ahead, trying to garner her control. Dragging her knees up to her chest, she wrapped her arms around them. "Your family...is there anyone back in Chicago?"

He was silent so long she thought he hadn't heard her. She glanced over at him. His gaze was fixed on some distant point high in the sky.

He suddenly seemed a million miles away. "Matt?" She almost hated to disturb him.

The sound of his name seemed to rouse him. He raised himself to a sitting position, carefully respecting the small distance she'd put between them earlier. "No," he said quietly. "No family." He appeared to hesitate. "Not in Chicago or anywhere else."

Angie frowned. "But you mentioned your mother this morning..." Too late she realized the path her statement led down. When Matt began to shake his head, she asked tentatively, "She's gone?"

He nodded. Angie waited for him to speak further, sensing that for once the tables were turned. That it was he who harbored secrets, he who held so much inside.

He suddenly looked older, and very tired.

The silence drifted between them, and Angie realized how much she wanted him to talk to her, how much she wanted to ease whatever had caused that somber, faraway look to settle in his eyes. Was this how Matt felt when she refused to talk to him about Evan? The thought had no sooner chased through her mind than she heard his voice.

"I had a brother once," he said softly, so softly she had to strain to hear.

"Did you?"

Pale streamers of light trickled through the tree branches, bathing his strong features in a kind of golden glow as he nodded. "Michael." A sad, wistful smile touched his lips. "His name was Michael."

Slowly, in bits and pieces, the story emerged of two brothers, raised in a tenement on Chicago's South Side by a mother whose husband had left one morning never to return.

It had been a struggle for survival.

"We never had enough money." He rested an arm on his knee as he spoke. "My mother did what she could." He shrugged, a silently eloquent gesture. "She had a lot of dreams for Mike, though, and I thought I could help, too. I got a job driving a delivery truck right out of high school. The only trouble was..." He paused, and she had the feeling he didn't really want to continue.

"Yes?" Her eyes encouraged him.

His face hardened. His mouth tightened into a thin line. "Neither my mother nor I were home much. Mike got in with a bad crowd." The hand resting on his knee tightened into a white-knuckled grip. "He was killed in a gang war when he was fifteen. My mother died three months later."

Of a broken heart. Angie's eyes closed. She didn't have to hear the words aloud to sense what Matt was feeling. She looked at him then and knew by the starkly rigid lines of his profile the battle he was exerting over his emotions.

There was a hollow sensation in her chest. She had never thought of Matt as vulnerable, yet he was a man who had been alone most of his life. A man who had reached out to her...

As if it were the most natural thing in the world, she bridged the small distance between them and laid her hand on his. It was a simple, consoling gesture, one she made without really being aware of it. She was reaching out to him.

Matt stared down at the small hand lying so trustingly, so comfortingly, atop his where it rested on his jean-clad thigh. His heart seemed to swell inside his chest with the powerful emotion that seized him. *At last,* he thought to himself, only barely able to believe it. *At last, she's starting to see how it is between us.*

"I'm sorry," she whispered, not knowing what else to say. "It seems so unfair for you to have had so little, and then to lose what little there was."

He was quiet for a few seconds. "I suppose it makes you appreciate what you do have."

"And reminds you what you don't," she said with a small sigh.

"True," he agreed, thinking of the two of them at this very moment. They were so close, yet there was still such a distance to bridge.

"I'm glad you told me," she found herself confessing. "I wish things could have been different for you, Matt."

His face softened as he gently turned his hand in hers and laced their fingers together. Their eyes melded. The emotion he saw reflected in those sapphire-blue depths stole his breath. For a heart-stopping moment he said nothing.

Then he brought her hands to his lips. "I'm not so sure I'd have changed anything even if I could," he told her huskily. "Because otherwise I might not be here with you right now." His lips sought the sensitive skin on the inside of her wrist. "My angel," he murmured. "My sweet, loving angel."

Angie froze.

"The girls," she mumbled, feeling deathly sick. "I'd better check on the girls."

As she jumped to her feet, Matt caught at her hand and followed her up. "Angie. Angie, what the hell. What did I say? What did I do?"

She hated herself for the confusion she heard in his voice. Time hung suspended for a tense, never-ending moment as she stared at him, her features pale and colorless.

"I'm sorry, Matt," she choked out. Her hands shook so badly

she clasped them in front of her to still their trembling. The words came out choppy and disjointed. "I don't mean to hurt you. Don't you see, it's not you...it's him! Him!"

And by him she meant Evan.

Matt's shoulders slumped. He had no way of knowing that his own face looked as if it had been etched in stone. As Angie turned from him and ran, powerful but conflicting emotions surged deep inside him. Anger. Hurt. Frustration.

But strongest of all was the undeniable certainty that he had made a mistake—a mistake that would cost him dearly.

TWENTY-FOUR HOURS LATER he still felt as if he were caught somewhere between heaven and hell. It was sweet agony to be near her but unable to touch her.

Angel... My sweet, loving angel... Because of something he'd inadvertently said, because of Evan, they were back where they had started. Even worse, Matt reflected testily on Sunday evening. Angie was more frigidly polite than ever before. It was a situation he was convinced would have tried the patience of a saint.

It was a good thing he had never aspired to such a lofty existence—he definitely wouldn't have made it.

Why did she stand so proud and aloof? What fueled her determination to keep him at a distance? Both were questions that nagged at him with such relentless persistence that he could think of little else.

The burnt child dreads the fire. He remembered the night he had said that to her. She had admitted she was afraid to let herself give in, to let herself love again. God knew it was still true. But not, he suspected, for the reasons he'd thought.

More and more, Matt was beginning to think there was more than just the memory of her husband standing between them. But what? *What?* Angie held the key. But Angie wasn't talking.

He leaned his head back against the sofa wearily, pondering the situation and wondering what, if anything, he could do to change it. He'd been struggling with himself all day long. He felt oddly out of step, unsure of which way to turn. One minute he was determined to demand that Angie confide in him, once and for all. The next he fought the urge to pull her into his arms and whisper that it didn't matter. Her secrets could remain hers—as long as nothing kept them apart.

But something *was* keeping them apart, and that was the whole damn problem. With a heavy sigh he got up and wandered around the living room.

They had spent most of the afternoon at the Crawfords, and he was glad for the opportunity to get her out of the house and get her mind off the letter she'd received Friday. After dinner they'd watched some of the home movies Bill had taken of both families. Angie had casually mentioned that somewhere at home she had a boxful of films taken when Kim and Casey were younger.

Matt wasn't surprised; Angie was the type of doting mother to catalog every stage of her children's development, both significant and insignificant. There were dozens of pictures, studio portraits and informal snapshots alike, crowded on one wall of her den. Atop the end table near the sofa were bronzed baby shoes. Just yesterday Casey had proudly pulled out her baby album and displayed footprints, handprints, even a lock of hair snipped when she was a year old.

Suddenly Matt stood stock-still. He sucked in a harsh breath of air, every nerve in his body tightened to an almost painful pitch of awareness.

Sentimental Angie. This time the words mocked him. He turned slowly, his eyes moving carefully around the room. All of a sudden he realized there was something conspicuously absent in Angie's home.

There were no reminders—absolutely none—of the man who had once been her husband. No wedding pictures or albums, no small mementos of love once treasured...

More than ever, Matt was certain that something wasn't right.

TWO VERY LONG BATHS and three bedtime stories later, it was time to head downstairs and face Matt. Lovingly, Angie tucked the blanket beneath Casey's chin. She reached over and smoothed the tumbled curls off Kim's forehead. Both were sleeping peacefully.

Moving noiselessly to the bedroom door, she realized there was no point in delaying it any longer. She had dreaded being alone with him all day. The tension between them had eased somewhat while they were at Janice and Bill's, but there had been several times today when she had glanced up to find him watching her with a dark, analytical stare that was unnerving. She wished she had some idea of what was going on in his head, but his expression gave nothing away.

That same prickly sense of unease gripped her once more as she paused near the entrance of the living room. Darkness had fallen. The room was lit only by a hazy path of moonlight that crept in through the windows.

She could see Matt in silhouette standing near the fireplace, his hands thrust into the pockets of his slacks. As if sensing her scrutiny, he slowly turned, his face all planes and shadows. Her heart thundered in her chest as she hurriedly switched on a light. The tension in the air was almost palpable.

Matt finally extended his hand. "Come here," he invited softly.

Angie swallowed. Certainly there was nothing threatening in either his tone or his manner, yet as she moved slowly across the room, she felt as if she was heading straight into a minefield.

His jaw hardened as she ignored his outstretched hand and sat down in the nearest chair, prim and poised. *So this is how it's going to be,* he thought silently, his feelings a curious blend of frustration and resignation. She was still putting up barriers between them. But he was going to get through that wall around her if he had to tear it down piece by piece. They had played the game by her rules, but no more, dammit. No more!

Still, he found himself giving her one more chance. "I noticed Bill and Janice's wedding picture tonight—the one hanging in their dining room." He paused, watching her closely. "I couldn't help but wonder about yours and Evan's."

If he had surprised her, she gave no sign of it. "Why?" she asked bluntly.

Matt shrugged. "No special reason, I guess." He wandered over to stare absently out the window. "How long were you and Evan married?"

Angie glared at his broad back. She knew what he was trying to get at, and she didn't like it. She didn't like it at all. "Ten years," she replied curtly.

"Ten years," he murmured. "All of them happily, I take it?"

She sucked in a harsh breath. Damn! she moaned silently. She should have realized Matt wouldn't be satisfied with the little she had told him. She clasped her fingers tightly in her lap as she tried not to let his words rattle her.

"You already know that," she started to say, but Matt cut her off.

"No, I don't know that, but it occurred to me tonight that I don't even know what the hell Evan looked like. And it also struck me as odd—damn odd—that the woman who is supposed to be so damn smitten with her dead husband doesn't even have a picture of him. No reminders whatsoever.''

He faced her once more, his eyes glittering angrily. ''Married for ten years, widowed for two and still in love with her husband. All along that's what you've wanted me to believe. Isn't it, Angie?''

Boldly he confronted her, his voice ringing with accusation. His eyes bored into hers, stripping away all pretense between them. Her tongue darted out to trace suddenly dry lips. She'd been right to be wary of him.

''Isn't it, Angie?''

Numbly she nodded.

''It was just an excuse, wasn't it?'' His voice was blunted with both hurt and anger.

''Yes,'' she whispered again and closed her eyes. That she had hurt him was something she had never even considered. She had thought only of herself, yet she knew that if the same choice had to be made all over again, it would have been no different.

A bitter oath penetrated the air. The confusion and conflict in her voice tore him apart, but there was such a wealth of pain and despair burning inside him he could fight it no longer.

Strong arms snaked out to trap her in her chair. He bent over her, his expression dark and relentless and piercing.

''Good Lord, Angie!'' he cried. ''What are you trying to do? Punish yourself because Evan is dead?''

For one paralyzing second she stared at him, her mind whirling. At Evan's name every nerve in her body tightened. Her stomach knotted into a sickening coil of revulsion. All this time she hadn't wanted to face up to her feelings about Evan. The anger at his abuse, the guilt she'd suffered by her decision to leave him. She had buried them in a far corner of her mind, refusing to examine them and let them go.

And then there was Matt. Was he right? she wondered giddily. By denying her secret longing for him, had she somehow been trying to punish herself because Evan was dead and she was alive?

Something within her snapped. She was furious with Matt for dredging up such painful memories, furious with Evan for stripping her of her pride, her dignity, destroying their love.

''No!'' she cried, her eyes sparkling wildly. Shoving him back, she jumped to her feet. She was only half aware of what she was saying. All her resentment at Evan was suddenly directed at the man before her. "I'm not trying to punish myself because I hated him! Do you hear? I *hated* him! I didn't want him in my life any more than I want you!"

Words. They were just words, uttered in the heat of the moment. In his rational mind Matt knew that. But because he was angry and because he was hurt, he struck out—just as she had struck out.

Her breath was torn from her lungs as he reached for her and grabbed her shoulders. "Dammit, Angie!" he muttered fiercely, giving her a little shake. "What will it take for you to see—"

He got no further. Launched from the shadows, a small body suddenly threw itself between them.

"Leave her alone!" a voice cried. "I won't let you hit her like Daddy did. I won't!"

Kim was pushing at his legs with surprising strength. Caught off balance, Matt regained it only to find she had thrown herself at him again.

Along with the flailing fists, the kicking legs, the pathetically furious little voice came a numbing realization. It hit him with shattering clarity, but for a fraction of a second, he was overcome with disbelief. Was it the product of an overly imaginative young child, or was it really true...?

One glimpse of Angie's haunted expression was all it took to know that it was.

CHAPTER FOURTEEN

IT WAS SUDDENLY so crystal clear that Matt wondered why on earth he hadn't been able to see it before. *Everything* pointed in only one direction: Angie's dislike of being touched, the fear he had sensed in her, especially at first, the way she clung to her conviction that she wanted no part of him, of *any* man.

And Kim. Only two days ago she had looked up at him, her eyes huge and solemn. *You won't hurt my mommy, will you?*

A wrenching pain ripped through him. But there was no time for his own emotions—he was still the target of an eight-year-old bundle of rage determined to protect her mother. From the corner of his eye, he saw that Angie had stumbled over to the sofa. She was staring blindly ahead of her, her face white with shock. Matt swore softly, torn between mother and daughter. He'd never felt so helpless in his life.

It was Kim who ultimately made the choice for him. She was crying, screaming. "Don't hit her. Don't hit her!" over and over. It wasn't hard to figure out that she was on the verge of hysteria.

"Kim." He spoke in a firm but reassuring tone, not wanting to frighten her anymore. She didn't even hear him. *"Kim!"* Finally he dropped to his knees and picked her up, wrapping his arms around her flailing limbs and gathering her small body up against his chest.

"It's all right, Kim. Your mom and I—we were arguing. But please believe me when I say I would never, *never* hurt your mom." He took a deep, ragged breath, marveling that he could speak at all, let alone calmly, soothingly. But something in his voice must have convinced Kim of his sincerity. Her sobs eventually gave way to a watery hiccough, but when she looked up at him, her drawn features were still filled with anger, fear and resentment.

Then suddenly her face crumpled. "He hit her." The pitifully thin voice quavered. "I had to go to the bathroom and that—

that's when I saw Daddy hit Mommy and she—she fell down the stairs. He—he hurt her, Matt.''

Matt drew in his breath sharply and glanced at Angie. She gave no sign that she had heard. The knowledge that Evan had abused Angie had been a shocking revelation. It had shaken him badly, and his throat worked silently as he saw the tormented anguish that lingered in her eyes. She hadn't known about Kim; that much was clear. For a child to witness such a brutal act, for Angie to have *endured* such a brutal act... His eyes closed.

This time he had to struggle to speak. ''I know, sweetheart.'' His large hand stroked Kim's hair gently. ''But no one is ever going to hurt her again. I swear.'' Cradling her limp body tightly in his arms, he picked her up and rose to his feet, praying that Angie would be okay until he could get Kim settled down.

The little girl clung tightly to his neck as he mounted the stairs. How he found the words to comfort her he never knew, but somehow he did. Still, it seemed an eternity before she finally drifted off to sleep.

Angie was another story. He had no idea what to say to her. She had fought him for so long that he wasn't sure what his own reaction would be if she turned away from him now. Now, when she so desperately needed someone to lean on. Someone to share her pain.

She hadn't moved from her place on the sofa. From where he stood behind her, Matt could see the soft swirls of golden hair that had escaped their prison and lay loosely on the tender curve of her nape. Oddly, those few curls only accentuated her vulnerability even further.

As he watched, she drew her legs up to her chest and wrapped her arms around them. Her head dropped forward so that her forehead rested on her upraised knees. She looked completely drained and lifeless.

The utter bleakness in that one action affected him even more deeply than anything in the preceding half hour. Matt felt an unfamiliar tightening of the muscles in his throat.

Swallowing convulsively, he moved to stand before her. ''Angie?'' His voice sounded raw, as raw as the storm of emotions churning inside him.

Slowly she raised her head and looked at him. ''Is Kim okay?'' Her whisper was reed thin.

''She's asleep,'' he answered quietly. His eyes never left hers as slowly he eased down beside her. If she turned away from him now, he didn't think he could bear it.

She didn't. With a strangled little cry she propelled herself toward him. Strong arms enfolded her with tender urgency. A rush of relief poured through him, so powerful that, for a fraction of a second, he went weak with it. His eyes squeezed shut as he absorbed the almost unbearable sweetness of what she had just done. She had finally turned to him of her own free will. But Lord, what it had taken for him to reach this point!

His arms tightened around Angie's trembling body. He buried his face in the fragrant silk of her hair, and for a long moment they clung to each other.

Finally she drew back. She gazed at him with dark and tormented eyes and opened her mouth to speak.

Matt had felt the tension invade her body. His fingers came up to silence her. "Not yet," he pleaded. "Just let me hold you a little longer." For just a moment he thought she would refuse. Then with a breathless little sigh she sagged against his chest once more, absorbing his warmth, his strength.

Long minutes later she finally stirred weakly. Matt kissed her softly on the temple, not resisting as she sat up in his arms. She didn't break the circle of his hold, though. She simply repositioned herself so that her shoulder was wedged in the crook of his arm.

Matt was well aware of what she was trying to do, but he didn't argue. He, too, knew that what was to come in the next few minutes would be easier for both of them if he couldn't see her face. His eyes dropped to where her fingers plucked restlessly at a fold in her slacks.

Sensing her uncertainty, he said quietly, "You didn't know that Kim saw Evan hit you, did you?"

She shook her head and dug her teeth viciously into her lower lip. A hollow silence ensued. She drew in a ragged breath and finally spoke, venting her thoughts aloud.

"I *should* have," she said tonelessly. What followed was in jagged bits and pieces. "She changed so much after Evan died, became so silent and withdrawn.... I thought it was because she missed him. I thought her shyness around men was because her father was gone, but she was probably scared to death. If she saw what he did to me—my God, she must have hated him as much as I did!"

He felt as if he'd been slashed to ribbons by the guilt in her voice. "There was no way you could have known," he told her quietly.

"But why didn't she tell me?" she cried.

He sighed. She was as tense as a taut metal wire, ready to snap with the slightest pressure. He eased her against him so that her back was flush with his chest. His arms encircled her, his forearms resting against her ribs.

"I don't know," he said finally. "Maybe for the same reason children who are abused don't let anyone know. Maybe she was afraid that somehow she would lose you, too." His hand blanketed hers where it lay on her stomach. "She'll be okay. She's young. She'll get over it in time." His fingers squeezed hers reassuringly.

It was a touch of utter familiarity, a touch that somehow gave her courage. She'd been so stunned by Kim's revelation, and at the same time so horrified that Matt would know her terrible secret, that she hadn't realized how perilously close she'd come to losing control. Even now the threat of tears hovered just beneath the surface.

It made the sudden quiet that descended almost unbearable. She knew what was coming next by the rigidness that invaded the arms that held her. Her heartbeat accelerated to a point just short of panic.

Matt had to force the words past the ache in his throat. "Kim said you fell down the stairs. How badly were you—"

This time it was she who cut him off. "He didn't put me in the hospital, if that's what you mean. My ribs were sore and I had some bruises." She paused to take a deep, uneven breath. "Nothing too terribly serious."

"You had no idea he was—" he hesitated "—violent?"

Wordlessly she shook her head. When it appeared she had no intention of saying anything further, he pressed on, gently but relentlessly. "Angie, please," he urged, his voice slightly ragged. "I have to know."

She hesitated, but finally she began to speak in a very low tone. "We'd been married for eight years the first time it happened. He...he slapped me once when he'd been drinking. He'd been off work for a while and...well, it wasn't the best of times. I think, too, he was a little jealous of my success." Her lashes dropped to veil her eyes. "He was as shocked as I was when it happened. We...we both cried afterward."

"Things were better after that?"

She was quiet for a long time. "Yes and no," she finally admitted. "It didn't happen again for almost a year, but by that time I knew I couldn't take it any longer. Evan was—" her shoulders lifted helplessly "—impossible to live with. He still hadn't found a job, and he was frustrated and angry—"

"And he took it out on you." Matt's jaw tightened as he fought a wave of blinding rage. If Evan Hall had been there before him, he had no doubt he'd have torn him apart with a great deal of pleasure.

Angie leaned her head back against his shoulder tiredly. "I don't know why I ever stayed with him as long as I did. I suppose I was trying to hold my marriage together. But the day came when I realized I just couldn't take it anymore. I suggested that we separate—" a shudder shook her slender form "—and that's when it happened again."

She turned in his arms and buried her face in the warm hollow between his neck and shoulder. "That's when Kim must have seen us," she whispered.

Trembling hands smoothed her hair. His voice was as unsteady as hers. "You didn't stay with him after that, I hope."

It took a moment before she could speak again. "I didn't intend to. He went on a hunting trip a few days after that, and..." Her voice faltered.

"That's when he was killed?"

She nodded. "I knew by then that a divorce was the only answer, but I was afraid to tell him." She hesitated uncertainly. She wanted him to know, and yet she didn't.

As if he sensed her need for encouragement, he linked his fingers through hers, and let their twined hands rest on his stomach. "Go on," he urged softly.

"While he was on his trip, I intended to take the girls and move out of the house. Before I had a chance, I learned he was dead."

Something in her tone made him tilt her face to his. He laid a lean finger along the curve of her jaw and he quickly scanned her face. "Good Lord." His eyes reflected both astonishment and a swiftly restrained surge of anger. "You feel guilty! How can you after what that bastard did to you?"

"I don't," she countered quickly, then just as quickly muttered, "Oh, God, maybe I do. Not because I intended to divorce him, but because I...when I found out he was dead, I knew I didn't have to be afraid anymore—afraid of what he would say, what

he might do to me. I felt relieved. I couldn't even cry for him.
All I could think was that there would be no more dread, no more
pain.'' Her eyes were dark with anguish but held a plea for understanding as she gazed up at him. ''What kind of person does
that make me? Am I as terrible—'' her voice caught painfully
''—as I sometimes feel I am?''

Matt felt her heartache as if it were his own. The hell she'd
been through with Evan hadn't ended with his death, he realized
grimly. In some ways it had only just begun.

His hands dropped to her shoulders, his grip light, reassuring.
''God, no,'' he said with a depth of emotion he couldn't quite
control; nor did he want to. ''That makes you human—just as
human as the rest of us.''

For a long time he simply held her, savoring their closeness.
Finally he drew back slightly. ''The other day,'' he said gently,
''I called you Angel and you ran away. Did Evan call you that?''

She silently nodded.

''Angie—'' his fingers tightened on her shoulders for an instant
''—all this...it's why you don't like to be touched, isn't it?''

It was a moment before she spoke. ''You...you noticed?''

His smile held no mirth. ''It was one of the first things I did
notice about you.'' He paused. ''Angie, he didn't...he didn't do
anything else, did he?''

He felt her stiffen beneath his hands. ''Like what?'' she asked
faintly.

Matt knew of no way to soften the words. The question was
wrenched from deep inside him. ''He didn't rape you, did he?''

He cursed himself roundly, knowing he was handling this
badly. But at the stunned expression he glimpsed in her eyes, all
that he felt suddenly rushed out.

''It wasn't only the fact that you don't like to be touched because you let *me* touch you. But all along I've sensed that you
were holding back, that you were afraid of letting yourself get
close to me.''

Angie inhaled sharply. ''You want to know if I...if I'm afraid
to make love,'' she whispered.

There was a burning ache in Matt's throat. ''That bastard has
taken so much from you,'' he said unevenly. ''Has he taken that,
too?'' At the stricken look on her face, he added quickly, ''It
doesn't matter to me, Angie. It really doesn't. But I...I'd like to
know.''

Angie swallowed deeply. ''I'm not afraid,'' she denied in a

low voice, then bit her lip. How could she explain what she didn't really understand herself? With the tight rein she had kept on her emotions, she had never let her dreams of Matt carry her to the point of lovemaking.

And now she did. She was no innocent when it came to the physical intimacies between a man and a woman. Loving was easy. *Wanting* was easy. But it meant nothing unless those feelings were returned in full measure.

Silence steeped the room. A dull ache settled in her chest. "Maybe I am," she heard herself admit huskily. "Not of the act itself, but..."

"But what?" A finger gently angled her face to his.

Angie had to swallow repeatedly before she could say anything. "Evan and I—we still slept together after...after he hit me," she confided. She couldn't bring herself to say they had made love—because they hadn't. "But not very often, especially the last year. When we did, it wasn't the same. Maybe I was still afraid of him. I'm not sure. I was always so glad when it was over because I felt so...so cold and empty inside."

Matt closed his eyes. He understood her deep-seated fear of rejection, but that she was afraid of being unresponsive to him was just plain foolishness—and he told her so.

She was thankful that the shadowy darkness in the room hid her burning cheeks. She started to move away from him, but Matt slid his arms around her and refused to let her go.

"You don't understand," she muttered, suddenly anxious to have it out and over with. "Evan said I was frigid. My God, the way he used to look at me!" She trembled. "He said I was inadequate. Only half a woman. He said..."

She was babbling. She knew it, but somehow she just couldn't stop. She was vaguely aware that Matt had turned her in his arms, aware of callused fingertips grazing lightly over each and every one of her features. But it wasn't until those fingers exerted a gentle pressure on her mouth that her voice trailed away.

"I don't care what that man said," he told her when he saw that he had her attention. His eyes never faltered from hers. "You're beautiful, Angie. Inside, outside, in every possible way there is." A finger lifted her face, and he lowered his until his lips rested just at the corner of hers. "You're more woman than any man could ever want, Angie Hall." He kissed her softly, sweetly, until he felt her tremulous response. "The only woman *I* want," he whispered when their lips finally parted.

Once again she was stung by his sensitivity, the heartfelt conviction in his voice. Wrapping her arms around his neck, she clung to him with all her strength.

"Oh, Angie." Closing his eyes, he rested his chin on her shining hair. His hand shook as he smoothed the tendrils away from her temple. "I only wish you'd told me all this long ago."

Deep inside, she realized she must have thought he'd think less of her. She felt so very grateful that he didn't.

"So do I," she whispered. Tipping her head back, she smiled at him poignantly.

A sudden thought occurred to him. "Who else knows Evan abused you?" he asked quietly.

Angie wanted to look away from him but found she couldn't. She was dimly aware that her hands were trembling. Somehow she managed to squeeze the words past the huge lump in her throat. "No one."

Matt felt as if someone had wrapped a huge band of steel around his chest. To think of Angie keeping all of this bottled up inside all this time. He suddenly understood why it was so important to her that a women's shelter be established in Westridge.

The constriction tightened further when he saw a diamond-bright teardrop suspended from her lashes. She made a valiant effort to fight it, the muscles in her throat working convulsively.

Matt could take it no longer. Her tortured soul needed to be purified, cleansed. Only then could the healing process begin. And he knew of only one way to do it.

He hauled her into his embrace, his arms both tender and rough. "Cry, babe," he muttered into the golden cloud of her hair. "Cry as much or as little as you want."

And she did. Warm, wet, salty tears of sorrow for a love once cherished, a love now mourned because it was dead and gone. Tears that slipped unheeded down her cheeks, tears that poured from an endless well inside her. She cried until she was exhausted, lying limply against a solid warmth that was the only beacon of light in a shadowy sea of darkness.

When it was over, Matt carried her up to bed. She had no strength left to protest as a voice softly commanded that she raise her arms, lift her hips. Soft white silk slipped down her body. But she was attuned only to an entirely different set of sensations—gentle hands, all the more comforting because of their very strength, a voice as feathery soft as down and a look so tender and caring she felt warm and secure as she'd never felt before.

The pins were removed from her hair, a brush quickly pulled through the loosened strands. She was all ivory and gold with her hair feathered over her shoulders, and her arms were bare beneath the cap sleeves of the gown. The scooped neckline offered tantalizing glimpses of the same smooth, honey-colored skin, skin that gleamed invitingly beneath the sheer material. Desire—sweet, warm and potent—surged hotly through Matt's bloodstream. The feeling was so intense it bordered on pain.

Pain because he wanted to make love to her as he had never wanted anything in his life. Pain because he ached to sweep her into a world of sweet oblivion, a world where there was no bitterness, no haunting reminders of the past...a world where only the two of them existed.

But he knew he didn't dare. Rest was what she needed right now...rest.

It took a moment before he was able to clamp the brake on that dangerous train of thought.

"Better?" When he was finally able to speak, he strived for a neutral tone, achieved it and then wondered how the hell he'd managed. Confining his attention to his hands and away from the lushly tempting curves of her body, he fluffed the pillow under her head.

Angie nodded. Her eyes were fused to his, and as he watched, a faint flush crept into her cheeks. He knew she was thinking of the way he had just impersonally undressed her, and he was both amused and touched by her reaction.

His own reaction changed to a far different one when she made no move to draw the sheet up over her breasts. This time he was the one who couldn't look away when she drew a deep, quivering breath.

He straightened abruptly. "Good night, Angie. I'll see you in the morning." He was astounded that he sounded so normal, even more so when he reached the door without looking back at her.

"Don't go."

It was a ribbon of sound, no more than a wispy breath of air. Convinced he'd conjured it up from the depths of his imagination, Matt's face tightened. Then he stopped and slowly turned.

The air was charged with a brittle tension as he stared at Angie. The heat reflected in their eyes melded, breaching the distance between them. He scarcely breathed, afraid she would disappear like misty beads of dew on a bright and sun-kissed morning.

Then she was there before him, his sensuous angel with the

golden halo of hair. He heard the soft whisper of her breath, smelled the musky, womanly scent of her.

A hand tentatively touched his chest. A second later the other crept up to join it.

"Please, Matt. Don't leave me." Quivering lips hovered temptingly, so temptingly, beneath his. "I...I need you."

I need you. It was a promise, a prayer, a plea... They were also the sweetest words he'd ever hoped to hear.

Deep within a flicker of hope burned brighter. But he couldn't touch her. Not yet. "I can't stay with you, Angie," he said very quietly. "Because if I do—" his voice reached an even lower pitch "—if I do, I don't know if I can stop myself from making love to you."

He thought she might flinch from his bluntness. But she didn't. She only continued to gaze up at him with eyes so blue, so full of trust that he felt oddly humble, strangely proud. And so filled with love he thought he might burst.

"I know," Angie said with a brave little smile. Very softly she added, "I thought you might say that."

His gaze roved over her delicate features. Her cheeks were still flushed from the tears so recently shed, but she had never looked more beautiful—or more vulnerable. He had to be certain, absolutely sure that *she* was sure.

His pose was relaxed, but inside he was trembling. "That doesn't scare you?" he asked, willing his voice to be steady.

In a slow but deliberate move, he settled his hands on her hips, aligning her body firmly against his. He heard her catch her breath at the implicit evidence of his desire for her, but she didn't move away. "Because if I touch you," he warned softly, "I don't think I'll be able to stop. For both of us, babe, make sure this is what you want."

Angie saw many things in his face as she looked up at him. He was so strong, so masculine, a man who had almost reached his limit but cared enough to give her one last chance to change her mind. She saw a man who gave unselfishly, without question.

She could be no less than honest with him. "I'm afraid," she whispered with a tremulous little smile, "but I'm even more afraid to spend this night alone."

It was enough. It would have to be, Matt thought giddily, for his control had just run out. His heart reached out to her...and so did his arms.

They were strong, those arms, but it was a strength tempered with tenderness as Angie found herself lifted and borne silently to the bed. Once there, she couldn't look away as Matt pulled his shirt off and tossed it carelessly across the chair.

His chest was wide and muscular, forested with tangled curls that dipped into the waist of his jeans. He possessed a dark magnificence that both thrilled and frightened her. A shudder passed through her as the side of the bed sagged beneath his weight. But whether it was from fear or some other nameless emotion, she wasn't sure.

In that very special way he had, she realized he must have sensed something of her tumultuous emotions. She was silent as he switched off the light and eased down close beside her. He touched her nowhere. He touched her everywhere—clear to her soul.

Their eyes cleaved together, and she saw so many things—tenderness, caring—that for a second she felt totally overwhelmed.

A slow silver flame burned brighter with each second that passed. The unmistakable hunger on his face seemed to warm her, calling forth the woman inside her that had lain dormant for so long...but no longer.

Her breath spilled forth in a rush, and she realized she'd been holding it. Anticipation swept through her like rich sweet wine. "Kiss me," she whispered.

He lowered his head. His gaze moved slowly, searchingly, over her face, as if to test the validity of her request. It finally settled on the parted softness of her mouth.

Dear God, she wondered frantically, *will he never...?*

His forehead rested against hers. "Do you know," he asked in a tone of utter seriousness, "how long I've waited for this moment?" He paused and took a deep, full breath. For the first time she realized exactly how great his restraint had been.

And she knew, as she had never known anything before, that being here like this with Matt was right...and good.

Her hands lifted to tunnel through his hair. "Do you know—" her voice was a feminine replica of his own "—how long I've been fighting this moment?" His mouth opened, but when he would have spoken, she gave a tiny shake of her head. "But I'm not fighting it anymore." One hand traced an unsteady path around his mouth. "I want you, Matt. The same way you want me."

Matt stared down at her for an endless moment. If he had

indeed harbored any intentions of calling a halt before things went any further, she had just blown that notion right out of the water.

"Oh, Angie." His voice was strained. It was all he could manage. "God, I hope you mean that," he told her fervently when he could finally speak.

It was all Matt could do to stop himself from loving her as fiercely and urgently as he ached to, but he reluctantly curbed the impulse. In spite of what Angie had said, he knew they had reached a critical point in their relationship. He intended to see that nothing happened to change that.

And so he held back the driving need to possess her, the searing passion pumping through his veins. "I want tonight to be perfect for you, perfect as it's never been before." He brushed the pads of his thumbs over her cheekbones as he cradled her face between his hands. "As perfect as I know it will be for me. Because with you it could never be anything else."

Leaning over her, he kissed her as gently, as thoroughly, as he could, putting all the tenderness he felt for her into that one sweet caress. Her lips trembled like the wings of a bird, but when her arms slipped around his neck, freely and without any urging from him, he knew for certain they were knocking on heaven's door.

They smiled at each other when he drew back, a silly, sentimental smile shared only by lovers.

Matt's was the first to fade away. His hand rose to cover the softer one curled lightly over his shoulder. "I love it when you touch me," he said quietly.

Wide blue eyes flashed up at him. "Do you?"

Her response was rather breathless. She was nervous, he decided. A twinge of remorse cut through him, overridden by the ache in his body that was by now almost a physical pain. But no matter what it cost him, suddenly he knew exactly what he had to do.

"We're going to do this your way," he said, smiling at her reassuringly. Then, remembering his words earlier that night, he couldn't resist adding teasingly, "You can touch as much or as little as you want." Still watching her, he leaned back against the pillows.

But he wasn't teasing, and they both knew it. There had been a time when Angie would have thought nothing of taking the lead during lovemaking. But that had been a long, long time ago, she reminded herself.

Consequently, the prospect of doing so with Matt was a daunting one. Daunting, but provocative—and irresistible.

He had removed his jeans, but he was still wearing his briefs, and she was suddenly glad. She edged up slightly so she could look down at him. There was an intimate glow of invitation in his eyes. Encouraged by that glow, she reached out and ran her fingers lightly over the curve of his collarbone, down over keenly honed biceps and back to his chest.

His skin was warm beneath the dense mat of hair that had always intrigued her. In an investigation that was both shy and bold, her fingers sought and found a flat brown nipple surrounded by a wiry nest of hair. In the moonlight she saw his eyes fill with a sublime pleasure. His expression reflected a thousand different emotions. She wanted to exclaim and marvel over each. She heard the ragged breath he drew, felt his chest expand with it and knew a heady sense of power unlike anything she'd felt before. She relished it, savored it, thanked him for it.

Matt felt as if every bone in his body had turned to water. The touch of her hands filled him with a thousand explosive sensations. Her fingers brushed, fondled, raked, teased and taunted as her mouth did the same to his lips. When a single finger pursued a relentless path downward from his throat to his navel, his heart beat a driving, pounding rhythm.

It skipped a beat when her finger paused for an unending, breath-stealing moment...then resumed its journey, tugging at the waistband of his briefs.

All his good intentions disintegrated. He couldn't help himself as he shifted his weight and crushed her body beneath his. It was sweet agony as her nipples burned twin peaks of fire into the hardened wall of his chest. But he forced himself to hold her, just hold her until the faint tremor in his limbs began to subside. He stared into her eyes for a long, breathless moment. Then his head slowly lowered.

Angie sighed as his mouth touched hers, at first the touch so reverent that she felt tears glaze her eyes. She felt him smile against her mouth, and for a heart stopping second she thought he had changed his mind. But soon the light grazing off his lips against hers became more urgent. His kiss deepened, and her lips parted in response. Her tongue flirted with the daring invader that breached the barrier of her teeth, joining in an intricate mating that left both of them gasping.

''God, Angie.'' The words came out hoarsely, wrenched from

deep inside of him. "I want you so much...so much." That need was magnified a hundredfold in the rawness of his voice.

She could feel the tautness in the arms that held her, in the velvet-and-steel fullness riding against her belly. At the thought the apex of her womanhood tingled with a heavy warmth.

Touching. Kissing. Caressing. Soon it wouldn't be enough, for either of them. She didn't care.

She drew away just enough to gaze up at him with shining eyes. "Make love to me, Matt." She caressed his roughened jaw with fingers that weren't entirely steady. "Make love to me."

This time there would be no stopping, and they both knew it. As if they had all the time in the world, Matt began to kiss her. Slowly. Leisurely. At every possible angle, in every possible way he had ever dreamed of.

When he did finally raise his head, it was to unhurriedly tug at the sleeves of her gown. She mindlessly obeyed his whispered instructions, and her eyes drifted shut as Matt slid the material down to her waist.

Her skin burned wherever he touched—the outward flare of her hips, the slender length of her thighs. And when her body lay bared to him, her eyes flickered open, anxiously awaiting his verdict.

He wasted no time in giving it. "You're beautiful," he breathed, extending a finger toward her breasts.

When he merely traced the deep cleft between their burgeoning fullness, Angie wanted to moan her frustration. The feeling quickly transformed into a delicious sense of anticipation as he settled his hands on her waist and slowly lowered his head.

His breath caressed her first. She felt its moist warmth like the first faint whispery wings of night. Her senses heightened by the deep, emotional pull between them, a ripple of pure sensation curled through her when his mouth finally closed over the aching peak. It built to a feverish pitch as he bathed the quivering bud of her nipple with moist heat. The same careful attention was applied to her other breast, and her world exploded into a million shattering sensations as he began a rhythmic tugging.

Never in her life had she felt more beautiful, more desirable, more alive. She wanted his mouth on hers, his tongue making wildly delicious magic with her own. She wanted his hands on her breasts, to feel him stroke the secret fire hidden deep inside her. She wanted his weight pressing into her, to feel him deep inside her to fill the empty void that cried out for him.

"Please, Matt," she begged. "Come to me. Come to me now."

Firm lips swallowed her husky entreaty. With a moan of sheer pleasure, Matt settled her bare breasts into the dark cloud of hair on his chest. Strong hands slipped under her buttocks, lifted, aligned his hips between the intimate cradle of hers.

The velvet strength of him sank slowly into moist, flowering petals of femininity. Matt closed his eyes at the incredible sensations bombarding him as her satin warmth surrounded him, made him whole. She was his...his at last.

Mindlessly he tangled his fingers in her hair. His eyes flicked open, and he stared into passion-drenched eyes. His voice stole softly through the silence. "I love you, Angie...I love you."

Then they were together, together with nothing between them. Hands touched and caressed; lips blended and merged. Her pleasure was his and his was hers as their hips indulged in a dance as old as time itself. Higher they climbed, ever higher, to a blissful place where hearts ran wild and free.

And then they were no longer two, but one. One body. One soul... One heart.

CHAPTER FIFTEEN

SOME TIME LATER Matt awoke. An oppressive heaviness hung in the air. Through the sheer ruffled curtain he saw that the night was starless. The heavens loomed dark and menacing. Lightning streaked across the sky, illuminating the storm clouds with an eerie silver glow for the space of a heartbeat.

He had expected to awake with Angie still slumbering in his arms, but he was alone. A cold sense of foreboding swept over him, and slipping on his pants, he went in search of her.

He found her in the dining room. She was sitting on the window seat, clutching a small patchwork pillow to her breast and staring out into the stark blackness of the night. She had slipped on a thin robe, and just imagining the honey-tinted sheen of her skin sent an electrifying rush of awareness through him.

But his intuition was right after all. Something was wrong. Something was very wrong.

She looked so lonely. There was a remoteness in the smooth lines of her profile that had him twisted in knots. He wanted to go to her, to take her in his arms and soothe her, comfort her as he had done once before that night. A flash of lightning lit up the room as bright as day, and he took a single step forward. She must have sensed his eyes upon her because she turned then.

The haunting bleakness in her eyes stopped him cold. He leaned a hand against the doorframe. "Can't sleep?" he asked quietly.

She shook her head and sat up straighter. He sensed she was gathering her courage.

Outside the wind began to howl. A pelting rhythmic rain began to fall against the windowpanes. In the corner a clock ticktocked.

The silence spun out between them. Matt waited...and waited. A sickening feeling of dread gathered in the pit of his stomach.

Finally Angie looked across at him. With the enveloping cloak of darkness, he had no way of knowing she'd spent the last hour fighting back tears—and not always succeeding. But there was nothing in her voice, no hint of emotion whatsoever as she said, "I'd like you to leave in the morning, Matt."

Matt couldn't quite control the fiery mist of anger that burned before his eyes. After all they had shared this night, she might have been a stranger. Her words were like a slap in the face.

His jaw clenched. "Why?" he demanded.

"Everything's been fine this weekend," she murmured. "The note—must have been a prank." She prayed he wouldn't see how difficult this was for her. "I don't see the necessity of having you stay any longer, so you needn't bother coming home with me after work tonight."

Matt's expression was stony. It irritated him that she pretended to misunderstand his question. His eyes never left her slender silhouette as he reached out to switch on the light. "It's not like you to beat around the bush, Angie. Why don't you just say what you mean? This is goodbye, isn't it?" His lips twisted bitterly. "In other words, it's been nice but don't come back."

Angie cringed at the mockery in his voice. His reaction was understandable; he was hurt and angry, and he was lashing out. "Please, Matt." She clutched the pillow she held even more tightly, as if it would somehow ease the dull ache in her breast. "This isn't easy for me. Just...just let it go."

The pleading in her voice cut him to ribbons, but there was a part of him that was furious with her for being so blind, so stubborn. Had last night proved nothing to her? They had been from hell to heaven, but it was a journey they had made together.

It should have counted for something...*everything*.

It was totally incomprehensible to Matt that last night had done no more than bring them full circle.

He took a deep breath to control his seething emotions, before he could speak. "Why are you doing this?" he asked intently. "You know how I feel about you. Do you really expect me to walk out the door and forget about you?" His eyes never wavered from her face. Softly, deliberately, he said, "We made love last night, Angie. Doesn't that mean anything to you?"

Her eyes darkened with the pain he was inflicting. "It was a mistake, Matt." But did she really believe that? She didn't know. Dammit, she didn't know! And that uncertainty was tearing her apart. Still, making love with Matt had opened her eyes as nothing else could have. She loved him. She wanted to give him everything. But her love was not so blind as it had once been with

Evan. And she was afraid. So very afraid of trusting that deeply again.

"It was a mistake," she repeated, her voice barely audible. In her heart she knew it was herself she was trying to convince. "It should never have happened. I know I wanted you...but I...I wasn't myself." She was making excuses; they both knew it.

It didn't stop Matt from feeling he'd been stabbed in the back. It was instinct, pure and simple, that made him want to react with anger, to show her that no matter what she said, her body wouldn't lie.

Yet somehow he damped down his own emotional upheaval and reminded himself of the anguish she had suffered in the last twenty-four hours...and what she had suffered with Evan Hall.

She needed him. She needed him as much as he needed her.

He moved slowly across the room until he was standing directly in front of her. He ached with the need to gather her close in his arms, but he sensed she would only turn away.

"I love you—" he began.

"Don't!" she cried sharply. "Don't say that again!"

It was those three simple words that had driven her from her bed and from the warm shelter of his arms. "I love you," he'd whispered between slow, mindless thrusts while he'd made love to her. She had listened with her heart and loved him with all her soul, but now those words had shattered her world.

She felt herself coming apart inside, but there was no stopping him. When she would have reached up to cover her ears, Matt's hands came out and held hers firmly at her sides, his grip unyielding but not hurtful.

"I love you," he continued quietly, as if she'd never spoken. "I love you and I want to spend the rest of my life with you." He paused for the space of a heartbeat. "I want you to marry me, Angie."

Angie couldn't look away from him. She could have wept from the depth of emotion in his voice, the tenderness in his eyes. Wrenching herself away from him, she jumped to her feet and ran across to the doorway. She wrapped her arms around herself, then slowly turned to face him.

Her lungs burned from the effort it took to hold back her tears. Her heart felt as if it were raw and bleeding. "I can't, Matt. Don't you see?"

"No. No, I don't." His eyes narrowed. "You love me, Angie."

"I never said that!" she cried wildly. She hated herself for the look of pain that flashed across his face, but she forced herself to stand her ground.

Matt had only to remember the way she had clung to him, her body arching beneath his, the sweet magic that had claimed them both, a magic that only came from such tender emotions as love.

It frustrated him deeply that yet again Angie withheld herself from him. Before it had been her thoughts, her feelings. And now? Now it was perhaps the most vital part of all, that which he treasured most of all—her heart.

It was ironic that she refused to say the words. But he decided this was not the time to force her to admit something he already knew.

Instead, he softly urged, "Talk to me, Angie. Tell me why you won't marry me. Is it because of Evan?" He saw her shiver slightly. His voice deepened to a rough whisper with the emotion that suddenly churned through him. "I'd never hurt you, Angie. Tell me you know that!"

His urgent plea wasn't lost on her. "I know that, Matt," she said quietly, then hesitated. "It's just that one failed marriage in a lifetime is enough. I'm not sure I'm willing to try it again."

Matt had a hard time believing what he was hearing. "You weren't the guilty party," he said curtly. "Evan was. If your marriage failed, it was because of him, not you."

There was a long silence. "Maybe," she finally agreed. "Maybe not." She took a deep breath, fighting for poise. "Even if Evan hadn't—" she struggled over the word "—abused me, I'm not sure our marriage would have lasted. For a long time I put Evan's needs before my own, but once I started working again, I realized that I had to please myself, as well." She gave a short, bitter laugh. "This may be the twentieth century, but a lot of men are jealous of the fact that women are invading their world."

Matt's jaw thrust forward. "And you think I'm one of them? That I'm jealous of your career?"

She met his anger with a steady calm. "Not in so many words. But can you deny that when you first took the job as police chief, you didn't resent you were working under a woman?"

He cursed himself for the dull red flush he knew was creeping up his neck. He had never dreamed she would throw that back in his face like this. "You're twisting things and you know it."

"I'm not sure that I do," she responded very quietly.

"I won't admit any such thing," he stated flatly. "I'll admit I was a little leery, but I certainly never resented you. And I wouldn't have taken the damn job if I hadn't thought that you were just as capable of doing your own!''

She emitted a weary sigh. ''I'm not going to argue with you, Matt. But even if you're right, there's Linda to consider.''

''Linda?'' He looked totally baffled. ''What the hell does she have to do with this?''

''You told me that part of the trouble between you two started when she went behind your back to her father.'' She hesitated. The closed expression he wore warned her of his reaction. ''We're talking about male pride, Matt. You didn't like being unable to buy her little things she wanted.''

His eyes narrowed. If she was saying what he thought she was... ''And?''

''And Evan was like that, too.''

The deathly silence that followed was somehow more shattering than a bomb blast. Matt dragged a hand down his face, wondering if this nightmare would never end. There was a painfully hollow sensation in his chest. He had the awful feeling he was about to lose Angie.

''You just said you knew I wasn't like him,'' he reminded her, his voice low and taut.

''I...I know,'' she whispered, turning her face aside. Knowing she was responsible for the torment on Matt's face cut into her like a knife.

It didn't make her decision any less agonizing. For all that he was kind and sensitive, he was also a demanding, strong-willed man. Any commitment between them would be total. There would be no half measures for a man like Matt.

''You don't trust me, do you? You don't trust me enough to believe that we could work it out.'' There was no anger in his voice. Instead, he sounded incredibly weary.

Her gaze flickered back to him. He seemed to have aged years in the space of a few short minutes. ''I can't Matt.'' Her shoulders lifted helplessly. ''And I'm not sure I'll ever be able to.'' She saw him through a hazy blur of tears. ''I never meant to hurt you,'' she choked out. ''Please believe me.''

His eyes bored into hers, creating a brittle tension that was almost unbearable for both of them. Time slipped quietly by.

He could have said, ''I'll be waiting for you when you change your mind." But he knew, as she did, that she wouldn't change her mind. Instead, he said, "I'll leave in the morning."

His footsteps never faltered as he walked quietly past her.

ANGIE DIDN'T GO in to the office on Monday. She asked Georgia to cancel the council meeting. The vote would have to wait. Instead, she spent the day at home, trying to recover from the strain of the past weekend. So much had happened—the note, finding out about Kim, and the agonizing scene with Matt—that for the first time in her life, she wondered how on earth she would cope with it all. But by drawing on some hidden reserve of unknown strength she knew she would manage.

Facing Kim wasn't easy, but she tried to act as normally as possible when she woke the girls that morning. She briskly shooed Casey into the bathroom, then sat down on the edge of the bed.

Kim was sitting up, her thin arms wrapped around her knees. There was a pinched, worried expression on her face that pulled on Angie's heartstrings, but she forced a faint smile to her lips.

"Are you okay this morning?" she asked softly.

Kim nodded, then spoke very hesitantly. "Are you mad at me, Mommy? Because of what I did last night?"

Angie's response was swift and immediate. "Of course not, sweetheart." She smoothed tumbled brown locks behind Kim's ears. "Did you think I would be?"

There was a tiny frown etched between the child's brows as she seemed to consider. "I...I guess not," she said finally, then seemed to relax a little.

Angie studied her quietly for a few seconds. The secret that she had held inside all this time couldn't be allowed to fester anymore. Kim carried far too many emotional scars already, and painful though it might be for both of them, they had to discuss it openly and honestly.

"Kim." Her voice was very gentle as she reached for one of Kim's hands and clasped it reassuringly between both of hers. "Sweetheart, we need to talk. Why didn't you ever tell me you saw—" she stumbled over the words "—your father hit me?"

Kim's eyes filled with tears. She didn't say anything for the longest time, and when she did, her mouth was trembling. "He...he scared me, Mommy. And then later...later I didn't like to think about it."

Knowing what Kim must have endured all this time was like rubbing salt in an open wound. A hard knot swelled in Angie's

throat, and she hugged her daughter fiercely. "I'm sorry, Kim."
Her voice broke painfully. "Sorry you had to see it."

"It wasn't your fault, Mommy." Kim's voice was muffled into
her mother's breast. She clung to her tightly. "Daddy was mad,
he was always mad. And I don't know why, but—but he didn't
need to hurt you!" she lashed out fiercely.

Daddy was mad, he was always mad. In spite of her tender
age, Kim had known that something was wrong. And Angie
hadn't realized her daughter had been so perceptive. *How could
I have been so blind!* she agonized silently.

It took a moment for Angie to gather control. "You're right,
Kim," she told her quietly. "What he did was wrong. But no
matter what, I want you to know that you can talk to me about
anything." She tilted Kim's chin up gently and searched her face.
"Especially if it's something that scares you. Because sometimes
it helps just to talk about it with someone else." Her smile was
faint, but her daughter seemed reassured. She could tell by the
way Kim's expression began to lighten, as though a thin, filmy
curtain had just been lifted. "Okay, sweetheart?"

Kim nodded, and just then Casey emerged from the bathroom.
Angie's youngest wasted no time in engaging her mother and
sister in a rip-roaring pillow fight. By the time Angie had the girls
dressed and sitting at the breakfast table, Kim was laughing and
giggling almost as much as her sister.

Still, the next few days were far from easy. "Why doesn't Matt
come over anymore?" Casey asked one morning at breakfast. She
had scarcely touched her food.

Angie winced at the wounded look in her wide blue eyes. Be-
fore she had a chance to respond, Casey spoke once more. "First
Spooky went away. Then Matt." Her bottom lip began to tremble.
"Don't they like us anymore, Mommy?"

Angie pulled her small body onto her lap. "Of course they do,
darling." She bit her lip, wondering how she could explain.
"Spooky...well, we just don't know where she is. And Matt has
been very busy lately."

"Looking for Spooky?" Casey stared up at her.

Nodding slowly, she smothered a feeling of guilt and quickly
changed the subject. That Spooky might be dead was something
she hated to think about.

But Casey wasn't the only one who noticed Matt's absence.
Kim expressed disappointment over the loss of her batting coach.

Their mother missed him, too—missed him dreadfully. Going

to work, knowing that Matt was in the same building made it even harder. She wasn't sure if she was angry or hurt at how easily he had accepted her decision.

The only contact she had with him was through Georgia. He let her know they still hadn't discovered the identity of the person who had sent the note, and he asked her to postpone the council's vote on the city hall issue until the following Monday rather than rescheduling it for later that week.

The whole business with the note had left her uneasy and on edge, but as the week wore on and nothing else happened, she began to breathe a little easier. And as she told Todd Friday afternoon, the issue was beginning to look up. Steve Jackson had mentioned to her only that morning that he would probably vote in favor of the city hall renovations.

Still, her mood was far from happy, and even Georgia moped around the office all week. Angie thought her own bleak spirits had something to do with it, but she soon discovered that wasn't the case at all.

Though Angie was glad that Sam and Georgia had found each other, she was the first to admit that the idea of Georgia involved in a mad passionate affair took a little getting used to. Georgia wasn't the type to supply every little detail of what went on between her and Sam, but over the past few weeks Angie had learned that things were progressing at a very nice pace.

"Going out this weekend?" Angie dropped a pile of letters she'd just signed back into the tray on Georgia's desk.

"Nope." Georgia slammed a drawer shut.

As she shoved her chair back and headed toward the filing cabinet, Angie's puzzled gaze followed her assistant. Suddenly she realized that she hadn't seen Sam hovering around the office at all during the past week.

"Uh-oh," she murmured, thinking aloud. "Something tells me there's trouble in paradise."

Georgia yanked a stack of folders from the cabinet and marched back to her desk. She eyed the younger woman over the rim of her glasses. "What makes you think that?" she retorted gruffly.

Angie raised an eyebrow. "I wasn't trying to pry, Georgia. But it just occurred to me that Sam hasn't taken you to lunch even once this week."

"That's because he's got more on his mind than lunch—a *lot* more!'' At Angie's startled look she heaved an impatient sigh. "For heaven's sake, not *that!*"

By now Angie was trying hard not to smile. "If not 'that,'" she chided teasingly, "then what?"

Georgia scowled. "Let's just say he's getting a little too serious."

Angie watched Georgia as she flitted around the office, straightening furniture that didn't need to be straightened, swiping dust off plants that weren't dusty. "Too serious?" she asked when it became apparent that Georgia wasn't going to offer anything more unless coaxed.

"He wants to get married!"

Angie was tempted to laugh at Georgia's aghast expression, but the hint of sadness mixed with the confusion in her eyes stopped her. "And you don't?"

"No!" Following that fervent denial, Georgia dropped into the nearest chair. "I mean yes, I do, but..." She began to wring her hands. "We had one heck of a humdinger over it," she finally admitted.

"Do you love him?" Angie asked calmly.

"Yes."

"And he loves you?"

"He says he does."

"Do you believe him?"

"Yes." Georgia's chin lifted a notch. "Yes, I do!"

Angie leaned a hip against the corner of the desk. "Then what's stopping you from marrying him?"

Georgia hesitated. "I'm forty-four years old," she said slowly. "I've been on my own for longer than I care to remember, I'm independent as hell." She shook her head. "I don't know, Angie. I'm not sure I could get used to making that kind of change in my life. Sam and I might end up driving each other crazy."

"That's where a little principle called give-and-take comes in," Angie reminded her. "You certainly won't know unless you try." She mulled silently for a moment. "I guess you have to ask yourself if you're better off with him or without him. And if worse comes to worst and you still can't decide, then maybe it's time to listen to your heart."

By the time she'd finished, Georgia was looking at her with an odd expression. "And maybe," the other woman added quietly, "it's time you listened to yours."

The room grew very still. She knew Georgia was referring to

the state of affairs between her and Matt. The reasons Georgia had just rattled off for refusing to marry Sam were ones that could easily have applied to herself.

What a fool she was. What a blind, hypocritical fool.

Finally she looked across at Georgia with a weak smile. "I'm a fine one to be dishing out advice, aren't I?"

Georgia got up and squeezed her shoulder. "If it makes you feel any better, he's just as miserable. Margie told me yesterday that walking into his office is like walking into a minefield."

But knowing that Matt was miserable didn't make her feel any better. It only made her feel guilty. It had never been her intention to hurt him—she'd told him that and she meant it with all her heart. If only she had been able to resist him. If only she had been stronger. If only he had listened to her from the start. If only...

BY SATURDAY MORNING there was one thing she was sure of— if she didn't find some way of getting her mind off Matt, she would end up a basket case. Even with the girls to keep her company, the loneliness at home was stifling.

The morning was warm, beautifully sunny and cloudless. Much too gorgeous a day to stay cooped up at home entertaining morose thoughts, Angie told herself. She called the Crawfords to see if they would be interested in a picnic. Bill was working overtime at the mill, but Janice and her children decided to come along, anyway. She packed a lunch, and they all piled into the Crawfords' station wagon and headed to a park just outside the city.

It was early in the afternoon when Janice glanced over at Angie. They'd spread a quilt beneath the protective shade of a gnarled old oak tree, and Angie lay on her back, her knees tucked up, her hands resting on her stomach. She looked peaceful and rested, but there was a telltale sadness in her eyes that was only too familiar to Janice. Over the past few weeks she'd followed the current state of affairs between her friend and Matt Richardson with delighted interest, but it was clear that lately something wasn't right.

"You know," Janice eased into the conversation, "that confession is good for the soul, don't you?"

Angie frowned good-naturedly, her eyes still closed. She'd known her friend far too long to pretend not to know what she was talking about. "We came for a little R and R, Jan. Let's not spoil it, hmm?"

Janice shrugged. The light, bantering tone didn't fool her. "Who can you talk to about a man, if not a woman?" She sighed when Angie wrinkled her nose. "And here I thought you'd thrown away your halo and clipped your wings not long after you met Matt Richardson."

Angie opened one eye and turned her head slightly. If Janice was trying to rile her, it wasn't succeeding, at least not yet. "What," she asked airily, "is that supposed to mean?"

Cross-legged, Janice swung around to face her. "It means that I thought you'd finally started living again."

Angie sat up. "Come on," she protested, brushing a stray blade of grass from her shorts. "What is this if not living? It's a beautiful day, I don't have to work and I'm not spending it cooped up—"

"Aha!" the other woman exclaimed triumphantly, a gleam in her eyes. "But what about tonight?"

Angie's mouth snapped shut. Janice's smile faded, as well, and she reached out to touch Angie's hand. "I'm not trying to pry," she said gently, "but I know when something's wrong. And I have a very good suspicion it has to do with Matt Richardson."

Angie nodded reluctantly.

"You're not seeing each other? Other than professionally?"

The shake of Angie's head was barely perceptible.

"Your choice or his?"

"Mine." Angie's mouth scarcely moved.

Janice's eyes were full of sympathy. "What's the problem? That is, if it's anything you can talk about," she quickly added. "Or *want* to talk about."

Eric had toddled over some time ago and now lay sleeping between the two women. In the awkward void of silence, Angie reached out and began to gently pat his back.

"There would be no problem if I'd never gotten involved with him in the first place," she reflected, then caught Janice's guilty expression. Hastening to reassure her friend, she summoned a wan smile. "Don't blame yourself. It would have happened with or without you trying to throw the two of us together."

Angie moved a finger up to caress the baby's chubby cheek. At her touch he blew out a bubbly sigh. Finally she looked up at Janice. "Matt thinks I don't trust him."

This time it was Janice who stretched out the silence. "Do you?" she asked very quietly.

In the next tree birds chattered noisily. High above, golden sunlight crept through the twisted jumble of branches and leaves. Angie looked out at the small pond nearby where Kim, Casey and Nancy splashed near the shore, the puppy yapping at their heels.

"I don't know," she said finally. "As much as I wish I could, it's just not that simple."

"Because of Evan." Janice paused to consider the situation, then spoke very gently. "I know how painful it was for you before Evan died. Bill and I couldn't help but see what he did to your marriage. Evan was...different. We saw the change he went through when he lost his job, the pressures he put on you. We saw him drifting away from all of us." The look she leveled at Angie was oddly probing. "But I hope you're not thinking of Matt in the same vein as Evan because they're nothing alike—and I think you should know that better than anyone."

It was a disturbing conversation, but nonetheless, the day's outing was just the therapy Angie needed.

Tired from all the activity, Casey had promptly fallen asleep the minute they climbed back into the car. When they arrived home Angie chided her good-naturedly, giving her a gentle slap on the bottom. "Come on and help like the rest of us. If you're tired tomorrow, you can take a nap."

The mention of a nap almost always guaranteed a state of instant wakefulness, and it didn't fail this time. Grabbing a thermos, Casey scrambled from the car and trailed behind Kim and Nancy toward the front porch.

Yes, getting out of the house had been just the thing she needed, Angie reflected as she and Janice followed the girls at a more leisurely pace. She definitely felt better. Maybe not good, but definitely better.

It made the scene that greeted her inside the house just that much worse.

Angie stood in the front hallway in stunned silence. She could only stare in helpless disbelief at the total destruction that met her eyes.

"My God," Janice gasped. "What on earth..."

The living room had been completely torn apart. Pictures had been ripped from the walls, cushions had been yanked from the sofa and chairs and thrown aside. Bits and pieces of glass and ceramics lay crushed and shattered on the carpet. It appeared as if a giant arm had swept across the room, ruthlessly crushing everything in its path.

A sickening wave of nausea swept over her. She became dimly aware that Casey and Kim were crying. Nancy looked just as frightened as she grabbed her mother's hand.

"It's okay, girls." Angie sent a wobbly smile to Nancy, then bent and hugged Kim and Casey, grateful that someone else demanded her attention. Gritting her teeth, she forced her mind to function once more.

"Angie." Janice hadn't moved an inch from her spot in the doorway, but her dark eyes scanned the room once more. "Maybe you should call the police."

Angie nodded. With both girls clinging tightly to her, she moved toward the small table in the corner. The fragile, spindly legs had been smashed to smithereens. She picked up the phone from the rubble, gratefully noting that the connection hadn't been severed. With trembling hands, she punched out a number.

It wasn't until a masculine voice answered that she realized who she had called. "Matt," she whispered. Weak with relief, she sank to her knees on the floor.

"Angie. Angie, what's wrong?"

She tried to tell him—she really did. But the only sound that emerged was a hoarse plea. "Matt," she choked out. "Please come...please."

"I'll be right there."

They were the sweetest words she'd ever heard.

CHAPTER SIXTEEN

EVERYONE JUMPED at the sound of footsteps pounding up the porch steps. The screen was nearly yanked off its hinges from the force used to open it. The front door burst open. A huge, distorted shadow loomed....

To Angie, no sight had ever looked quite so good as Matt's big frame filling the doorway. "Matt." Her shoulders sagged with relief. She made her way toward him on legs that felt like melted candle wax. "Oh, Matt, thank God you came."

His arms immediately closed around her. In the seconds before he was surrounded by four other obviously frightened females, Matt saw the wreckage that littered the living room and entryway.

"Good Lord." He sounded as shocked as he looked. "What on earth..."

It was Janice who managed a sickly smile, bouncing the baby gently against her hip. "I already said that, Chief." She went on to tell him they'd been gone all day and returned less than ten minutes ago to find the house like this.

His fingers tightened briefly on Angie's shoulders. He could see that she was badly shaken. Her face was deathly pale, and he could feel her trembling in his arms. The youngsters, he noted, didn't look quite as fearful as they had when he walked through the door. He smiled reassuringly at them, then looked over Angie's head at Janice.

"Did you phone the police yet?"

She shook her head. "Angie wanted to wait until after you came. I called Bill, and he's outside checking to make sure there's no one still around."

Just then another door slammed, and Bill walked in from the kitchen, his face grim. He nodded briefly to Matt. "Everything's okay outside, and nothing's been touched upstairs." He looked at his wife. "Show him the note yet?"

He stiffened. "Note? What note?"

Angie finally drew back to gaze up at him. She was still pale, but her eyes were clear. "We found another one," she murmured in a low voice so the children wouldn't hear. "Stuck to the wall with a knife." How she prevented herself from shuddering, she wasn't sure.

The contents were much the same as before—but it was clearly a warning. Matt's jaw jutted out as he read. He didn't like this whole setup. Not one damn bit.

"You and the girls are coming home with me. And you're staying until we've found out who's behind all this."

His voice was quiet, but there was a steely determination in his eyes. Angie could tell he was waiting for her to explode. But she didn't. She knew he was right. It would be best if she wasn't alone. Besides, she just didn't feel up to another argument with him. She began to tell him so, but Janice cut her off before she could say a word.

"He's right, Angie. I think we'll all feel you'll be a lot safer if you're with Matt." Her look turned imploring. "And this time I'm really *not* trying to knock your heads together!"

"I agree," Bill put in. "You shouldn't be taking any chances, Angie."

Angie's laugh was wobbly. "Hey, don't I get a say-so here?" She held up her hands in a conciliatory gesture. "Before all of you decided to gang up against me, I was going to say that it's probably for the best if I don't stay here." Her gaze slid to Matt's. "Now can we gather a few things together and get this show on the road?"

IT WAS LATE when Matt hung up the phone in his kitchen. He remained where he was, silently assessing the figure sitting at the table.

"Coffee?" he asked, covering his concern with sudden efficiency. Without waiting for an answer, he reached into the cupboard and brought down two cups. After filling them both from the pot on the counter, he walked back to the table and set one before her.

Angie accepted the offering, marveling that Matt was so calm, so offhand. She still felt as if her insides were no more than a mass of gelatin. It was hard to believe the girls were now safe and asleep in the spare bedroom upstairs. She was, however, very grateful for his calm reassurance.

"Thanks," Hesitantly she smiled at him. "For everything."

He nodded. "We'll have a team out to check for fingerprints and talk to the neighbors first thing in the morning."

In spite of herself, Angie shivered. Just thinking about the havoc at her home made her feel cold inside all over again. "Think it will do any good?" she asked, trying her best not to sound glum.

"I wouldn't bank everything I owned on it, but let's hope so."

For her own peace of mind, she attributed his pessimism to caution. Tracing a finger around the rim of her cup, she smiled rather weakly. "Three women and a puppy may cramp your style, Chief Richardson."

He didn't say anything for the longest time. When she finally glanced up at him, she saw such tenderness that her heart turned over. "I'll take my chances, Ms Mayor," he murmured. "I'll take my chances." Rising, he held out a hand. "You must be exhausted. Let's get you to bed, okay?"

Angie unthinkingly placed her hand in his and let him pull her to her feet. Their eyes met and merged, melded by a force neither could deny. She wanted nothing more than to lose herself in the dark warmth of his mouth, the strength and security of his arms.

In that moment the feeble defenses she had forged against him crumpled. She was so tired of fighting—fighting Matt, fighting the confusion in her heart. Perhaps someday she would succeed in sweeping him from her life. Someday...but not now.

A finger beneath her chin eased her face upward. "How are you holding up?" he asked very gently. "Truthfully, now."

She was touched at the deep concern reflected on his face. "I'm fine," she murmured.

"Really?" His eyes searched the pale curve of her cheek, then lingered on the dewy softness of her mouth.

"Really." Her body responded instinctively to his nearness. Her arms found their way around his waist. She leaned her head against his chest as if it were the most natural thing in the world to do. "But only because you're here," she whispered.

Matt smiled at the faint shyness he heard in her voice. "I'm glad you called me." His breath stirred her hair as he rested his chin on her head. "You scared the hell out of me, though. All I knew was that something was terribly wrong, and I thought something had happened to Kim or Casey." He paused. "The minute you saw what happened, all of you should have left, Angie. Whoever broke in could have still been inside the house."

"I know," she admitted sheepishly. "Janice and I were both so stunned I couldn't think straight. Especially after I found the note."

"That reminds me," Matt said with a frown. "The city hall issue is on the agenda for Monday's council meeting, isn't it?"

She nodded. Pulling back, she looked up at him worriedly. "Do you think we should postpone the vote again?"

"No... No, I think you should go ahead with it."

Something in his voice made her curious. "You know who it is, don't you? Who, Matt?" she demanded urgently. "John Curtis?"

"We don't know," he said cautiously. "But whoever it is, he's been pretty damn careful so far."

A prickly unease ran down her spine. "Then why do you think we should go ahead with the vote?"

He shook his head. "Angie, please, no more."

Her eyes remained locked on his face. His closed expression revealed nothing, but suddenly something clicked. "Wait a minute," she said slowly. "Whoever is behind this...you're trying to smoke him—or her—out of hiding."

Before he had a chance to respond, one of her hands, which had been resting lightly on his waistline, eased around toward his back.

"Your gun. You're wearing it again." Her breath fluttered unevenly. Since the night she'd told him how Evan had died, Matt hadn't been carrying it—at least when he was with her.

But tonight he was. She tried not to be alarmed, but her attempt at a smile fell flat. "I'd like to say you're not scaring me, but I think I'd be lying."

"Dammit, Angie." Muttering roughly, Matt hauled her tightly against his chest. "After what you've been through, that's the last thing I want."

Held so tightly against him, his heart drumming steadily under her ear, she felt as if some of his strength radiated into her. "I'm okay. Honestly," she assured him and managed a tremulous but honest-to-goodness smile. "Only between all the excitement and coffee, I probably won't be able to sleep a wink tonight."

His thumb traced the fragile line of her cheekbone. "Are you propositioning me again, Ms Mayor?"

"I'm not sure," she responded quietly, a vaguely troubled light appearing in her eyes. "But I do know I don't want to be alone tonight."

His warm lips touched her forehead, closed her eyes with wispy, feathery brushes, before settling fully on her mouth. It was a kiss filled with tenderness, meant to comfort, and Angie felt a storm of emotion fill her heart near to bursting. She was dimly aware that she was handing control over to Matt, but at this moment she trusted him every bit as much as she trusted herself.

She clung to him wordlessly as he scooped her into his arms and carried her up the stairs to a room swallowed by darkness. She felt the softness of a mattress beneath her, the touch of his hands on her body, his whispering voice instructing her to slide over.

"Hold me," she pleaded.

She was instantly cocooned in warmth, blanketed in security. The only thing she could think of was how right—and how good—it felt here in Matt's arms. And somehow she had never been more grateful for this man who gave everything and demanded so little.

He kissed her eyelids closed, drew the covers up over her bare shoulders. "Go to sleep, babe."

Even though Angie was convinced it would be hours before she could relax, she fell asleep almost immediately.

Instead, it was Matt who lay awake long into the night.

ANGIE DISCOVERED she didn't particularly care for the feeling of being a hunted animal. It was hard not to read ominous signs into anything the least bit unexpected—the sound of a car door slamming, the phone ringing, a floorboard creaking. But for the girls' sake, she managed to act fairly normally.

Kim and Casey stayed at the Crawfords' place most of Sunday afternoon, and she and Matt went back to her house to begin cleaning up. While the damage wasn't as bad as it had appeared at first sight, it was nonetheless a tedious chore. She was both angry and frightened that someone had invaded the privacy of her home and rifled through her personal belongings. By the time the day ended her nerves were shot.

Monday was a little better. The city council meeting was set for seven that night, and she was anxious to have the vote on the city hall issue over and done with. Perhaps then she could get back to normal. Still, if the vote didn't turn out as she hoped, she knew she would be very, very disappointed. Her tormentor, whoever he was, would have gained exactly what he wanted.

Which only brought her around to why. *Why* was someone so set on building a new city hall that he would slash tires, abduct her cat, vandalize her yard and ransack her home? What was in it for him? Matt thought it was for money. But perhaps that wasn't it at all. Maybe *she* had been the intended target all along, the city hall issue only a ruse.

Around and around her mind roiled. Her temples were throbbing when she pulled a small bottle from her desk, dumped a couple of aspirin into her palm and swallowed them with a glass of cool water.

She had just eased her head back tiredly when a knock sounded at the door. Todd Austin walked in.

"All set for the big meeting tonight?"

"I'd better be." She smiled wanly. "Besides, I don't have much choice, do I? Much as I hate to admit it, though, I hope we don't have another stalemate on our hands."

Todd wandered over to glance idly out the window, his hands in his pockets. "It'll be close, all right," he agreed. "I did a little unofficial checking and it looks like it could go either way. So—" he turned and lifted his brows "—looks like everything's riding on you."

Angie didn't say anything. The last time she'd spoken with Steve Jackson, he'd indicated he would support the renovations, but there was always the outside chance he had changed his mind. If the council was indeed split down the middle once more, she would have no choice but to cast the tie-breaking vote.

"Well," she said quietly, "we'll just have to wait and see, I guess." She looked across at him. "You'll be there, won't you?"

Todd nodded. "I do need to pick up a few reports I forgot at home this morning, though." He paused. "I don't suppose you could give me a lift? My car's in the shop till tomorrow afternoon. We could grab some dinner on the way back."

Angie checked her watch. It was nearly four-thirty. "I can give you a ride home and back, if you like. But I'll have to say no to dinner." She hesitated. "I'm meeting Matt Richardson here in about forty-five minutes."

"I see." His expression seemed to tighten. "He's staying for the meeting?"

"Yes." There was an awkward silence while Angie scanned his face anxiously. Then he seemed to relax.

"No problem," he told her. "We'll be back in plenty of time."

Angie collected her jacket and satchel, then stopped briefly by

Georgia's desk to tell her she was leaving. When she and Todd neared her car, he asked, "Mind if I drive?"

With a shrug she handed over her keys. She'd been a passenger often enough in Todd's car to know that he was a capable driver.

The car was hot and stuffy from sitting in the sun all day. Rolling down the window, she enjoyed the feeling of the breeze cooling her face as Todd pulled out into the flow of traffic.

She frowned, though, when she happened to observe that his grip on the steering wheel was so tight his knuckles showed white. Beads of perspiration dotted the grim line of his lips.

"Todd?" Her voice was sharp. "Are you all right?"

He didn't seem to have heard her. "You're going to vote for restoring city hall, aren't you, Angie?"

"If it comes to that, yes." Her tone was puzzled. "But you already know that, Todd."

"I wouldn't if I were you." His eyes narrowed to pale slits. "No, Angie, I think you're going to have a change of heart. You'll vote for a new building...with the right incentive."

At first Angie found his words incomprehensible. Then, in spite of the heat of the day, she suddenly felt as if the temperature had plunged below zero.

There was a feral gleam in Todd's eyes, a harshness in his voice she'd never heard before.

"You," she whispered, stunned. "You're the one who slashed my tires, who broke into my house—it was you!" A burning rage replaced the icy numbness in her veins. She balled her hands into fists on her lap. It was all she could do to stop from hurtling herself at Todd's throat.

"Don't forget about the cat. You'll never find her, you know. I dumped her halfway to Seattle." His laugh was bitter. "I had to do something, didn't I? I had you right where I wanted you till you got it in your head you wanted to renovate that damned old building. But I wasn't worried. I could have talked you into anything—*anything*—until *he* came along!"

"Who? Matt Richardson?" The car veered around a corner. She gasped when her shoulder bounced painfully against the door.

Todd's lips curled. "Damn him, anyway!" he swore viciously.

Angie stared at him, her mind reeling. Surely he wasn't saying he was jealous. There was more to it—much more. "I don't understand, Todd. Why...why did you do all those terrible things? What difference does it make to you whether or not city hall is renovated?"

"A hell of a lot! Money, Angie. It all boils down to money. Me and Jerry—we got it all worked out."

"Jerry?"

"Jerry McKinley. McKinley Construction." He shot her an impatient glance. "He planned to submit a bid for the new building..."

Angie went numb. "And in your job, you would have had access to all the bids."

"Now you're catching on. In exchange for a sizable fee, Jerry gets a little freebie." Todd laughed maliciously. "There's no way anyone else could turn in a lower bid, right? Bingo, Jerry gets the contract—"

"And you get your pockets padded." Her stomach began to churn. Now she understood Todd's reasons for wanting to deepen their relationship. He hadn't wanted her for herself; he'd only wanted to *use* her. Greed had been his only motivation.

"My God, Todd," she muttered. "I can't believe you tried to terrorize me into changing my stand. Don't you know me any better than that?"

"I know you, all right," he snarled. "And you'll do anything to protect those brats of yours! Do you know where they are right now, Angie? Who they're with?"

She stared at him dumbly. She couldn't believe that Todd would really... But he'd already kidnapped Spooky, a terrible voice reminded her. And he was tense, so tense. She could feel his desperation.

The tires squealed as the car screeched to a halt. Angie focused dimly on the traffic signal before them, the long stream of cars.

She lifted her chin defiantly, wondering if her lips were trembling as much as she thought they were. "You won't find them," she said clearly. "They're not at home."

"They're at the Crawfords. I know it—and so does my friend."

Pure panic clawed its way up to her throat. Her head swam dizzily, and for a sickening moment she thought she might pass out. "They're fine," she said jerkily. "If something had happened, Janice would have called...."

Her voice trailed away. There was no way of knowing if Janice *had* called. And she couldn't watch Kim and Casey every second. If either one happened to be near the street... They were so young. It would be so easy to pull a small, unsuspecting child into a car.

The light turned green. Her head jerked back as Todd accelerated. "Todd, be reasonable," she pleaded. "You can't expect to get away with this."

His hands gripped the steering wheel fiercely. "I can and I will!" he shouted. "As long as you do what I tell you."

"Even if I did, sooner or later someone would find out." Angie braced her hands on the dashboard. Fear sharpened her voice. "Todd, listen to me!" They careered around a corner, and she cracked her head on the window. If he was trying to scare her, he was doing one hell of a job.

The Mercedes sped forward, darting and weaving through the traffic. Horns blared, brakes squealed. And still they moved, faster and faster.

"Todd, please!" Angie grabbed for the emergency brake, knowing her effort was hopeless even as she lunged across the seat.

She heard the sickening sound of metal on metal. A sharp cry filled the wildly spinning void around her.

Then everything went dark.

MATT STEPPED into the mayor's office at precisely five-fifteen. Georgia was standing at her desk in the process of clearing the day's clutter.

Without breaking his stride, he started across the room. "Hi, Georgia. Angie still holed up inside?"

Georgia's voice stopped him halfway.

"She's not in there, Chief." She squinted up at the clock on the wall. "Left here about four-thirty."

Matt turned with a frown. He was a little surprised she hadn't let him know she was leaving. "Did she go home?" he asked. "She was supposed to meet me here."

"She said she'd be back. Todd Austin's car is in the repair shop, so she gave him a ride home," Georgia shrugged. "She must have got caught in traffic."

"The repair shop?" There was a distinct edge to his voice. "I saw him drive up and park over on Oak Street less than two hours ago." He hadn't given it a second thought at the time. But most of the city's employees parked in the lot adjacent to the building or on the street directly in front of it. Now chilling needles of apprehension raced up his spine.

"Maroon sports car, some kind of foreign make?"

He nodded, a tense look on his face.

"That's his, all right," Georgia confirmed.

Matt felt as if he'd been struck between the eyes with a hammer. "It's him!" He banged a fist on the desktop, suddenly furious with himself—and with Todd Austin. "Dammit, it's him!"

He had just slammed his car door shut and was shoving the gearshift into reverse when he heard the crackle and buzz of the police radio. Matt gunned the motor. He was scarcely listening as a call sputtered through, dispatching a unit to the scene of a traffic accident.

It wasn't until the officer requested a DMV check on the vehicles involved that Matt gave it a second thought. And then he broke out in a cold sweat. His stomach lurched sickeningly.

One of the cars belonged to Angie—and an ambulance had just been summoned.

MATT WAS NEVER SURE how he got to the scene of the accident in one piece. Over and over, agonizing thoughts ran through his mind. How badly was Angie hurt? Had she been thrown from the car? Through the windshield? His stomach tightened. What if she was...

He yanked the steering wheel toward the curb. With a spray of gravel, a whining squeal of the brakes, the car screeched to a halt.

Matt jumped out, his eyes quickly scanning the area. The street had been blocked off. There was a small city park on one side, a grocery store on the other. The site was teeming with police vehicles and bystanders.

Then he spotted Angie's car. The front end of the vehicle resembled an accordion; the rear door on the driver's side was almost completely caved in.

The ambulance was nearby, parked beneath a tree. Two blue-shirted paramedics were just sliding a stretcher through the double doors. There was a white blanket draped over the stretcher, but Matt could see that the victim was a woman.

Matt felt his heart stop. He rushed over to the ambulance just as the driver was closing the second double door at the rear of the van.

"Wait!" He was dimly aware of his voice cracking. "The woman inside...how serious is it?"

The man shrugged. "Likely a concussion, I'd say. She smacked her head on the steering wheel pretty good. Fractured arm, too.

Don't know about internal injuries yet. Have to wait till we get to Emergency to find out.'' He started around the side of the vehicle, then turned back. "You know her?''

Matt nodded tersely.

"You can follow us to the hospital if you want."

There was a sickening feeling in the pit of his stomach, a kind of fear he'd never known before. He took a moment to gather himself, watching as the ambulance pulled onto the street. The sight of the overhead lights flashing in the brilliant sunshine seemed almost obscene.

He felt a tap on his shoulder. "Why is it you're always a little too late to get in on the action?'' a voice behind him asked.

He turned and for a second he thought he was dreaming. But when a warm, yielding form walked straight into his arms, he knew that he wasn't.

"Angie. Angie, I thought..." He couldn't go on; he could only look at the flashing lights of the ambulance rounding the corner, his throat clogged with emotion.

She ran her fingers over the sharp angles of his cheekbones. "I'm fine. See?'' She pointed to a small bruise on her right temple. "My only battle scar." Her slight smile faded. "Todd side-swiped that car—'' she pointed to a mangled sedan behind him "—and the driver's the woman they just took to the hospital.'' She didn't tell him that, before she had blacked out, they had spun around on the sidewalk and narrowly missed hitting a tree.

Matt hugged her fiercely, then drew back to gaze down at her. His hands rested lightly on her shoulders. "Todd's behind this whole thing, Angie,'' he began.

"I...I know. He told me. He vandalized the yard, took Spooky and dumped her miles out of town. And you were right, Matt. It was all for money." In a low voice she told him of Todd's plan. She ended with a shiver. "He threatened to do something to Kim and Casey if I didn't vote for the new building.''

Matt froze once more. "They're fine,'' she assured him quickly. "A dispatcher has already checked with Janice.''

Her smile was brave, but there was a telling glaze of moisture over her lovely blue eyes. Matt aimed a silent curse at Todd Austin.

At precisely that moment he saw a uniformed officer leading Todd toward a police cruiser. He then decided voicing his outrage would be much more satisfying.

"I'll be back in just a minute," he told Angie. Dropping a light kiss on her forehead, he moved away.

Briefly noting the name tag worn by the officer, he dropped a hand on his shoulder. He nodded pleasantly toward the caged back of the cruiser. "Mind if I have a word with the suspect, Officer Stevens?"

The man turned with a frown, but the look changed to one of respect as he saw who had made the request. "Sure thing, Chief."

Sullen and stony, Todd Austin stared straight ahead, handcuffed wrists dangling on his knees. Without a word Matt opened the door, grabbed him by his lapels and unceremoniously hauled him from the back of the vehicle.

A number of spectators looked on with interest at the spectacle that was about to unfold.

Matt towered over the other man. With his feet braced slightly apart, big hands curled into fists at his sides, Matt was indeed a formidable figure. "Do you have any idea what I'd like to do to you, Austin?"

Todd sneered. "I almost got away with it, Richardson. You had no idea it was me who was terrorizing your precious little—"

"Shut up." The incredibly soft tone belied the savage light in the police chief's eyes.

"Oh, come on," Todd taunted. "Are you afraid somebody's gonna find out about you two?" His laughter was malicious as he jerked his head toward Angie, who was watching silently a short distance away. "Instead of bragging about what you'd like to do to me, why don't you tell us what you wanna do to her? What you've already done—"

But Matt had heard all he wanted. He lunged toward the other man.

"Matt, don't!" Angie pleaded, determinedly tugging at his arm. "He's only goading you. Don't you see that?"

The harshly threatening expression slowly faded from Matt's face. He stared down at Angie, suddenly aware that there was something different. She looked rather scared, undeniably concerned, but there was also a depth of emotion in her eyes that hadn't been there before—at least when she looked at him.

He released Todd so abruptly the other man fell back against the trunk of the car. He nodded briefly to Officer Stevens. "Get him out of here."

A wave of intense feeling swept through him as he caught Angie's hand in his. "You're right," he said softly. "He's not worth it. But I will say he's damn lucky you *weren't* hurt, or it wouldn't be the jail he'd be spending the night in.''

Right now all Angie wanted was to forget this whole mess. ''Let's go home,'' she murmured. The smile she directed at him was weary yet tender.

Matt's eyes dropped to where her hand had settled into the crook of his arm. He was just about to tease her when a voice called, ''Hey, can we get a shot of you two?''

They both turned to see a photographer from the *Bulletin* waving at them. Angie gave a tiny moan, but Matt grinned devilishly.

''Sure thing,'' he promised. Before she had a chance to protest, he pulled her into his arms and ducked his forehead down to hers. ''Ms Mayor and the Chief may make the front page yet,'' he whispered just before he gave her a kiss guaranteed to knock the socks off anyone who cared to look on.

Angie didn't mind in the least.

CHAPTER SEVENTEEN

THE EPISODE didn't quite end there.

Janice, of course, had to hear all about it. At nine o'clock that night Angie, Matt, Bill, Janice and four youngsters were still gathered around the kitchen table at the Crawfords' house.

"I can't believe it. It was Todd Austin all along!" she exclaimed for what seemed like the hundredth time. "When the police called to see if Kim and Casey were all right, I couldn't imagine what was going on." She shook her dark head and grinned at Angie. "Didn't I tell you once that having a big-time cop from Chicago was like having Kojak in town?"

"*Ex*-cop from Chicago," Matt reminded her. His fingers curled around Angie's, as if to remind himself that she was really okay. "And I'd hardly call myself the hero in this story, anyway," he added wryly. "As usual, though, there's never any shortages of bad guys."

He was talking about Todd.

Beside him, Angie found herself lost in thought, scarcely listening to the conversation. In spite of the contempt she had for Todd's planned manipulation, she felt rather sorry for him. He was bright and intelligent, and he'd had so much going for him. He should have been grateful; instead, he'd found himself blinded by the need for more.

She had also discovered something else tonight. She suspected she was very, very lucky. Matt loved her, but instead of accepting and nurturing that love, she had chosen to turn her back on it, and him, because she was afraid. She could only hope it wasn't too late. But from the warmly possessive light shining in Matt's eyes the past few hours, she didn't think it was.

"Mommy." Kim cast a worried look at the puppy, who was sniffing around the corner of the kitchen. "I think Patches needs to go outside."

At the sound of her name, Patches began wagging her tail. Matt laughed and got up. "I'll bet she does, too." He scooped the pup up in one big hand, then glanced at Kim. "Coming, Kim?"

Not only did Kim tag along on the trip outside, but Casey, Nancy and Bill went, as well. Janice took Eric up to bed, and there was a rather smug expression on her face when she came back.

Angie shook her head. "All right, Janice Crawford. I've seen that look before. What's on your mind?"

Janice grinned. "I was just thinking of that night you went to dinner at the Sheraton right after Matt was hired."

"You gave me a big lecture on needing a man in my life again," Angie recalled dryly. "And you said something about going out and making something happen—snagging a rich husband, I think it was."

"I really never thought that you would!" Janice said with a laugh.

"But I haven't!" A smile began to blossom. "At least not yet," she added. "And Matt isn't rich."

Janice waved a flamboyant hand. "One out of two isn't bad." She eyed her friend slyly. "He *has* asked you to marry him, hasn't he?"

She nodded.

"And *this* time you're going to accept, aren't you?"

Angie shook her head. Janice knew her very well—almost as well as Matt. "If he asks me again, I will," she confided rather breathlessly.

At that moment Kim and Casey ran through the door, the others trailing behind. "Mommy!" Casey shrieked. "Mommy, look who we found!"

A ball of dirty, scraggly fur was dropped into her lap. Startled, at first Angie thought they'd dragged in a stray cat, but as she glanced down at the animal, she noticed a familiar-looking streak of silver beneath the grime.

"Spooky! Spooky, how did you ever find your way home!" The cat yowled indignantly as Angie hugged her tightly. She wasted no time in wriggling free and jumping to the floor. For all her dishevelment, the way she preened while walking across the kitchen was no less than queenly.

When Patches ran after her, yipping playfully, Angie glanced over at Matt, who had resumed his place beside her. "We may have a slight problem here," she murmured. "I don't know if Spooky will like sharing the house with a dog."

Matt laughed. "I wouldn't worry if I were you." He nodded toward the two animals. Spooky had turned golden eyes toward Patches, her tail waving lazily in the air. Then with a bored yawn she padded from the room. Patches sat down on her haunches and stared after her, but the next minute she was playing happily under the table once more.

"One big happy family," Angie commented with a secretive smile. "I hope you're right."

As if Matt sensed what was on her mind, he said quietly, "I think it's time we headed home." His eyes dropped to where Casey had crawled up on his lap, her lids drooping wearily.

Once they were sitting in his car, he asked, "You don't mind spending one more night at my place, do you? It's a little late to get all your things together now, anyway."

Angie murmured her agreement, but she smiled to herself in the darkness. Did she mind one more night with him? Quite the contrary. She was counting on it—very definitely counting on it!

Nor was she the only one with that thought firmly in mind. Still, he knew that when they were finally alone, they had some talking to do first.

He was sitting on the top step of the stairs when she closed the bedroom door. He'd left her alone to put the two girls to bed, knowing she needed some time with them to reassure herself that they were safe and well.

"Everything okay?" he asked as she approached.

Angie nodded and sat down beside him. "I'm still finding it hard to believe this whole thing wasn't a nightmare. When I think of what Todd did..." She shivered. "It's scary to realize that I honestly thought him capable of harming Kim and Casey. Never once did it occur to me he might be bluffing."

She was silent for a moment. "But then I'm grateful he wasn't put to the test. I'm not sure I really want to know just how far he would have gone to get what he wanted."

"At least it's all over now."

"Not quite," she reminded him. "The city council still hasn't decided the fate of city hall."

Matt's eyes gleamed. "Don't you have any faith in your powers of persuasion?"

Her heart began beating a little faster. There was the faintest hint of suggestion in his voice. "Maybe what I need is a trial run."

"Maybe." He smiled his approval. "Looking for a guinea pig?"

"I think I've already found one." Somehow she managed to match his light, bantering tone. "Do you think I could possibly persuade *you* what a fool I've been—especially concerning matters of the heart?"

He crossed his arms over his chest and propped a shoulder against the wall. He couldn't believe his ears. His heart skipped a beat, but then it began to soar as the budding hope within gained momentum. "I think it could be arranged," he murmured.

At his playful tone Angie's eyes began to gleam, as well. "You're very agreeable tonight, aren't you?"

"I should hope so." His voice dropped to a conspiratorial whisper. "Actually, I'm hoping to snag myself a wife. Know anyone who might be interested?"

For a moment Angie just stared at him, trying to absorb the reality of what he was saying. She had hurt Matt, hurt him deeply, struck a blow to his pride. In a way, she had proved herself no better than Linda. Because of that there was a part of her that was afraid he would be unable to forgive her.

Her fears, it seemed, were groundless. She was scarcely able to believe she'd been given a second chance with this man.

"What?" Matt cocked an eyebrow at her. "Not so agreeable now that the shoe is on the other foot?"

A rush of blinding joy swept through her. "Matt," she finally choked out. "Matt..." She was laughing, she was crying.

She was in his arms, and nothing had ever felt so right. All the pain, the doubt and uncertainty of the preceding days disappeared like mist beneath the burning rays of a blazing sun. The touch of his hand as he smoothed strands of hair from her tear-dewed cheeks was so tender, so filled with love, that she felt her eyes glaze over once more.

"Oh, Matt," she whispered. "How can you ever forgive me?"

Matt shook his head. "It doesn't matter—" he started to say.

"But it does." Looking at him, she saw all that he was—an intensely masculine man whose warmth and sensitivity equalled his strength. The man she loved.

"In the short time I've known you, you've given me so much," she told him. She hesitated but an instant. "Remember the time you said that someday soon the day would come when there were no secrets between us?"

There was a time—was it only hours ago?—when he had suspected he was very, very wrong. But he nodded, sensing how important it was for Angie to say what she had to tell him.

"When Evan died, I was very bitter," she said quietly. "I tried to remember the good times, but somehow all I remembered was how terrible it was at the end." Hard as she tried, she couldn't control the painful catch in her voice. "It was easier after a while, but I know now that all along I've been running. Running away from facing up to my feelings about Evan, and then lately—" her eyes held his "—running from the way I felt about you."

Matt understood her need to explain, the need to let go once and for all. The need to make peace with herself and with the dark shadow of Evan's memory.

"You're a strong woman, Angie," he told her gently. "A survivor."

"I'd like to think so," she agreed with a faint smile. "But it's taken me a long time to put aside the bitterness and realize that Evan is a part of my past while you—" she turned slightly and slipped her arms around his neck "—are my future."

Matt didn't delay sampling the lips she offered so temptingly. Still, he eyed her quizzically when at last he raised his head. "What made you change your mind?" he asked.

"It wasn't *what* so much as *who*. You've had allies in Georgia and Janice almost from the start." Her fingers toyed with the dark hair just above his collar. "But it was Georgia who really started the ball rolling. We had quite a conversation several days ago."

"Oh?" He raised an eyebrow. "About me?"

"It didn't start out that way," she confessed. "But that's how it ended up." She went on to tell him of Sam's proposal, Georgia's uncertainty and how she had told Georgia that, if all else failed, she should listen to her heart.

At that, Matt shook his head. "Don't tell me she threw that little piece of advice right back at you."

Angie nodded.

"A woman of wisdom," he murmured, pleasantly surprised. "I'll have to make sure I never tell her I first thought of her as an old battle-ax."

A faint frown had appeared in Angie's eyes, and he knew she was still thinking of Georgia and Sam. "They'll work it out," he reassured her. "Which reminds me, you still haven't told me whether or not you'll marry me."

She laughed, that unrestrained tinkling sound he so loved to hear. "What do you think?"

Light as her tone was, there was a world of emotion reflected in her eyes. Matt's arms tightened around her, and for a moment he simply absorbed the wonder of her nearness, the warmth of her body.

"I think—" he planted nibbling little kisses along her jawline "—I may have to rely on my own powers of persuasion." His mouth finally reached hers.

She smiled against the deepening pressure of his lips. "I think they're working already," she murmured.

Matt's laugh was shaky. "Let's hope so." He raised his head, and their eyes melded. "Do you love me, Angie?"

His voice fell into a hushed void. When she finally spoke, she repeated the question almost whimsically. "Do I love you?" Her hands dropped to rest lightly on his shoulders.

"Because of you, I've learned a lot about myself," she told him very softly. "I need a man who feels the same way I do. A man who isn't afraid to let me know he's as vulnerable as I am. A man who loves the same way I do." She paused for the space of a heartbeat. "I need you, Matt. I want to share your life, have your children. And...and I love you more than I ever thought possible."

The world spun crazily. Matt's heart soared skyward. Then he pulled her to him fiercely.

She could only cling to him, caught up in the same battle to control the overwhelming intensity of emotion that consumed them both.

"Oh, Angie." Her name emerged as an uneven groan. "I think I knew it even before you did. But just so I know for sure—" he lifted his head to look at her but didn't lessen his desperate embrace "—tell me once more."

Angie felt her heart burst with joy. Knowing that his pride had never meant less to him, aware that he didn't give a damn that she saw his tears, only made her love him all the more.

Her heart was so full she could hardly speak. Cradling his lean face in her hands, she somehow managed to force the sound past the lump in her throat. "I love you," she said in a voice that shook with emotion. "I love you."

Through laughter and tears, through hope and joy, over and over she told him of her love for him. She didn't stop until Matt captured her mouth firmly beneath his, trapping the sound in the back of his throat.

It was everything a kiss should be—tender, urgent, possessive and warm. Angie didn't realize Matt had carried her into the bedroom until she felt the mattress beneath her. Matt's body followed her down, and with an infinitely adoring touch, he began to undress her.

When she did the same for him, Matt felt his bloodstream explode. His pulse came quickly as her hands pushed him to his back, the touch gentle but firm with intent.

The golden web of her hair teased his skin before twin peaks of fire angled across his chest. Her lips hovered just above his as one slim thigh nestled gently between his.

Matt tangled his fingers in her hair. "Are you trying to drive me crazy?" he asked teasingly, his eyes feasting on the soft curve of her mouth.

Her smile was bold and sensuous, faintly mysterious—the smile of a woman who knew all too well the effect she had on him. "Is it working?" she countered, raking a hand through the dark curls on his chest.

"Like a charm," he responded sultrily.

The next second Angie found their positions reversed. She was so startled that she stared up at him wide-eyed. Matt laughed at her surprise. Then his eyes dipped to her mouth and lingered there.

"I love you," he said, his tone very quiet. His mood had swung from teasing to one of the utmost seriousness.

Suddenly the world seemed to narrow into a dark velvet void where only the two of them existed. "And I love you," she whispered.

His mouth lowered as she raised hers. The contact was unhurried, tender but quickly became a fire flowing between them. The breath rushed forth from her lips to his, and his to hers. Desire, hot and urgent, tightened Matt's body with a full and aching need.

Angie felt the unhurried glide of his tongue tracing her lips before delving within, and she responded with a wanton artistry that delighted them both.

"Oh, Matt," she breathed, trailing her fingers along the steely hardness of his back. "You make me feel so..."

"What?" His voice was thick. He lifted his head and stared down at her, his eyes silver bright.

"I don't know." She gasped as a pleasantly rough fingertip brushed across the beaded tip of her breast. When she was finally able to speak, she murmured, "You make me feel...whole."

His fingers stilled in their quest. The room grew suddenly

hushed as he lifted a hand to trail gently across her cheek. "It's funny you should say that because that's how I've felt with you almost from the start." His expression was more tender than she'd ever seen it. "For the first time in my life, I feel as if I really belong."

Then there were no more words, and none were needed. His hands were everywhere—stroking, seeking, arousing her to a pitch of intensity she'd never known before. His mouth slid down to cover the achingly erect tip of her breast, tracing scorching circles of fire around her nipple. A hand drifted lower to slide into the springy softness between her thighs, caressing her with a sensually tormenting motion that made her clench and unclench her fingers against his shoulders. His breath was labored and hot against her skin, and she could feel as well as sense the rigid control he exerted over himself. But always beneath the raging storm of his desire were the ever-present elements of tenderness and caring he had shown her.

Never before had Angie been more aware of it, and it only made her all the more determined to give as he was giving.

She could stand his erotic ministrations no longer. Driven by a powerful tide of longing, she shifted beneath him and began a mindless undulation of her hips that she knew would drive him wild.

"Angie..." His breath tumbled out in a rush.

She responded by parting her thighs. Eyes closed, she surged upward in search of vital male warmth, moaning her satisfaction when she found it.

Matt gasped with pleasure as her fiery softness surrounded him. Unable to help himself, he gave in to the myriad sensations bombarding him. Cradling her hips in his hands, he caught her to him and bound them together. Angie's eyes drifted open, and smiling directly into her eyes, he began the slow, rhythmic motions of love.

A long time later she stirred weakly in his arms. Through love-sated eyes, she gazed up at Matt. "I just realized," she said rather sleepily, "that I didn't think to have someone notify the city council about tonight's accident. I wonder how long they sat in the council chambers."

Matt brushed a strand of gold off her temple. "If anyone asks," he said, his mouth twitching, "we'll just have to tell them the mayor was otherwise engaged."

"Otherwise engaged?" she repeated, then seemed to consider.

"I guess I am, at that," she murmured, then added, "Blair Andrews will have a field day with this, you know."

"Why's that?" He ran a hand lazily over her bare hip.

"Stay tuned for the latest of Ms Mayor and the Chief," she quoted, her eyes dancing with amusement. "Somehow I don't think she expected it to end this way."

Matt leaned over and dropped a kiss onto her mouth. "I hate to disillusion you, but this is only the beginning."

HE COULDN'T HAVE MADE a more accurate prediction. They were married five days later.

It was a simple, quiet ceremony, attended by those closest to them. Neither Angie nor Matt felt the need for fanfare. The spiritual binding of heart and soul was already strong and enduring. With the shadows of the past behind them, they wanted only to sanction their union as quickly as possible.

The following Monday evening Matt met his bride at the door. Kim and Casey had been in bed for the last hour. A blue-black darkness had settled over the earth, but the smile on Angie's face as she stepped inside was more radiant than the brightest day of sunshine.

Matt's eyes dropped to the two champagne bottles she held. He didn't have to ask how the city council had voted on the fate of city hall.

"Two?" he found himself teasing. "Have I driven you to drink already?"

Angie wrinkled her nose at him and lifted one of the bottles. "This one is to celebrate our anniversary."

"Three whole days." His eyes glinted as he followed her into the kitchen. "I can't wait to see what you come up with on our twentieth."

"Day or year?" She directed the question over her shoulder as she set the bottles on the counter, then opened a cupboard to search for some glasses.

Coming up behind her, he slid his arms around her waist. "Years, of course," he whispered, dropping a kiss on her nape.

A pleased little smile hovered on her lips. "You'll just have to stick around and see, won't you?"

Matt turned her in his arms and smiled down at her. "That," he said in a husky voice, "is something I have every intention of doing—for a lifetime." He claimed her mouth in a long, leisurely kiss, then finally asked the question he knew she'd been dying to hear since the minute she'd walked in the door. "What are we celebrating with the other bottle of champagne?"

"Any number of things," she responded airily.

"Such as?"

"Such as the fact that city hall will be getting a face-lift after all!"

"And Westridge will be getting a women's shelter, too?"

She nodded, her eyes dancing impishly. "You're a smart man, Chief Richardson," she proclaimed sweetly. "Now I know why I hired you."

"To tell you the truth—" his eyes took on a provocative gleam "—I'm much more pleased that you married me." And he proceeded to show her exactly just how pleased he was.

Some time later they both lay stretched out on the bed upstairs, basking in the warm afterglow of their lovemaking, Angie's head pillowed comfortably on Matt's shoulder. "Sure you don't mind postponing the honeymoon a few weeks more?" Matt asked softly. "I know your presence at city hall is vital right now, but..."

She laughed and tugged playfully at the dark curls on his chest. Angie and Matt planned a trip to Arizona to visit Angie's parents. They had offered to look after Kim and Casey so that the newlyweds could be alone for a few days. But the girls would be with them during the two-day drive.

"You can ask *that* after the last thirty minutes?" Then in a more serious vein she added, "Are you sure you don't mind the girls tagging along the first few days?"

"Idiot," he admonished softly. "I love those kids almost as much as I love their mother." Threading his fingers through the flowing fullness of her hair, he guided her mouth to his for a deep and lingering kiss, letting her feel all the love in his heart.

Angie's eyes were shining when he finally released her. "I hope you know," she said rather breathlessly, "that we never even touched that champagne I bought."

The tip of his finger dipped just inside the moist warmth of her mouth. He carried it from her mouth to his, and smiled. "Essence of Angie. Much better than champagne."

Just then the bedside phone rang. Angie switched on the light and answered it. From the one-sided conversation he heard, Matt gathered it was someone inquiring about how tonight's city council meeting had gone.

"That was Georgia," she told him when she hung up a few minutes later. Then she added mysteriously, "I know what we can do with those two bottles of champagne."

A silly grin edged her mouth at his surprised look as he suddenly made the connection. "Wait a minute," he gasped. "You mean—"

She nodded. "Georgia and Sam are leaving for Reno in the morning. To get married."

He shook his head good-naturedly at her unnecessary addendum. "Just one more reason for you to gloat tonight, isn't it?"

"Maybe," she agreed. The teasing light in her eyes faded. With the suddenness of their marriage, she hadn't wanted to rock the boat too much where Kim and Casey were concerned, so Matt had moved most of his things into her house for the present. But in the last few hours she had been thinking.

"How would you feel about selling your house," she asked carefully, "and turning this one over to the city?"

In that very special way he had, Matt understood immediately. "For the women's shelter?"

Angie nodded. "I thought maybe we could buy another one."

"I see," he said slowly. "Not your house or my house, but *our* house."

She felt a familiar warm glow in her heart when he cupped his hand behind her neck and drew her down so that their lips met briefly.

"I like the sound of that," he said softly. "Almost as much as I like the sound of Mrs. Matt Richardson."

"Funny," she murmured against his lips. "So do I."

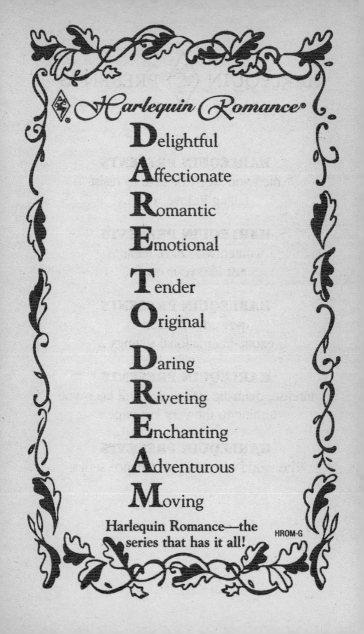

Harlequin Romance®

Delightful

Affectionate

Romantic

Emotional

Tender

Original

Daring

Riveting

Enchanting

Adventurous

Moving

Harlequin Romance—the
series that has it all!

HROM-G

HARLEQUIN ✦ PRESENTS®

HARLEQUIN PRESENTS
men you won't be able to resist
falling in love with...

HARLEQUIN PRESENTS
women who have feelings
just like your own...

HARLEQUIN PRESENTS
powerful passion in
exotic international settings...

HARLEQUIN PRESENTS
intense, dramatic stories that will keep you
turning to the very last page...

HARLEQUIN PRESENTS
The world's bestselling romance series!

Harlequin® Historical

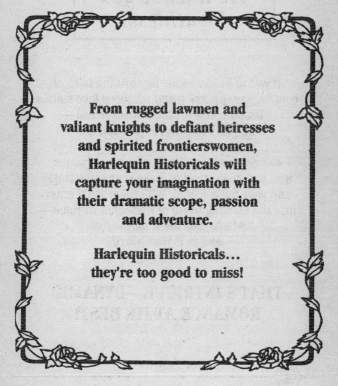

From rugged lawmen and
valiant knights to defiant heiresses
and spirited frontierswomen,
Harlequin Historicals will
capture your imagination with
their dramatic scope, passion
and adventure.

Harlequin Historicals…
they're too good to miss!

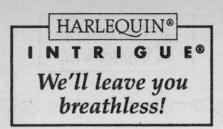

HARLEQUIN®
I N T R I G U E®
We'll leave you breathless!

If you've been looking for thrilling tales of
contemporary passion and sensuous love stories
with taut, edge-of-the-seat suspense—
then you'll *love* **Harlequin Intrigue!**

Every month, you'll meet four new heroes
who are guaranteed to make your spine tingle
and your pulse pound. With them you'll enter
into the exciting world of Harlequin Intrigue—
where your life is on the line
and so is your heart!

THAT'S INTRIGUE—DYNAMIC ROMANCE AT ITS BEST!

HARLEQUIN®
I N T R I G U E®

INT-GENR

LOOK FOR OUR FOUR FABULOUS MEN!

Each month some of today's bestselling authors bring
four new fabulous men to Harlequin American Romance.
Whether they're rebel ranchers, millionaire power brokers
or sexy single dads, they're all gallant princes—and
they're all ready to sweep you into lighthearted fantasies
and contemporary fairy tales where anything is possible
and where all your dreams come true!

You don't even have to make a wish…
Harlequin American Romance will grant your every desire!

Look for Harlequin American Romance
wherever Harlequin books are sold!